the
begin
and
end
of
us

the
beginning
and
end
of
us

ROSE JAMES

Bookouture

Published by Bookouture in 2019

An imprint of Storyfire Ltd.
Carmelite House
50 Victoria Embankment
London EC4Y 0DZ

www.bookouture.com

ISBN: 9-781-83888-126-9
eBook ISBN: 978-1-83888-125-2

For Jenna, Rachell and Margaret,
and for You, μου.

Prologue

Now that I've made up my mind to do this I don't really know where to start, so I'm just going to jump straight in and see what happens. My name is Aphrodite. Like the goddess. Well, *I'm* not like the goddess… at least, not exactly. Not like the mythological version: an idealised, perfect woman who made gods and men fall in love with her wherever she went. I'm thankful for that. Sounds like a major headache if you ask me. But if there was a real person who inspired that myth, then you might say I am a bit like her. I'm of this world, but not entirely part of it; there's the human part, and then there's… something else.

It's entirely possible that no one will ever read the words I'm about to set down on these pages, but that doesn't matter. I think, like most of us, I'm just trying to make sense of it all. And it feels like the right time to do this now, at the start of a new chapter in my life.

If you're reading this and it dawns on you that you shared some of this story with me, I hope it will help you make sense of what happened too. I hope you're happy, wherever you are now – that you found whatever it was you were looking for and that it was everything you hoped it would be. Sometimes the things we think we want don't turn out exactly the way we expect when viewed up close. Sometimes they're even better, but most often – at least in my experience – they become doorways that lead to whatever happens next: not the end of the road but the beginning of another part of the journey. Perhaps I have a different perspective on that, given everything I've been through. Being something more – or maybe less – than human brings with it a certain clarity.

Anyway, I'll get to that later, but let's just say for now that I'm more than I first appear to be, just like the others of my kind. Oh yes, there are others, although I have no idea where they are and I probably wouldn't know one of them if I tripped over them. You have no idea how lonely that can be.

But hey, I am what I am. Love has been my reason to exist, my function, for almost as long as I can remember. Without it I would never have started on my Path. Like I said, I'm not *the* Aphrodite, but I am akin to her in a way.

I've had so many loves, and every single one was different – some chaotic and all-consuming, others gentle as summer rain. You might be thinking that I'm talking about promiscuity, not real love, but you'd be wrong. I was created to love completely and devotedly, without judgement or reserve, until... until my purpose was fulfilled. And although at times that has felt like a curse, deep down I know it's a blessing: to have loved – and been loved by – so many.

I'll be honest, some of those loves have affected me more profoundly than others. I don't mean that I loved one person more than another, but some loves go beyond being something you *experience* and become part of who you *are*. They become embedded in the very essence of your being, until you can no longer separate them from yourself. Those loves linger on, long after the people you shared them with have slipped from view, and you carry them with you for the rest of your life, whether you're aware of it or not.

So, these words are my parting gift to you, my loves. A memorial, of sorts – a thank you, and a final farewell. I dedicate it to all of you. Just know that I meant every bit of it, and always will.

First Love

You were the first. I know that now, although I could never have guessed what that meant back then. It seems such a long time ago, but it can't have been more than… actually, it *was* a long time ago. But I still remember every detail.

I was sixteen years old, impossibly innocent and desperate to grow up. We'd been friends since we were what, six? We were children together, just learning the rules of the world and our places in it. I wasn't Aphrodite then, and you weren't who you are today, but there must have been something of my later self in that naïve little girl. I know that, in hindsight, because of everything that's happened since.

Hearthfire – our home and school since we were children – seems a world away now. It wasn't like anywhere else I've ever been. It had a feeling about it, an elusive enchantment that went beyond the towering grandeur of the old, red sandstone walls; beyond the endless adventure of poking around the musty outbuildings and spooky cellars; beyond the ever-shifting beauty of the grounds that swept down and away from the house, beginning as a broad, well-tended lawn and gradually metamorphosing into the untamed tangle of the Fairy Wood with its ash trees, wych elms and hazels. It was something more than the closeness of our wild extended family – the Elders who were our teachers, carers and confidants; the dozens of brothers and sisters who laughed and played and fought and cried together, every day and every night for all those years. We were distinct from the rest of our species – other and apart – and Hearthfire was *our* place, our sanctuary, so I suppose it makes sense that it was different too. It held itself apart from the world, just as we were held apart.

There were exactly forty of us children, all around the same age, and even now I still feel a pang of regret when I think of the friendships we all had to leave behind. Well, at least *I* had to leave them behind. I suppose some of the others might have stuck together after they left, but it's not as if there's anyone I can ask, not now. Since I left it has just been me and the world. All contact broken. All ties severed.

I would have liked to have said goodbye, though, at least to you. But then, you were the reason I had to leave. You set the ball rolling. I know you didn't mean to, but the result was the same in the end.

I think it started the year before I left, the summer after my fifteenth birthday. That night when we snuck out and escaped to the woods, with some pilfered snacks and apple wine. The wine was far too potent for two untutored teenagers, and we were drunk before we were halfway through the bottle.

You had your guitar with you, as always, and we sat on the big, flat rock by the stream – the one we sometimes perched on to net sticklebacks – and sang and laughed and drank our wine. Neither of us cared that I was a girl and you were a boy; we were Adam and Eve before the Fall, still innocent and unselfconscious in each other's company. We were the best of friends, brother and sister, although maybe closer than real siblings because we never argued over anything.

My other best friend, Hannah, was your girlfriend at the time. I always envied her a little, not because of you but because she was the one with all the brains, which might have explained why she refused to sneak out with us. She was the sensible one, I suppose.

It's funny but it didn't seem wrong that we were out alone together in the dark; that wasn't how we were. I miss being that young!

Eventually we ran out of songs to sing and food to eat, and we crept back through the pale, early dawn, arms wrapped tightly around each other to fend off the chill. My hair hung loose around my shoulders like a warm woollen cape, and you made a show of spluttering occasionally when the wind whipped a few stray strands of it into your mouth.

Partway across the lawn I complained that I was too tired to walk any further, and you made me stand on your feet, my back to your belly, and walked the rest of the way straight-legged like some kind of clunky, stiff-jointed robot. Your arms clamped me tightly against you so I wouldn't fall off, and the guitar hung upside-down across your back, held on by the strap around your chest.

We reached the door to the girls' wing, which I'd wedged ajar earlier with a spent toilet roll tube, and you stopped so I could disembark. I turned to smirk at you triumphantly, delighted by the success of our clandestine mission, before carefully pushing the heavy chunk of studded oak back on its hinges to avoid the squeak.

Just as I was about to step through into the familiar gloom you reached out and stopped me, and I looked back to find you grinning broadly, the shaggy waves of your sandy-brown hair stirring gently in the chill morning breeze. I half-turned towards you, and for just a second it felt like we were on the edge of some marvellous discovery... but then it was gone, and you tweaked my nose and jogged away around the side of the building, heading for the boys' door.

Looking back, that must have been where it began. That tiny less-than-a-heartbeat in which I felt something *other* than everything I'd felt before. I was young enough that it didn't trouble me, but I know now what it was. It's happened many times since that day, although never quite as sweetly.

It's funny how something that seemed so insignificant at the time has stuck with me for so long, but since then I've learned the meaning of those moments. I've had to; they're what I've built my life on.

Where was I? Oh yes, so, the summer passed without further incident. Autumn was a riot of colour and scent, and I felt like I had suddenly learned to *feel* more than I ever had before. Everything was so much brighter, sharper, like when you wake up from a dream and realise how foggy and unclear it was compared to real life.

You broke up with Hannah at All Hallows', which upset her greatly, and I didn't speak to you for a while even though we saw each other every day. I don't know why I was annoyed at you – you hadn't done anything to me, and I'd always been closer to you than her, but I felt like I owed it to her to be loyal in the face of male treachery.

I'd forgiven you by the first snowfall, with all the fickleness of youth, and although Hannah thought it was insensitive of me I took to spending a lot of my free time with you again. What can I say? We were drawn together. And I had more fun with you anyway.

Winter was beautiful, as it always was at Hearthfire. The sugar-frosted leaves crunched underfoot, and the great swathe of sky alternated between mottled metallic-grey and that startling shade of blue that looks like the colour of pure air. In spring we danced like hares across the dew-soaked grass, consumed by the sensations of the sap stirring in our veins and the warmth of the new sun on our faces.

I remember looking up at you one day, as you sat on your usual perch in one of the old oak trees that stood in regimented file along the western perimeter wall, swinging your feet back and forth and tapping out a

rhythm on your thighs. Between one blink and another you looked…
different, and that split second of sweetness from the year before came
sweeping over me, intense and terrifying as a summer storm.

The feeling refused to go away for the rest of the afternoon, and
it was still tormenting me when the dinner bell rang in the evening.
When I woke the following morning I thought I might be free of it,
but the second I saw you at the breakfast table I was flooded with a
sickening sense of longing, an urgent buzzing in my bones that didn't
seem to switch off no matter what I was doing or who else was around.
For the next few days my face felt hot whenever we were close, my
mouth went dry and my limbs became clumsy and unruly, as though
they were no longer under my command but that of some external,
malign force that was bent on making me look a complete idiot. I
didn't know what was happening to me.

In the space of a week you were no longer my childhood friend,
co-conspirator, faithful companion and brother of my heart, you were
you: an impossible, unsolvable puzzle that I struggled to comprehend.
Our friendly games became something else; our secrets were suddenly
sacred and unbearably vital; the sun would rise or set on a chuckle or
a frown. I hungered for your smile with every breath of my body and
jealously guarded every moment I could spend with you without the
irksome presence of another person – any person.

You definitely felt it then too. I know you did. I know it because
of what I am.

One day, as we were chasing each other across the lawn, you seized
my hand to pull me off-balance and I fell against you, only just keeping
upright by grabbing hold of your T-shirt and spinning us both in a
circle. We came to a stop face-to-face, breathless and waiting, and I
wanted to let go of you but my hands refused to move from your chest.

I don't know who leaned forward first, but I know that when our lips met with a clumsy bump and the salty taste of sweat, it was what we had both realised would happen in the end – what we had both wanted to happen, even if we hadn't admitted it to ourselves.

We stopped kissing and looked at each other, shy for the first time in our lives. I was very aware that I was touching your body, and although the sensation was pleasant there was a part of me that wanted to make a throwing-up face so you'd laugh and stop being so intense.

'Um, sorry,' you said, without letting go of my waist.

I grinned. 'Why?'

'I… I don't know why I did that.'

You looked guilty, the way you'd looked when you were caught stealing from the kitchen. The thought made me giggle.

You relaxed at the sound, and a tentative smile twitched across your lips. 'I just… felt like kissing you.'

'Well, I liked it,' I said, trying not to laugh too much in case you thought I was laughing at you.

'Oh. Really?'

I nodded, fascinated by the soft, downy hairs on your chin.

'Coz, I've wanted to do that for ages.'

'Really?' I echoed you. 'How long?'

You blushed. Neither of us had moved. I think we were scared to in case the spell was broken.

'Well, you know when I broke up with Hannah—'

'What?' I felt a twinge of guilt that she would find out I'd kissed you and be upset, but then it melted away as I realised I didn't care.

'Was that *why* you broke up with her?'

'Yeah.' Now you looked really sheepish. 'I felt harsh, but… I just really like you.'

'I like you too,' I said softly, the truth dawning on me at the same moment the words came out. 'It's just… weird. Coz we've been friends so long. I just never… *thought*. You know?'

You nodded and I saw your gaze flicker down to my lips and back up again. Your arms tightened around my waist and your fingers tapped a quick staccato rhythm against my spine. You always drummed them when you were nervous.

I shifted my hands to your shoulders, elated by my own daring.

'Can I kiss you again?' you asked, in your deepening man-voice.

I felt a surge of hormones so fierce that my fingers flexed involuntarily, and before I knew it your lips had found mine again, and it was strange but wonderful, less clumsy this time and so much better because I'd liked you for so long and now I knew that you felt the same about me.

We stood together in the sun with the rich, sweet scent of honeysuckle infusing the air around us, discovering new facets of each other that we'd never dared to imagine before, kissing and smiling and blushing with shy adoration, whispering promises that we fully expected to keep – assuming, like all young lovers do, that the rest of the world would simply get in line, that the universe was on our side.

But it wasn't, was it? That was the beginning and the end of what we were. That was how I became… me.

After that first kiss, it was less than a day before I found my full purpose. I had less than a day to revel in the new, blissful sensation that was the touch of your fingertips on my face. Less than a day to stare wonderingly into your eyes and notice the flecks of purple I'd never seen before. Less than a day to savour the soft and thrilling sweetness of your lips, as we redefined the boundaries that had existed between us for most of our young lives.

That night Elder Maia came for me, and I never even got to say goodbye. I was becoming Aphrodite, and they had to get me out of there.

It still makes me sad to think of it, even though I understand the reasons why they couldn't let me see you. It was the way it had to be, but… it all seemed so unfair, to be forced out into the world just when I'd found the biggest reason to stay. Though it might have been worse if I'd known it was coming.

In the deepening twilight, Maia led me across the pale gravel of the forecourt and up to the solid double gates under their filigree arch, set into the high brick wall that had formed the outer limits of my world for as long as I could remember. She pulled the right gate open with hardly any effort at all, the unresisting steel swinging back silently on well-oiled hinges.

Beyond there was a tiny walled courtyard with a stone building on the far side, like a gatehouse but with only a single door for an entrance. I stared at it for a moment, puzzled to find the gates didn't open directly onto the street as I'd always imagined they would. Then I realised what the building was. The smooth, worn stone that looked far more ancient than its surroundings. The weathered door decorated with obscure, primitive characters, so faded as to be barely discernible.

The Forge.

Maia led me to the centre of the courtyard and turned to face me. Her dark eyes were sad, but her smile was kind and encouraging.

'So…' I glanced nervously at the building. 'What do I do now?'

She exhaled slowly through her nose and patted my hand. 'It's not my place to tell you, anymore; we have nothing more to teach you. It's time to tread your own Path now, little lamb. Follow it bravely.

The Path of Love isn't easy; in some ways it's the most painful of all, and only the strongest of us are chosen to walk it. There will be times when your courage will fail you, but keep faith.'

'Love?' I gazed up at her. *I'm to be the Keeper of Love?* The thought made my stomach clench with excitement and apprehension.

Maia nodded, and for a moment I thought she was about to cry, but she straightened her back and cleared her throat, and when she looked back at me her eyes were dry. 'You have so many beautiful things ahead of you. And remember your purpose. Remember what's at stake.'

'What if I can't do it?' I asked, consumed by a sudden dread. I understood perfectly the responsibility that was being laid upon my shoulders – had spent my life preparing for it – but never before had it seemed such a monumental thing, and now my mind was filled with a thousand burning questions that I had never realised I needed answers to.

She shook her head. 'You won't fail. You can't. You have been chosen to walk this Path, and you won't be released from it until your purpose is fulfilled.'

'But… what happens if I *never* fulfil my purpose?'

A frown clouded her face. 'You know what would happen.'

I swallowed hard. I did know what would happen, it was just… somehow I hadn't quite believed that it could happen to *me*. It was one of the first things I'd ever learned here: the Keepers are the light and the hope of the next generation – the ones who mark out the Paths for the rest to follow. If a Keeper fails, their Attribute is lost to humankind, forever. So… no pressure or anything.

'Without you, there is no future,' Maia continued quietly. 'Without *you*, my dear, there is no love in the world, and without love…' She stared at me, and for just a second I saw a deep fear flash across her features. But then her expression cleared and she smiled at me again. 'But you shouldn't worry, sweet child. You were born for this Path. And you have the strength of all the past Keepers inside you; they will guide your steps.'

I let out a long breath and straightened my shoulders. *Of course I won't fail. This is my destiny.*

The door before me seemed to loom out of the thickening shadows, almost as though it were floating in space, unsupported by anything but its own strange power.

Maia tucked my hair back behind my ear. 'I promise, you'll know when you've found what you're looking for. There's no mistaking true love; it's not like anything else in the world. Stay true to your Path. And always remember the Hearthfire burns within you, wherever you go.' She kissed me on the forehead and stepped aside, releasing me.

It struck me that after this moment I would have to leave you behind forever – that I would never see you again, no matter how hard either of us wished it.

'Can I really never come back? Not even to visit?'

She didn't say a word but her expression told me everything. I knew the answer anyway: *There is no going back.*

I forced a smile and took a shaky breath, before turning away from her for the last time and letting my feet carry me up to the door that would open the way to the rest of my life. My fingers rested against the timeworn carvings, and I paused on the threshold as the image of your face floated across my inner eye.

I wish it didn't have to be this way. I willed the thought to fly to you so you'd know how hard it was for me to leave you behind. It was too late to go back. Already, it was too late. So instead I continued on, towards the future and away from you.

That was the night I lost you, and gained myself. From that moment on I was Aphrodite, the Keeper of Love. And I was alone.

*

I don't remember much about the weeks that followed. I existed in a dreamlike state for a long time, with no real knowledge of what I was doing or where I was going, and no clue how I was supposed to start on my Path. It's bittersweet, thinking back to that time, because, of course, I had already taken the first steps along it. I floated through space on a current of feeling, my mind replaying what I had learned and what it would mean.

The first thing that intruded on my consciousness was a sound. It was some weeks after I left Hearthfire – in fact, it must have been around midsummer because the sky had that particular warm shade of blue that only exists for a month of the year. The sound I heard was a song that was playing on the radio in a shop. Just as I was passing by the entrance the music came drifting out to me, and although it was only faint it brought me to an abrupt standstill. I stood, trembling, listening with every pore and hearing every word as though it was sung to me alone, like the universe was sending me a message.

That song brought back every second I had spent with you, every whisper and shriek of glee, every prank and promise, every touch and kiss and sweet, luminous glance. I felt a searing pain in my chest, reaching up to choke me as molten tears poured from my eyes. The music enfolded me as lovingly as your arms had, such a short time ago. It was 'Kiss the Rain' by Billie Myers, and it spoke of every aching beat of my poor, bruised little heart.

So, you see, you started all this, First Love. And although I don't think it was necessarily part of the plan for me, you started something else too. Because for everyone I've loved since you, there has always been a song – actually, in my mind, they've become Songs, capitalised – sometimes more than one. That's how I know when I've found someone who needs me. That's how I know when it's time to move on. The Songs are like a soundtrack to my life, signposts for me to follow when I don't know which way to turn. Perhaps it's a frail little way to impose order on something that often makes no sense at all, but it helps. It strings together all the stepping stones that make up my Path and forms a chain that I can follow back to the beginning.

Music is the friend I can always turn to for help, or for consolation when there is no help to be had. It's the only constant I have, in a life that's ever-changing. I know what it means now. I know why the music has stuck with me through everything, and you do too. But that part of the puzzle wasn't solved by then. All I knew was that I had lost something dear to me at the very moment in which I'd found it.

I'd like to say that losing you was the worst pain I've ever suffered, but sadly that wouldn't be true. Still, it was the first pain, and I'll never forget it.

I never got the chance to say it then, but I can say it now: Goodbye, First Love. No matter what came after, you will always be my dearest treasure.

Hidden Heart

Hidden Heart. You were in every way a revelation to me. I met you almost two years after my first foray into the outside world, and you opened my eyes to everything I could be... and everything I couldn't. I still dream of you sometimes. Not like in the beginning, but every once in a while I'll see your face as I wander the corridors of my mind and it makes me smile a little. And ache a little.

My time with you didn't dawn on me slowly like the turning seasons, but crashed into me all of a sudden, with no warning and no escape.

We were in New York City, at a party – my party, as it happens. Well, more my housemate Lizzie's party, but since I was living there I guess it was mine too.

I'd moved into her apartment on the Lower East Side about a month earlier, right at the end of March, after meeting her on a subway car. Normally nobody ever talks on those things, but I'd been sitting next to her and reading *The Bell Jar*, and as soon as she spotted it we got chatting. The rest is history.

She'd helped me get a job at a coffee house on Delancey Street, which was managed by a friend of hers from college. She was a few years older than me and far more worldly, and her parents were pretty well-off, although she never said so outright. She ran her own jewellery-making business from home, and alternated between long hours of intense concentration and brief explosions of energy, like a Mentos mint that's been dropped in a bottle of Coke. These days she might be thought of as a hipster, but this was the 90s and they hadn't been invented yet.

I felt out of place around all her loud, animated friends; they seemed so much cooler than I could ever hope to be, but I was determined to find a way to fit in. They always seemed to be having so much fun, and I figured that if I could work my way into their group, I could have lots of fun too.

I'm not sure why I'd decided on New York, exactly. I think after spending most of my life in semi-isolation, I wanted to go *big*, take the plunge. And I must have felt, somewhere deep inside me, that it was where I needed to be. I suppose it was the obvious choice for someone on a quest to find a love that could define a generation: might as well begin in the place where anything and everything is possible, right?

I loved living there: everything was bigger, brighter, faster; the people were slick and snappy, always in a hurry to get where they were going; the buildings loomed up all around – glass and steel and concrete pillars holding up the sky, alongside beautiful old gothic-style churches, proud monuments and elegant brownstones. Even the subway, with its flickering sepia lighting and musky odour of engine grease and stale sweat, had a certain glamour to it, at least in the beginning. If you're going to be on a subway, better the New York City subway than any other.

And the lights – well, the lights were something else. Glowing orange streetlights and soft yellow rows of windows, crisp white shop fronts and brightly beckoning bar signs in red, blue, green; flashing, migraine-bright neon and the fever dream of Broadway – a colossal mass of bulbs and tubes that outshone the stars, both in number and luminosity.

But I think what I really loved was the part of the city that lay beneath all that – below the concrete skin and flesh, the steel bones:

feeding through the arteries. The thing I loved most was its heart. Its lifeblood. New York is a city built on hope and hardship; on toil and struggle and suffering; on faith, triumph, the joy of success and the devastation of failure. New York is the land of dreams – those yet to be realised, those that have come true and those that have been crushed beneath its boot-heel – and of families, real people, forging their own realities in that unrelenting furnace of life. It was all right there to experience: a microcosm of humanity. I couldn't imagine anything more enchanting.

On the night of the party I was still a little overwhelmed by it all. I was sitting on one of the sofas in our bohemian-style living room, trying to keep up with conversations that were way over my head and that I could barely hear over the music streaming from the stereo. The room was lit by a few artfully positioned lamps, their soft light filtering out through the many-coloured scarves that were draped over the shades, and incense and cigarette smoke drifted lazily through the air, heightening the sense of otherworldliness. Even the people on the other sofa, just across the coffee table from me, looked ghostly: shadows flitting in and out of existence.

I was feeling a bit queasy, partly because of the cocktails Lizzie had been plying me with all night and partly because I was experiencing this strange sensation, like the world had been nudged slightly off-centre. I couldn't put my finger on it, but there was definitely something funny in the air.

As I sat there, surrounded by strangers whose lives seemed impossibly beyond my reach, I desperately tried to think of a way to insert myself into one of those conversations. What could I talk about? I didn't even know anything about myself, never mind the rest of the world. I remember worrying that I'd messed everything up already.

How could I be the Keeper of Love if I was too scared to even introduce myself to anyone?

I gave myself a mental slap and looked around the room.

There must be something I can talk about. I just need to think of an opening… come on, anything!

A song that I recognised began to play and I felt myself relax. With it came an odd sensation of déjà vu, like it had triggered something I was supposed to remember. I sat completely still, listening raptly, waiting to hear some clue in the words. I knew, in the quiet place in the centre of my being, that there was some message in it, and that my hearing it wasn't a coincidence.

It was a typical 90s song, sweet and simple with an underlying feeling of optimism. I know now that it was a Song, and that it's by Donna Lewis: 'I Love You Always Forever'. I was captivated by it. I saw all the images in my head as the words rang in my ears, and a wonderful sweet rush flooded my body.

A warm leg leaned against mine, and when I glanced up and saw you my stomach did a backflip. You were absolutely the coolest, most beautiful man I'd ever seen. You looked like you'd been pulled straight out of a surfing documentary: tanned face, sun-kissed blond hair that brushed the tops of your shoulders, and ocean-green eyes like a Caribbean lagoon. You were wearing one of those loose-fitting linen shirts with a pocket across the front and light stonewashed jeans with a hole in one knee.

As I looked at you, locked in my breathless paralysis, I felt like I was teetering on the brink of some profound chasm of revelation… but then it snapped closed and I was left feeling slightly sick and extremely nervous.

'Hi,' you said, meeting my gaze and flashing me a smile that seemed to make the room grow brighter.

'Hi yourself,' I answered, aware that I was grinning like an idiot. I tried to tone it down but found that my face was stuck that way.

You studied me for a moment, with a thoughtful expression that narrowed your eyes into two slivers of sparkling turquoise.

'You sound like you have an accent.'

I found myself laughing in response, without any clear idea why. I guess I was more tipsy than I'd thought.

'Doesn't everyone?'

Your smile broadened as you tucked a lock of hair behind your ear. 'Yeah, I guess so. I never really thought about it.'

'I take it you're from here?'

'No, I'm from Boston. Well, outside Boston, actually. Not much of a city boy until I came here.'

'Me neither – a city girl, I mean; I grew up in... the country.' *I sound so lame!*

'Huh. Two hicks in the big city. Probably the only ones Liz knows; you've seen the rest of her friends, right?'

I stole a glance at the people nearest to us: I could see your point. Everyone else looked so polished. Even the ones who were trying their hardest not to.

'Maybe she thought we needed to be introduced?' I heard the comment leave my mouth but had absolutely no idea where it had come from. It sounded flirtatious and confident, two qualities I was unaware of possessing.

Your eyes had widened with pleased surprise and were now dancing with humour, along with something else I couldn't quite place...

'I'd have to agree.'

I shrugged, as if I didn't care either way.

You laughed then, and the vibrant sound filled my ears, blending with the gentle pulse of the music.

I took a sip of my drink, despite the churning in my stomach, and locked gazes with you over the rim of my glass.

'Ouch, you're a mean woman,' you said. 'Not gonna make this easy for me, huh?'

I raised an eyebrow and said nothing, letting my expression answer for me. To tell the truth I was a little disconcerted at being referred to as a woman. I still felt very much a girl, and that was the first time anyone had told me any different.

'So, how long have you been in New York?' you asked, propping your elbow against the back of the sofa and leaning your cheek on your hand.

'Just a few weeks,' I answered. 'You?'

You snorted and looked away. 'Too long,' you said, taking a deep swig of beer from the bottle in your hand.

You seemed to ruminate on something, your perfect eyebrows knitting together to form a perfect frown, but then you snapped back to the present with a jolt, gave a brief, apologetic smile and went back to contemplating my face.

'So, what's a nice country girl of, what, twenty?'

'Eighteen.' I blushed, wondering if you really thought I was older or if you were just teasing me.

'Eighteen… doing hanging out with a bunch of pretentious assholes from the East Village? Shouldn't you be out raising hell somewhere?'

'Well,' I laughed nervously, 'I do live here. I'm Lizzie's flatmate.'

'Ahhh, *you're* the new girl.'

'Why do you say it like that?'

'Like what?'

'Like you've heard something about me.' I kept my tone light but my heart was racing. What had people been saying? Had I done something wrong already?

'Well, I *have* heard rumours,' you said, beckoning me towards you and glancing around conspiratorially.

I could tell from your expression that you were only teasing, and I relaxed, relieved. Obviously no one had been saying anything bad. In fact, they probably hadn't been saying anything at all, but I decided to play along. Any excuse to get closer to you was fine with me.

'Apparently,' you said with mock sincerity, 'anyone who touches you turns into a love-crazed lunatic, and then they run off into the night, never to be seen again.'

'Oh.' I nodded sagely. 'Yeah, that's true, that does happen a lot.'

'Really?'

'Mmm-hmm. It's this curse that was placed on me by an evil witch. I've come here to try and find a cure.'

'Wow. What a nightmare.'

'Yeah, it's really bad.' I toyed with a loose thread on the woven Afghan throw that covered the back of the sofa. 'An affliction, really.'

'I bet.' You watched my hand, momentarily entranced by the movement of my fingers. 'That's a real shame.'

'It is?' We looked back at each other in the same instant. 'Why's that?'

You didn't answer for a moment, but then you slowly moved closer, until we were almost sharing the same breath.

'What the hell,' you murmured, the words whispering over my lips. 'Totally worth it.'

I felt your mouth closing over mine, and an electric thrill rippled across every hair on my skin, as though the air around us was charged with latent energy. I let that feeling envelop me, fascinated by the sensations of your lips against mine, your tongue exploring my mouth, your fingers sliding beneath my ear.

Eventually we broke apart, and I was vaguely aware that my drink had been in my hand the whole time. Your eyes were locked on my face, and I read something in them that I'd never seen before, at least not directed at me.

'What's your name?' you asked.

'Aphrodite.' I held out my hand and laughed giddily when you assumed an expression of stern formality and clasped it in yours, shaking it firmly with strong, slender fingers.

'Huh. Cool name. Good to meet you, *Aff-ro-die-tee.*' You slowed down a little over the sounds, like you were trying them out for size, and your lips twitched with humour as you spoke.

'Good to meet you too. And nice job on the pronunciation.'

'Thank you. I'm an *educated* hick.'

I didn't let go of your hand, daring you to release mine first. Instead, you pulled me towards you again, relieving me of my glass and placing it on the table, your gaze never leaving mine.

Your mouth was hungrier this time, and your arms moved around my shoulders and waist, drawing my body to yours so that I felt your warmth through the thin fabric of my dress. I combed my fingers up through the hair at the back of your neck, gratified by the little shiver that ran through you in response to my touch.

I think that was the first time I realised the power I have; it scared and excited me in equal measure. I enjoyed the feeling of your firm back under my palm, and I imagined sliding my hand up under your shirt and pressing my fingers into the skin beneath… I broke off again, feeling self-conscious, suddenly remembering we were surrounded by people.

Just then the bottom dropped out of my stomach, and a cold sweat broke out on my forehead. I put my fingers to my lips, anxious that they would give me away.

'Are you OK?' you asked, and the question made me realise how thoroughly *not* OK I was.

'Um.' Saliva filled my mouth and I had a sudden, compelling urge to bolt. 'I just have to—'

I leaped up from the sofa and rushed down the hallway to the bathroom, clamping my hand over my mouth and desperately hoping no one was in there already. I almost sobbed with relief to find the door open, and I didn't even manage to close it before crouching over the salmon pink toilet bowl and retching more violently than I ever had before in my life. I heard a sound behind me but I couldn't spare the time to turn and see who it was. I was about to add abject misery to my list of ailments when I felt a cool hand on my back, and I heard Lizzie's low voice speaking somewhere above my head.

'Whoa! Are you OK?'

I groaned in answer before spewing up another bowlful of stomach contents.

'Damn. I should have kept an eye on you.'

I began to laugh, despite myself, and sat back on my heels, reaching up to pull the handle and flush my shame away. I was relieved to see that Lizzie had closed the door behind her.

'You did!' I croaked. 'You're the one who got me drunk in the first place!'

'Well, I didn't mean for you to hurl it all up again.' She sounded half-amused and half-outraged, but I could tell she was glad that I was coherent enough to answer back.

'No. Me neither,' I said ruefully, wiping my face with my hand. 'Things were just getting interesting.'

I heard footsteps in the hall outside and stared up at her in panic.

'Hey, is everything OK in there?'

It was definitely your voice. I spread my hands in silent helplessness. There was no way I could bring myself to face you just now.

'We're fine,' Lizzie called. 'Just had a little too much… fun.'

I felt bad. I didn't want to be *that girl* at the party. I wanted people to like me, not think I was some stupid kid who couldn't handle her alcohol.

'Is there anything I can do?' you called through the door again.

I was mortified to have made such a fool of myself in front of you. The fact that you were being nice about it only made it worse.

'No, we're good,' Lizzie assured you. 'We'll be out in a minute.'

I hid my head in my hands. Lizzie reached down and rubbed my back, making gentle sounds of sympathy.

'I'm fine,' I mumbled. 'I just… need a minute.'

'No, you need a breath mint.'

She ran the cold tap and filled a cup for me to drink from. I took a cautious swallow and wiped some water across my face, then tentatively pulled myself up and perched on the side of the bathtub. I felt horrible, but better than I had a few minutes before. It seemed like the worst was over.

Lizzie sat beside me on the edge of the bath, tucking my hair back behind my ear.

'I told you I'm not a big drinker.' I smiled wanly.

'No, you weren't kidding… Don't worry, we'll work on it.'

'Ugh!' I answered, screwing up my face in disgust. 'I'm never drinking again.'

'You should go lie down.'

I nodded, feeling dejected. 'Hey, can you do me a favour?'

'Sure, what do you need?'

'Just…' I sighed. 'Can you just make sure he doesn't see me like this? I'm such a mess.'

The look she gave me was pitying, but also a little amused. 'No problem. I got you covered, girl. You just get some sleep and feel better, OK?'

I hid behind the door as she pulled it open, and I could hear her talking to you further down the hallway before your voices receded and were swallowed by the music in the living room.

I peeked out to check the coast was clear and hurriedly shuffled across the narrow span of bare wooden planks to my room. I closed the door behind me and stood in the semi-darkness, my eyes growing accustomed to the gloom and tracing the outlines of my bed with its filigree headboard, the dressing table strewn with make-up, the oval mirror on top with its feather boa trim, and the dark lump in the corner that was actually a chair, buried under an avalanche of clothes.

The wedged heels I'd borrowed from Lizzie were pinching my toes, and I yanked them off and sighed as the tender skin met with the smooth coolness of the floorboards. My feet sank into the rug as I took the few short steps to my bed, and with intense relief I flopped down on the soft mattress and let my body relax, safe in the knowledge that Lizzie would take care of everything.

Well, that wasn't exactly the start of a beautiful romance, was it? The only way I could have messed it up more would have been if I'd actually thrown up on him.

I wallowed in the shame of it all for a while but soon grew drowsy, and thoughts of my disgrace were replaced by recollections of the new and thrilling feelings that had awoken within me in the moments leading up to that cringe-worthy conclusion. I let myself be lulled by the sweet caress of memory, and I slipped into pleasant dreams of sea-green eyes and soft lips from which I never wanted to wake up.

*

It was several weeks before I saw you again, but not a day went by in between when I didn't think of you.

It was a Saturday morning, and I was walking down Delancey Street on my way to my new job, my gaze flitting between the bright patchwork of awnings, billboards and hanging signs that swung above the shop doorways, and the scrum of noisy traffic that lurched past in halting, erratic spurts, filling the air with industrious rumblings and honkings and the acrid tang of exhaust fumes.

As I threaded my way through the bustling crowd I felt a nudge against my elbow, and I glanced up to see you walking along next to me.

The street seemed to vanish and I stopped in my tracks, blinking in thrilled surprise.

'Hey, stranger,' you said, flashing that impossibly self-assured smile. 'I thought it was you.'

'Hi,' I answered, my mind scrambling to find something clever to say but instead just tying itself in knots.

'Mind if I walk with you?'

'No, of course not.'

'Where are you going?'

'Just work.' I gestured at my uniform and felt suddenly self-conscious. The bright red skirt felt far shorter than usual, and the breeze was stirring the fabric around my legs in an alarmingly lively manner.

'Oh. Well, I'll keep you company... I was actually hoping I'd run into you.'

Your eyes were focused on the pavement ahead, and I was glad you didn't see the sudden blush that bloomed across my cheeks.

'Oh... really? I thought maybe—' *No! Don't remind him about the puking!* 'Um... How come?'

'Well, just... I wanted to see how you were. You know, after the um...'

I cringed and you laughed, but not unkindly.

'I can't believe I did that.'

'Hey, it happens,' you said, giving my elbow another gentle nudge.

'Ugh, well, I wish it didn't happen to me!'

'Yeah, we all do when it's us. We never learn though.'

We walked in silence for a minute, and I tried to filter out the smells of rotting food and car exhaust to focus on the more pleasant aromas of bacon, fresh bagels and rich ground coffee that wafted in brief spurts from the coffee houses and food trucks as we passed. Even at that time of the morning the air was already growing warm, and I felt sorry for the food vendors sweltering away in their metal boxes, surrounded by hotplates and spitting griddles.

As we approached Marco's – the coffee house where I worked – I desperately tried to think of something to say that would lead to me seeing you again. Thankfully, you spared me the trouble.

'What are you doing later?'

'Um... nothing.' The amount of effort it took to sound casual was ridiculous.

'Do you want to do something? Together?' You smiled hopefully.

We came to a halt outside, and I gave a laid-back shrug. 'OK. I'd be up for that.'

Yes, yes, yes, yes, yes!

'Great. What time do you get off?'

'Around four?' *Why am I saying that like it's a question?*

'OK, sounds good. I'll meet you here?'

I couldn't help but grin as I nodded my assent. I was ecstatic that you were asking me out, especially considering the disaster that had been our first meeting. I drank in the details of your face – the sharp cheekbones and full, expressive lips, the perfect arches of your eyebrows and the soft waves of spun gold that framed your features like a painting… I had never wanted anything so much in my life.

You glanced at the wine-red awning, digging your hands into the pockets of your jeans. 'Cool. See you later.'

I nodded again, attempting to school my expression. 'OK. See you later.'

Your next move caught me completely unawares: you took my face in your hands and gave me a soft, lingering kiss that turned my insides to goo, then pulled away and looked at me, running your thumb across my cheekbone.

The world was tilting off-centre again, like it had the night we met, and as I gazed into your eyes I felt something inside me opening up, unfolding, like a spring flower in the sun. It was such an intimate thing, sharing those breaths with you – the air between us mingling, ours and no one else's. It wasn't the clumsy, furtive exchange of two teenagers; it was direct, immediate and adult. My first grown-up kiss. The whole of reality had been suddenly reduced to the outline of your face.

'Have a good day,' you said, releasing me.

I had no words to respond, so I simply swallowed, nodded again and somehow retained enough composure to turn and walk into work, my legs threatening to buckle beneath me with every step I took.

I spent the day floating in a semi-stupor. It was the longest six hours of my life.

You were standing waiting for me outside when I clocked out, and my stomach did a little dance as you looked at me, smiling.

'Hey. How was work?' you asked.

I shrugged. I didn't want to talk about work.

'Come on, I've got a surprise for you,' you said, holding out your hand for me to take.

I slipped my fingers through yours, and the thrill of touching you again sent a delicious flood of warmth through my whole body, starting in the middle of my chest and emanating outwards like rays from the sun. I noticed that you had a large, full-looking backpack with you. You saw me eyeing it and tapped the side of your nose, saying nothing.

I felt like skipping as we made our way through the seething mass of people, and I tipped my face back to savour the kiss of the late-spring sunshine on my skin. It was a gorgeous day, and even though the afternoon was fading it had the feeling of a bright summer morning – all promise and anticipation.

Your presence seemed to augment my senses, and I was aware of every colour in the tapestry of life around us; the sound of every voice, car horn and rumbling engine; the myriad smells of sweating bodies, hot tarmac, fresh coffee and a million other things I couldn't identify. More than anything, I was aware of the places where my skin touched yours – our palms pressed together, our fingers intertwined, our forearms lightly touching and the arteries in our wrists pulsing against each other. All the while, my mind was whirring, spinning almost as

I bounced along beside you. I couldn't help trying to guess what you had in store for me; I was tingling with excitement.

I didn't have long to wait. We reached Washington Square Park and made our way across the lawn, among the tall, leafy trees that created a cool oasis of green shade only a breath away from the busy streets. We found an unoccupied spot on the springy grass, within sight of the tall white spear of cascading water that shot straight up from the fountain in the heart of the park. You pulled off the backpack and produced a blanket from inside, shaking it out and laying it neatly on the grass.

'Are you hungry?'

'Starving!'

'Well, that's good; otherwise I'm going to have to eat all this by myself.'

You started unpacking the bag. There were fresh bagels with cream cheese, smoked salmon and cucumber; plump cherry tomatoes, still on the vine; olives in a lemon and herb marinade – which I couldn't bring myself to eat since I still hadn't acquired the taste; fresh orange juice; huge chunks of cherry pie and some delicious, rich coffee in a thermos flask.

'Wow,' I said, once it was all laid out on the blanket.

You shrugged, like it was no big deal, and handed me a plastic plate. 'Dig in.'

'Wait,' I hesitated, peering at you suspiciously. 'Are you just making sure I don't have an empty stomach in case we end up drinking again?'

You laughed. 'You're funny.'

I flushed, pleased by the remark, and proceeded to tackle the nearest bagel.

We ate and drank, swapped stories of our childhoods and compared notes on our experiences of life in the big city, bonding over our mutual otherness. Of course, I didn't mention anything about my unusual upbringing; I just kept my tales of home suitably vague and missed out the parts that might seem too strange to pass unnoticed.

'So, what do you do?' I asked, after swallowing a large mouthful of cherry pie. The crystallised sugar made my teeth tingle, and my fingers were covered in red, sticky goop, which I licked off as you answered.

'I fix up cars.'

'Ahh, mechanic? I wouldn't have guessed.'

I didn't want to talk about what you did for a living; it was such a banal thing to say, but my nerves had got the better of me and it was the first thing that had sprung to mind. What I was really interested in was what made you laugh and cry and rage, what you longed for in your soul, what you loved – more than anything I wanted to know that – but I didn't know how to ask. Where was that playful tease from the party? She'd been great, until…

'No?' You raised an eyebrow, inviting further comment.

I sat back, resting my hands on the blanket behind me and studying you. *Come on, calm down. Focus. You managed it before; stop overthinking everything and just talk.*

'You seem a bit too… suave,' I mused, beaming as you snorted with amusement. *Yes!*

'Suave?' You shook your head before tilting it back, your gaze traversing the blue sky above as you considered my assessment. 'What did you think I was, a secret agent?'

We both laughed at that and I was pleased to have tickled you.

'Maybe. Or a poet or something.'

'A *poet*?'

'Yeah. Not a pretentious one, though, a real one. Well, maybe a *bit* angsty, but still good.'

'Angsty, huh? You might be right about that. Not about the poet thing, though; words are not my department.'

'Hmm, well, that's what I would have guessed.' I took a sip of orange juice and studied you surreptitiously while you cast a glance across the park. You didn't look like a mechanic to me – but then, what did a mechanic look like? There was something else... 'So what *is* your department? You don't seem like a nuts-and-bolts kind of guy.'

You shrugged. 'This and that. I like playing around with machines so it suits me OK.'

What am I not getting? 'Well, I still think there's a poet in there somewhere. Or a musician maybe; you look like you should be the lead guitarist in a band.'

'Nope. Never picked up a guitar in my life. I'm really not all that interesting.'

'Yes you are!' I flushed as you caught my eye. I hadn't meant for that to come out quite as vehemently as it had, but it was too late to take it back now. 'I think you are,' I followed up quietly. *Does my face look as red as I think it does?*

You sighed, cocking your head to one side and regarding me with something bordering on affection. 'I like you.'

Such a simple statement, but to me it was like a choir of angels breaking through the clouds and pouring symphonies of heavenly music down into my waiting ears. To think that someone so gorgeous, and cool, and just... *gorgeous* was into me – *liked* me – made my skin tingle all over. And the fact that you were a few years older made you that much more *want*able; of all the women you could have chosen to take on a picnic, you chose me. Me! I could have squealed for joy.

Instead I shrugged and gave you a cheeky smile. 'You're OK.'

You let out an exasperated growl and buried your face in your hands.

And suddenly, I felt like I was the one in control.

We stayed in the park until sunset, watching as the clumps of people started to thin out and the buildings became a sea of glow-worms twinkling against the deep blue-black of the sky. You threw the blanket around my shoulders as we made our way back across the grass, and I was touched that you'd thought of it.

As we turned onto Bowery Street I sensed that the date was coming to an end. I wasn't ready to say goodbye just yet, and in a rush of boldness I decided to make my wishes known.

'I want to see where you live,' I said, nudging you with my elbow.

You looked down and draped your arm around me. 'Yeah?'

I nodded, feeling my stomach knot with excitement. I couldn't believe I'd really said that out loud, or that you might actually agree. And if you did, then did that mean we would… *Am I ready for that? What if I chicken out?*

'What, now?'

'Sure, why not?' I said, as though I was simply agreeing to your suggestion. 'No time like the present.'

Oh crap, this is really happening. But also – yay, this is really happening! I'd never been so direct about anything before. I felt like I was jumping off a cliff into unknown waters; it was thrilling.

You chuckled, amused by something you chose not to share, and nodded obligingly. 'OK. It's not far. You mind walking?'

I shook my head, smiling happily. I would have done just about anything to remain in your presence at that point.

Your place was about twenty minutes away from mine and Lizzie's – down towards the East River, a stone's throw from the Manhattan Bridge. The evening was clear, and the rest of existence seemed to fade away as our feet ate up the pavement. We chatted and laughed, and the city transformed around us as the evening lull gave way to the growing hum of nightlife.

Girls in high-waisted jeans and tight, cropped tops skipped past in groups of three or four, interspersed with little knots of young men with long, dishevelled hair, backwards baseball caps and oversized plaid shirts. Every once in a while we passed other couples – lost in their own little bubbles – and families in sports shirts or evening dress, making their way towards whatever the night had in store.

Before I knew it, we were there: Your Place. Suddenly, it all seemed very real.

You lived on the fifth floor of an apartment block with two other guys, both of whom happened to be out that night. The living room was clearly a man-cave, dominated by a giant, worn leather sofa, which was flanked by two matching armchairs and faced the big-screen TV that sat on a stand by the wall. A couple of games consoles were tucked beside the stand on the laminate wood floor, and in the centre of the room stood a large, square, battle-scarred coffee table. The walls were a sage-green colour and were dotted here and there with posters of grunge bands and Tarantino films, and the whole place carried a faint aroma of weed and beer. I thought it was ridiculously cool.

The kitchen was visible through an opening in the wall, and a kitchen counter separated the two rooms. In front of that stood a large stereo on a low table, with stacks of CDs piled up on the floor underneath.

You grabbed a couple of beers from the fridge, handed one to me and flicked the stereo on. I didn't recognise the music – something mellow and bassy – but it was exactly the kind of thing I would have expected you to like.

I followed you across the living room, pausing as you snatched up a tobacco tin from the coffee table, and over to one of the window seats, where we sat looking out at the lights of passing cars and the people on the twilit street below us while you rolled a joint. I watched your fingers move, entranced by their deftness. I sipped at my drink to calm my nerves, but then reminded myself not to overdo it and set the bottle down at my feet on the floor.

You slid the top half of the window down, letting in the cool evening air, and crossed your legs in front of you before sparking up the joint and leaning your forearms on the frame, blowing a thick swirl of smoke out into the night.

I admired the shape of your shoulder and watched the play of light on the muscles of your arm as you brushed some stray tobacco off your jeans. The glow from the streetlights seemed to sharpen your features, adding contrast to the planes and shadows of your face. There was nothing I disliked about you; you were flawless. Your face could have been the face of a film star. And you were so cool...

'So. Aphrodite,' you said, turning your head towards me, 'what made you move to New York City?'

I reached for the joint when you offered it and took a tentative drag; I wasn't used to smoking and I was afraid of what would happen if I had too much, but I wanted you to think of me as an adult, not some inexperienced kid. I wanted to prove that I was your equal – worthy of your attention – so if you were getting high then I was getting high with you.

I passed it back to you, considering the question as I exhaled and leaning my back against the windowpane.

'I just... wanted to explore, I suppose. This seemed like a good place to start.'

You nodded, frowning thoughtfully as your gaze skimmed the façade of the building opposite us. 'It is a good place to start.'

'What about you? Why did you move here?'

You shrugged. 'Small town blues, I guess. And work.'

You passed me the joint again and I held onto it for a moment, studying you.

'Not enough cars to fix back home?'

'Not much of anything back home. And I... well, there were other reasons, but things didn't work out.'

A flicker of bitterness passed across your face, and your eyebrows drew together for a brief second, creating a crease of deeper shadow. I had an urge to reach out and smooth it away, but it was gone as suddenly as it appeared.

'Why, what happened?' *A woman?*

'You have an insatiable curiosity.' You didn't sound annoyed, more amused, and the darkness that had clouded your features evaporated completely as you regarded me in the silence that followed that comment.

The air stirred between us as the night breeze whispered through the window. I suppressed a shiver as it played across my skin, my imagination replacing the currents of air with the gentle flutter of kisses. I couldn't help but look at your mouth then – at your lips which seemed eternally on the verge of twitching with humour. I really wanted to kiss them, the way we'd been kissing the night we first met, like nothing else existed in the whole wide world.

You were so close I could detect the sharp, clean scent of your aftershave, so close I could see the soft blond hairs rising along your arm in response to the breeze. I remembered the feeling of those arms around me – firm and inescapable – and I wanted nothing more than to feel that again; all I had to do was lean forwards a little...

I realised you were still looking at me and I reined in my wayward thoughts, dragging my mind back to the conversation at hand.

'Yeah.' I took a drag and passed the joint back, feeling more relaxed now that my brain had ceased its whirring. The world had grown softer around the edges. 'Like the Elephant's Child.'

'You know Rudyard Kipling?'

'Of course. And if you do too then I was right about you: you're not just a nuts-and-bolts kind of guy.'

Your eyes crinkled at the corners when you smiled, and the breath caught in my chest as I took in the million tiny details that, together, made you so unutterably beautiful.

'You're smart, you know that?' You raised one eyebrow slightly.

'Yep.' I grinned, knitting my fingers together and stretching my arms out in front of me until my shoulders clicked. Why did everything suddenly feel so wonderful?

'And modest.' You were teasing me now. I could see the laughter in your eyes but it didn't matter because you weren't being unkind.

I nodded solemnly. 'I totally underestimate my own brilliance.'

There it was again – the uncertain, self-conscious girl was being shoved to one side by a confident flirt, and I could only sit back and watch in amazement as that part of me took over.

My mock-arrogance must have caught you off-guard because you choked on the lungful of smoke you'd just inhaled and covered your mouth with your forearm, consumed by a fit of coughing. Your eyes were watering when it finally passed but you still looked amused, shaking your head as you wiped away the tears and taking a couple of deep breaths before throwing me a look of mild admonition.

I responded with an expression of wide-eyed innocence and you broke into a chuckle, dropping the act. I liked hearing you laugh; it made me feel warm and light-headed... although that time it could have been the weed.

You finished the joint and threw the end away, a tiny red dot sailing through the air and out of sight. You sat still for a moment, searching the darkness, then turned to look at me with that expression I'd seen as we had sat on the sofa in my apartment.

And then you leaned in and kissed me softly on the mouth.

The contact stirred my insides instantly, and I sucked in air through my nose as I felt your arms encircle my waist. I could hear the blood rushing through my head, and for a terrifying second I thought I might pass out, but then the adrenaline kicked in and I was suddenly and completely rooted in the present, every nerve in my body tingling so insistently I thought I might explode.

You pulled me closer and I slid onto your lap, wrapping my legs around your waist. Your kisses became more urgent and I could feel my body responding, aching for more, more, more as your hands pressed and pulled at the skin beneath my thin cotton T-shirt. I gasped as your lips fluttered across my neck, tracing the line of my jaw before returning to my mouth. I started pulling at your clothes, clumsy in my eagerness, impatient to feel your naked skin against mine.

Your fingers clenched around my thighs and you stood upright, lifting me with you.

'Come on,' you said. 'I'll show you my room.'

We carried on kissing as you half-carried, half-walked me down the short hallway to your bedroom, shoved open the door and let us both topple onto the soft, yielding mattress. My fingers were in your hair, raking your shoulders and back, unbuttoning your jeans and clenching spasmodically against your straining flesh. My heart pounded joyously inside my chest and my blood sang with happiness as I finally got to experience what it was to be loved by you – and in the soft yellow light that spilled through the doorway you taught me things about myself I had never even imagined. In those moments I felt more alive than in all the years of my life that had gone before.

You ran a bath afterwards and we soaked for a little while, before we were swept up once again in a wave of desire and sent a frothing flood of water all over the bathroom floor. We paused long enough to laugh at the unwitting destruction we were causing, but were far too preoccupied to spare it more than a second's thought.

In the morning I woke to the sound of thumping on the door. I was completely disorientated, thinking it must be Lizzie, then realised where I was and shook you gently awake.

You smiled a self-satisfied smile and stretched like a cat beside me. I was instantly aware of how naked I was – how naked we both were, bare skin brushing up against bare skin – and of the sour taste in my mouth, the clamminess of my armpits and the tangy, rich scent of you… or maybe of us. I was shy of you seeing my body now that it was light, and tucked the sheet more securely around my chest. It was an intriguing experience, waking up next to someone: in a way it felt like a continuation of the night before, an extension of our date, but also completely different. It was strange and wonderful, and… precious. I didn't want it to end. I wanted to stay forever and ever, and forget anything else existed.

'Yeah?' you called at the door thumper.

'Hey, man, what the hell happened in the bathroom?'

I giggled and you snorted with amusement. The little wrinkles around your nose made me blush as memories of the night before flooded my mind… the way your face looked when you were—

'Sorry! I'll clean it up later.'

'Oh.' The voice sounded uncertain. 'You got company?'

I nibbled on your neck and slid my hand under the sheets, inhaling the scent of your skin in the warm spot I'd discovered just beneath your ear. You groaned softly and turned to me, forgetting to respond as we lost ourselves once more.

It was past noon by the time we finally decided to get up, and I was desperate for a pee. I pulled on my T-shirt and a pair of your boxer shorts before bolting for the bathroom, waving a cheery hello to your two housemates as I scooted across the living room behind the sofa.

'Hi!' I called, glancing over my shoulder. 'Nice to meet you!'

One of them had a game controller in his hand and the other was twiddling idly on a battered guitar. I must have taken them by surprise since neither of them said anything in response, and I heard your laughter follow me as you emerged from your bedroom.

After I'd washed my face, gargled some mouthwash and dragged my fingers through my hair, I went back into the living room to find you sitting in one of the big, sagging armchairs, a freshly rolled joint in one hand and a cup of coffee in the other. I squeezed in beside you, smiled shyly at your friends who were sitting at either end of the sofa and looked over at the TV to see what game they were playing. I didn't recognise it; all the first-person shooters looked the same to me.

You nodded towards a mug of steaming coffee on the table in front of me and I gratefully retrieved it, sipping carefully as I watched the figures on the screen. You offered me a smoke as well but I waved it away; I couldn't quite face the idea of smoking first thing in the morning – well, first thing in the afternoon. You shrugged and passed it across to the guitar player before slipping your arm around my waist and pulling me deeper into the chair.

'Aren't you going to introduce us?' asked the guy playing the game, his voice heavily accented in a thick Brooklyn drawl. He had short, dark hair and a beard to match, and he looked like he'd be tall when he stood up. He didn't look away from what he was doing, but turned his head slightly to indicate he was listening.

'Oh yeah, this is Nick, that's Alex and this is Aphrodite.'

'This is who?' asked Nick, sparing me a cursory glance.

'*Aphrodite,*' I repeated shyly. 'Aph is fine.'

'Cool name. Where'd you pick that up?' asked Alex, twanging out a chord before giving me a thorough inspection. He had a pierced eyebrow, and a curly brown mop of hair which protruded from underneath his loose grey beanie.

I hesitated, a little flummoxed by the question, but you came to my rescue. 'Where do you think, idiot?'

I swallowed nervously but Alex just laughed, and I took an instant liking to him. I had a feeling we were going to be friends.

'OK, stupid question. What I should have said was, "My, what an unusual name, how extraordinary."' He put on a hoity-toity voice while he said it, like a bad English accent, and I giggled.

Nick took the joint from Alex and passed him the controller, then sat back on the sofa and studied me more closely. 'Do I know you?'

'Umm. Maybe?'

'Where d'you work?'

'At Marco's Coffee House. Down on Delancey?'

'No, that's not it... Oh, wait, weren't you at Liz's party?'

I sighed and rested my chin on my hand, knowing what was coming as soon as I responded. 'Yeah... I sort of... live there.'

'Ohhhh!' His eyes lit up with malicious amusement. 'You're the roommate, huh?'

'Yeah, yeah, laugh it up,' I said, beckoning with my hand.

'Well, that's one way of putting it,' Nick answered, folding his arms across his chest and grinning. He glanced from me to you and back again. 'Be honest, was it because of this guy? I'd be throwing up too if he tried sticking his tongue down my throat.'

'No,' I answered mildly. 'Actually, it was a relief to meet someone from out of town; I've heard you New Yorkers are terrible kissers.'

You burst out laughing and held up your hand for me to high-five. 'Touché!'

'Don't knock it 'til you've tried it, sweetheart.' Nick winked at me.

'Hey!' you protested, forming a barrier around me with your arms. 'Stop making moves on my woman, asshole!'

My woman? When did that happen?

I was delighted to hear it but I wasn't sure how seriously you meant it, and a quick glance at you did nothing to enlighten me; I had absolutely no clue what was going on inside your head.

You took me to get breakfast – or lunch I suppose – at a deli on East 5th Street, and then walked me to the park where I was meeting Lizzie for some sunbathing. It took us a while to pick her out among the scattered clumps of park-goers that dotted the swathe of lawn, but eventually I spotted her, stretched out on a blanket alongside Mikey and Julia, whom I'd met a few times before, and a couple of her other friends.

I really wished you were sticking around for the afternoon but you said you had stuff to do, so after chatting to everyone for a couple of minutes you stood up, dusted the grass off your jeans and leaned over to give me a kiss goodbye.

'Thank you,' you whispered in my ear.

I must have flushed red because my face suddenly felt hot, and I peeked up at you.

'Thank *you*,' I answered cheekily, and maybe a little more loudly than I had intended.

You chuckled before bidding everyone goodbye, and the second you were out of earshot Lizzie sat up from her sunbathing position and swiped at me with her hand.

'Oh my God! Did he just *thank* you?'

I blushed all the way up to my ears as I received appraising looks from two of the girls who were sitting with us.

'Mind your own business!' I replied, glaring at her.

'Man. Here I was thinking I needed to look after you when I should have been asking for tips! Are all the guys you sleep with so polite the next morning?'

I let out a snort and quickly covered my mouth with my hand, dismayed and delighted, as always, by her bluntness.

'*All* the guys? How many do you think I've slept with? And no, since you asked; he's the only one who's ever said that. He's special.'

She lowered herself back onto her elbows, squinting up at the sky and cocking her head to one side like she was listening for something.

'Well then, aren't you the lucky one?' She lifted a leg and poked at my calf with her toes. 'Look at you, smiling all over your face. You look like the cat that got the cream.'

I grabbed at her foot, threatening to tickle it, and tried not to look too pleased with myself. She was right though, that was how I felt. My heart soared every time I thought back over the last twenty-four hours.

*

The next few weeks were an intoxicating blend of intense delight when I was with you and even more intense longing when I wasn't. On the days when I couldn't see you I usually called you after work, and you always sounded happy to hear from me, even though it was only ever me doing the calling. You rarely came to mine and Lizzie's apartment except for the occasional party, but it didn't matter because Nick and Alex had decided I was acceptable company, and I spent nearly every Saturday night and Sunday afternoon hanging out and playing video games in your living room. I liked them better than Lizzie's friends, who were always nice enough to me but for her benefit more than mine. I never really felt like I fitted in around them; they were all up-and-coming twenty-somethings with business degrees and respectable parents. They drank wine and ate olives and hummus, watched arthouse films and liked jazz fusion – well, they said they did, anyway. They were kind and they did their best to include me in conversations, but most of it was way over my head.

But it wasn't like that with you guys. I felt like we were all on the same level. Alex was a bartender at a cocktail bar in Little Italy, and Nick worked as a driver at his uncle's delivery firm. None of us were rich or sophisticated, but we knew what we liked and we definitely knew how to have a good time.

It turned out Alex was a pretty decent guitarist, and even though his guitar looked like a piece of crap, apparently it was actually quite a good one. He'd often be strumming away in between turns on the PlayStation, or sometimes we'd all be sitting around talking and he'd be plucking out sweet little melodies in the background.

One night, as I was kicking Nick's arse on *Street Fighter*, Alex started playing a song I knew and I began to hum along, unaware that I was singing at the same time as frantically mashing buttons. After one last burst I finally managed to get my character to pull off a super combo, depleting the last of Nick's health and sending his character sprawling on the floor.

I threw the controller down on the sofa and raised my arms. 'Ha ha! You lose!' I looked around at the three of you, and you were all staring at me in silence. 'What?'

'When did you turn into Aretha Franklin?' Alex was looking at me as if I'd suddenly become a completely different person.

'Huh?' I glanced at you, hoping for clarification.

'I didn't know you could sing,' you said, giving me a soft little smile. There was something sad and almost wary about your expression, as though you weren't sure what to make of me in light of this new information.

'Oh. Well…' I sat back against the sofa cushions, hugging my knees to my chest. 'I mean, yeah, I can sing – everybody can *sing*… Why are you guys looking at me like that? Stop it, it's weird.'

Nick grinned, whacking me companionably on the leg. 'You're in the wrong job, sweetheart. You need to get up on a stage.'

You were still watching me, your hands poised over the book on your lap that you were using to make a joint on. You realised I was studying you and shrugged off whatever was on your mind, throwing me an encouraging smile. 'Seriously, babe, you should get up there with Alex at the open mic night. They'd love you.'

'You think?'

I'd never considered it before. I wasn't a singer… I wasn't anything really, not in the way other people were. I didn't have any career aspirations; that wasn't part of my Path.

'Definitely!' Alex said, his fingers plucking out a sweet, sad chord. 'Here, try this one…'

*

Over the following months Alex took me along to quite a few open mic nights, and you were right, they did seem to love me. I started to enjoy being up onstage; it was fun, once I got over being scared, which I think happened around halfway through the first song. I only ever went if you were willing to go too; I never wanted to do anything that would take me away from you, and seeing your face in the crowd always made me feel less nervous.

Alex started teaching me a little bit of guitar too, although it was far harder than it looked and I was pretty terrible at it. I stuck to singing for the most part – to everyone's relief, I think – and we became quite a slick little double act, if I do say so myself.

You were always praising me and insisting I go to practice, even when I wasn't really in the mood, and you were careful not to disturb us when we were playing in the living room, but sometimes I had this sneaking feeling that you were less than thrilled when I was enthusing about a new song or a special moment onstage. It definitely wasn't anything to do with Alex – he wasn't into girls so that was never an issue – more the music itself, or maybe just the fact that I was good at something… I don't know. I'm still not sure if it was even really there, but after everything that happened I wonder if there was a part of you that struggled with that side of me. Maybe you were worried it would take me away from you.

A few times I tried encouraging you to try out something new – art classes or community theatre or martial arts – but you always just shrugged and changed the subject, and that was the end of that. You didn't really have any hobbies apart from playing video games, and I thought it strange considering how smart you were that you never seemed to want anything more out of life. I didn't question you about it, or about anything really; you could do no wrong, so if you were content working as a mechanic and hanging out with your friends then obviously that was the right decision.

As the weeks passed by, with the summer greenery fading into the russets and yellows of autumn, I started to believe that I truly meant something to you. Even though you were never one to talk about your feelings – at least not the ones beneath the surface – whenever we walked down the street together, or sat next to each other, or lay half-asleep in bed, your fingers were always laced through mine, like you wanted reassurance that I wasn't going anywhere.

I cared more about that than I'd ever cared about anything in my young life; I was enthralled by the feeling of being totally immersed in another person. Looking back, I think I was more in love with the idea of you than who you really were. After all, I didn't *see* who you really were; I didn't see that you were human just like everyone else, with your insecurities and flaws and regrets. Part of that was because you hid them from me, but even if you'd confessed every dark, ugly secret and fear in your heart it probably wouldn't have registered. You were everything I thought I wanted – my dreams distilled into a perfect, irreproachable being – and nothing would have persuaded me otherwise, not even the truth. It felt like we belonged together, like we had a connection that would last forever and ever. You were the centre of my universe: the star around which I was happy to orbit. If that wasn't true love, what was?

One thing I'd never been prepared for during my time at Hearthfire was how incredibly *real* it all felt. I was hopelessly and helplessly in love with you – as I suppose any girl that age would have been – but it was more than that. I think what I'm trying to say is that I never expected it to be so all-consuming, to occupy every thought at every moment of every day. I hadn't understood that to be a Keeper meant you *became* the thing you embodied: I didn't just *feel* love, I *was* love. And I was still such an innocent. Blissfully naïve. I'd spent years being taught theories and principles, but I didn't have the first clue about *life*, about real connections with real people, or about pain. I'd felt it, once, and at the time I thought that meant I understood it, but I really had no idea back then just how much the heart could hurt. That's not something you can teach in a classroom.

One Friday, after I finished my shift at Marco's, I walked down to meet you at the garage where you worked so we could go for pizza before heading to your place. When I got there one of the other guys directed me round to the back, and I spotted you from across the yard, peering under the rear wheel arch of a sleek red coupé, while a guy on a long sliding board on the ground pointed something out to you underneath the chassis.

You glanced up as I approached and touched the guy on the elbow, excusing yourself, before making your way across the oil-stained concrete.

'Hey, babe,' you said, wiping your sleeve across your forehead, which only served to smear more dirt over the existing layer of grime.

'Hey,' I answered, wanting to kiss you but uncertain whether I should in front of your workmates. 'You ready to go?'

You nodded. 'Almost. Just got to finish up here and get this crap off my hands.' You held them up and frowned at the black streaks that coated your arms up to the elbow.

'And your face,' I said, pointing with amusement at a smudge on your nose.

You reached out, threatening to wipe some of it off on me, and I danced away, laughing. You dropped your hands and beckoned me closer with a finger, and I warily approached to lay a kiss on your lips, which were probably the least grimy part of you.

You stood looking at me in silence, contemplating. 'You wanna see something cool?'

I nodded, intrigued.

'Come on.' You turned and waved me after you.

We crossed the yard and you led me into a large shed, past several vintage-looking cars to a shadowy area right at the back. I followed you over to a large, boxy campervan that was painted in patches of green and black, like camouflage.

You glanced back at me, your expression strangely apprehensive, before taking hold of the handle on the side door and yanking it open.

My jaw dropped as I peered inside. 'Wow!'

It was obviously in the process of being converted, but I could see the layout taking shape. Large sections of MDF had been cut and inserted to create shelving at head height, a long, bench-like seat underneath the opposite window and a little square cubicle further towards the back. A small wood burner squatted in one corner by the rear doors, the chimney rising up to the roof where a hole had been cut for it to fit through.

'This is awesome!' I said, grinning enthusiastically. 'Whose is it?'

You reached up and patted the roof in a protective sort of way.

'It's mine,' you said. 'I've been working on it.'

'Well, I really like it. It's going to be great when it's finished.'

'Yeah.' You smiled – a small, bittersweet smile. 'It's my ticket out of here.'

My heart stopped at those words: you weren't showing me because you wanted to impress me or confide in me; you were showing me because you wanted me to know that someday – maybe soon – you were going to leave. And I wasn't going to be invited along for the ride.

I suddenly remembered all those tiny fragments of conversations – the very first time we met, the night you took me to see your place, the day I started singing, and every time I'd asked you about your life before New York – when I'd seen glimpses of the unhappiness that lay beneath your cool, untroubled surface. I didn't know why those moments should spring to mind now, but they made me deeply uneasy; they made me think you'd been planning to leave all along, and I was just, what, a distraction? Something to keep you occupied until you were ready to begin your life in earnest?

There was no way, at that point in my life, that I could possibly have understood your need to escape. There was no way I could have known how small and stifling the world can feel when it's full of disappointed hopes and dreams, even a world as mad and vast as New York City seemed to me then. But I get it now. You needed an exit plan. You needed to know there was hope – for happiness, for something better, hell, just for something different. For you, that van was the last remaining link to the life you'd dreamed of having when you'd moved to New York. All your other plans had fallen apart around your head, and all you had left was that one, precious relic of a time when you'd felt that anything was possible – that the future was yours for the taking.

I pretended to be excited about the idea of you going travelling. That was the adult reaction, right? The selfless, loving reaction: to care more about your happiness than about keeping you for myself.

'I love it,' I said, plastering a grin across my face. 'It's so… you.'

'Thanks, babe.' You took a deep breath and glanced around the van's interior. 'Still a way to go but it's coming along.'

We stood in silence, lost in our own thoughts, but then you leaned over and kissed me, and I wondered if I was overreacting. Maybe I was just panicking over nothing.

*

I told Lizzie about the van when I got home on Sunday evening, unsure how I should feel and wanting someone to tell me it was all OK, that there was no need to stress out… and honestly, yes, that you weren't really going to go away – that it was just a pipe dream that would never actually come to anything.

'No way! He showed you?' she said, raising her eyes to stare at me across the kitchen table.

She was in the middle of twisting a piece of fine silver wire into a dainty spiral with her pliers. She'd received a last-minute order for a matching set of jewellery that was intended to be a birthday present, and she was in full weekend work mode, wearing loose grey sweats and a huge pink plaid shirt that came down almost to her knees.

I nodded in response to her question and picked up a tiny glass bead from one of the plastic compartments in the tray on the table, rolling it around between my thumb and index finger a few times before dropping it back among the others.

Lizzie studied me for moment, her eyebrows drawn together in puzzlement, before returning to her work. I offered her a coffee and heaved myself up from the chair, crossing our small, Moroccan-style kitchen to the coffee maker in the far corner. I leaned against the counter top as the coffee brewed, and watched as she began to thread a minuscule bead onto the finished coil.

'Did he tell you what it was for?' she asked, not looking up.

I shrugged, scratching my thumbnail over a loose flake of some unidentifiable food that was stuck to the edge of the worktop.

'Well… I assume for going travelling in. But he said… all he said was that it was his ticket out of here, whatever that means.'

'Hmm… Nothing else?'

'No.' I looked at her sharply. 'Why?'

'Ah, jeez.' She sat back and dropped her pliers on the table, rolling her shoulders to release the tension. She turned towards me in her chair, raking her fingers through her long blonde hair and blowing the air out between her lips. 'OK, don't freak out.'

'OK.' I stood up straighter, hugging myself tightly. I had a strong feeling I was about to freak out.

She got up and finished off the coffee, handing me mine before returning to her seat.

'Well, it's like this.' She took a sip and cleared her throat. 'So, when he first moved here, there was… this girl. His girlfriend. Sophie.'

'Sophie.' I cradled my mug against my chest, watching her through the thin coil of steam.

'Yeah.'

'From Boston?'

'Right. Her folks had a place here though, and she wanted to go to college here. That's how we all met him, through her.'

'He moved… to be with her?'

'Uh-huh.'

She was squirming a little at the questions, but I needed to know. I wanted to understand, even if it was hard to hear. It couldn't be any worse than my imagination, could it?

'So, he dropped out of MIT—'

'What's MIT?'

She gave me an incredulous look. 'The Massachusetts Institute of Technology?'

'Wait, *the* MIT?' It was worse.

'Yeah. I think he got in on a scholarship or something; the guy's crazy-smart. He didn't tell you that?'

I couldn't even answer. I could barely shake my head. *Seriously? He went to* MIT*?*

'Oh, God. OK. Well, he did.' She was sitting sideways on her chair and she propped one foot up on the seat, clicking her fingernail against the side of her mug. 'Anyway, he came here with her, and they bought that van so they could go travelling together, and... well, he started working at the shop so he could fix it up and so he wouldn't have to live off her parents' money – which, by the way, they had a *ton* of – and then... she left. Just boom! Gone. One day she was here, the next day she wasn't. She moved back to Boston and told him not to follow her. I think he had like a week to find somewhere to live, it was brutal.'

'Wow,' I mumbled. I didn't know what to think.

'But hey, listen, that was like two years ago. Things change. And I don't know if this helps, but he's never shown *anyone* that van before.'

A tiny flame of hope flared in my chest. 'Really?'

She nodded.

'No one?'

'Not a soul. It's like this big secret project or something. Like... the Holy of Holies, y'know? I didn't even know if he still had it, honestly. He hasn't mentioned it in a really long time.' She slurped at her coffee.

'So, this van is kind of important, right?'

Lizzie didn't comment, but she nodded along.

'And he doesn't show it to anyone, because, what, it's too painful?'

'Maybe.' She shrugged. 'But he showed it to you. That's not nothing. In fact,' she continued, raising her index finger away from the mug,

'I'd say that's a pretty big deal. Maybe even…' She chewed her bottom lip, turning a thought over in her mind.

'What?' I prodded.

She shook her head, studying my face as if she might find an answer there. 'Maybe he wants you to go with him. Maybe… he's in love with you.'

I stared back at her. I wanted so much for her to be right, but I was still so unsure of myself that I couldn't quite trust that what she was saying made sense. I don't know why I found it so difficult to believe; it was exactly what I was put on this Earth for, I knew that, but even knowing it didn't compensate for the fact that I was so young, and so… clueless.

She smiled wistfully, taking another sip of coffee. 'I think so, honey. I think maybe it's love.'

I felt completely elated, but frightened at the same time. I didn't know what scared me more, the idea that you were going to up and leave without me or the thought that she might actually be right.

Lizzie and I had a big party the weekend before Christmas, and we all got roped into playing Truth, Dare, Kiss or Promise. I ended up having to kiss both of Mikey's feet, and you were dared to run around the block in nothing but your underwear and boots, which must have been horrendous in that merciless cold but you did it anyway.

Lizzie's new boyfriend, Steve, was staying over at our place, and Alex and Nick were both out of town, so you and I had been making the most of having your apartment to ourselves before you headed to Boston to spend the holidays with your family. It almost felt like we were living together, which was the best Christmas present I could have asked for. If I'd been braver I might have said we should make it a more permanent arrangement, but instead I had to content myself with playing house. I was still far too timid to suggest something that momentous.

At one point, as we were walking back – sometime around 3 a.m. – you got a wicked glint in your eye and started pulling me across the street in the wrong direction. I was too surprised to protest and I could tell you had some mischief in mind, so I trotted along after you, clinging to your arm to avoid slipping in the snow.

We ended up in front of the railings that surrounded the little park we always passed between your place and mine.

'What are we doing here?' I whispered, gazing around at the icy street. There was no one there to hear us, but it felt like we were up to whispery sort of business.

Your only answer was an exaggerated shrug and an expression of wide-eyed innocence that didn't fool me for a second. You hopped over the railings and held out your hand, and I somehow managed to scramble in after you. We skidded down the shallow bank on the other side and skirted the wide, open field, our shadows thrown out across the pockmarked snow by the yellow glow of streetlights.

It was so beautiful, I felt like we'd been transported to a magical fairyland, like Narnia… like Hearthfire.

You pulled me into a little copse of trees, and after leading me between the shadowy trunks for a minute you drew me close to you and kissed me in a way I'd come to recognise, softly at first and then with growing insistence, the clouds of our breath mingling in the freezing air and swirling around our faces like a mist. You worked your hands under my clothes and I gasped as your cold fingers found my skin, but then it ceased to matter as the pleasant sensations took over.

When we got to your apartment we dashed straight to your room and stripped off our wet clothes, not even bothering to turn on the light in our haste to get under the covers and get warm. My teeth were still chattering as I clambered into bed beside you and huddled under the layers of duvet and thick woollen blankets. We pulled them right up over our heads and turned to face each other, our breath slowly warming the space between us as our shivering gradually subsided.

Despite how tired I was I stayed awake for a while after you fell asleep, my head still spinning from the party and the exhilaration of our adventure in the park. I couldn't believe we'd been together a whole seven months. Not long really, in the grand scheme of things, but to me it felt like forever. I was young enough to think that word meant something.

*

The weeks following Christmas were uneventful, and the New Year blues seemed to settle over everyone. Lizzie broke up with her boyfriend and grew kind of snappish with me, which wasn't like her but I figured she'd get over it soon enough. They hadn't been together that long.

Alex and I played our first little gig at the end of January. Granted, it was to a half-empty room in the middle of the week, and he snapped a string partway through so we had to stop while he replaced it and retuned his guitar, but it was fun.

I felt a change coming over me during that time. It was a slow, creeping change and one I didn't really notice at first, but looking back I think it was the beginning of my transition from a girl into a young woman. I grew more self-assured, less awkward and insecure, and I questioned things more, even you. I was still hopelessly in love with you, but it felt... different. I felt less like an eager puppy chasing after you and more like your equal.

*

It was sometime at the beginning of February when you told me that you loved me. I was just about to leave your place one morning, and you kissed me goodbye and looked me in the eyes, and just said it, super-casual: 'Love you, babe.'

And what was my response to this immense confession, this heartfelt sentiment that is my reason for being on this Earth? Did I utter some soppy, sweet reciprocation? Did I swoon like the lovestruck teenager I most certainly was? Nope. I looked back at you, seemingly cool as a cucumber, and just said, 'I know you do.' That was it. I think I may have smiled too.

I spent the entire walk home berating myself.

*What is wrong with you? How long have you been waiting for him to say that? And then he finally does, and you COMPLETELY blank him!...
'I know you do'... What IS that?*

I told Lizzie when I got home, expecting her to squeal at me in delight – or at least laugh at me for being an idiot – but she seemed preoccupied and offered me nothing more than a low, morose grunt. I didn't think she'd been that bothered about Steve, but I realised she must have taken it harder than I'd thought. Still, it wasn't fair that she was taking it out on me, and I wondered if she was being like that with everyone or if I'd done something to upset her.

My one year New York anniversary came and went, and you and I got drunk and had sex to celebrate. I mean, we would have done that anyway, but it was special anniversary sex, with strawberries and stuff.

Lizzie and I had made up by then and everything seemed perfect. I really felt like I'd carved out a life for myself, like I had something lasting and good that I could cherish and hold onto... Silly me.

It was only a couple of weeks later when you dropped the bombshell.

*

It was a Monday. I was at work. Nothing out of the ordinary had happened, until just after 11 a.m. when I got a text from you saying you wanted to talk. Completely unawares, I rang you to see what was up, and I could instantly tell that something was very wrong.

'Can I come see you?' you said, your voice strained and quiet.

'Umm, I'm sort of at work.'

'I know... um, sorry. It's important, babe.'

I looked at the clock. The lunchtime rush would be starting soon, but I really wanted to find out what was going on.

'Let me call Steph and see if she can cover for me. Is everything OK?'

'No,' you said, your voice quieter than ever. 'I... I can't see you anymore.'

I couldn't answer. My brain was doing so many different things at once that it felt empty, at a standstill, like an overloaded computer that had finally crashed.

'Aphy? Call Steph. Let me know when you can finish.'

I hung up the phone, staring numbly at the rota on the wall. I called my friend Steph, one of the other baristas, and somehow managed to convey the urgency of the situation without having a total meltdown. She made it there just after midday and I sent you a text as I was leaving, already having to wipe away tears so I could see what I was typing.

You met me in the middle of the street, about halfway between the coffee house and your apartment. You looked pale and exhausted, like you'd been crying too, and the self-assurance that had always seemed such an essential part of you was completely absent. It was as if you'd become a different person overnight.

'Can we go to the park or something?' you asked.

I nodded, not caring where we went as long as I could be with you.

Neither of us spoke as we walked. My insides were churning and my eyes were stinging with tears. The bright sunshine seemed to mock me as it gleamed on the rain-soaked pavements.

You spread your coat out on a bench for us to sit on, and I nearly laughed. It seemed like such a pointless touch of consideration when you were in the process of putting my heart through a meat grinder.

'Listen, babe, I'm really sorry.'

I pinched my lips together. All the arguments that had filled my head had evaporated, leaving nothing but a desperate longing for you to hold me and tell me everything was going to be alright.

'Then why are you doing this?' I whispered hoarsely.

'I can't explain. It's just…' You trailed off, looking more unhappy than anyone I'd ever seen.

'You said you loved me.'

'I do.'

'Then whatever it is, we'll work it out.'

You looked at me, and for one heart-stopping moment I thought you'd reconsidered… but then you shook your head, and the chasm of despair opened up to swallow me.

'It's not that simple, Aphy. This isn't about you, it's just… I'm not in a good place right now, OK? I need some time by myself. I need to figure out what to *do* with my life, and this is just… It's not fair on you. I'm not the person you think I am.'

'Is this about Sophie?' I regretted the words the instant they left my mouth, but I couldn't take them back. 'I'm not her. I *want* to be with you; I want to make you happy.'

You gazed at me, and your sea-green eyes seemed to glow with emotion. 'It's not about Sophie. It's about me. I've messed everything up. I keep messing everything up.'

'Then let me help; I want to help!'

'I slept with someone else,' you said, choking on your own words. 'I'm sorry, I just… I didn't mean for it to happen but it did, and it made me realise I can't be here anymore. I hate this city; my life just feels *empty,* all the time—'

'Empty? How can you say that?'

Didn't I mean anything to you at all? After everything we'd shared, everything I'd felt for you, you had been with someone else… as if what we had didn't even matter.

'I'm so sorry, babe. I'm a shitty person, OK? You need to understand that about me.'

I let out a soft sob. 'I don't care,' I said, gripping your hands, clinging to you as though you might blow away. 'I forgive you. Just… just stay with me. I love you.'

You looked away from me, your face twisted in anguish but your mouth set in a resolute line. 'I can't. I need to be on my own. Please don't be upset.'

I choked on a bitter laugh that grated in my throat. 'Oh, OK, I'll just cheer up, shall I? I'll just get over it – there, all done, problem solved.'

'Aphy—'

'Don't,' I said, releasing you abruptly and standing up. I wanted to fling something at you, slap you, tear at you with my fingernails, but I couldn't bear the thought of hurting any part of you. 'Don't *Aphy* me. I can't…' I swallowed a sob. 'I just can't.'

I turned on my heel and walked away, the tears falling freely down my face and turning everything to gold as the sunlight dazzled my eyes.

*

I called in sick the next day. And the one after that. I played 'I Love You Always Forever' over and over again until the words lost all meaning, and lay on my bed crying endless, bitter tears. Lizzie brought me coffee and made me sandwiches, even though I really wasn't hungry and didn't care if I wasted away. She ran me baths and sat beside me on my bed, sometimes talking, sometimes just holding me so I could cry silently into her chest.

The days grew warmer but I still felt chilled inside, like the snow had settled in my bones. I was inconsolable. I felt betrayed, discarded and furious, and if I'd been able to argue you back into loving me, I would have done.

I felt like you were abandoning me, but now I understand what you meant when you said it wasn't about me. You were stuck going nowhere, and the longer you carried on pretending everything was OK, the more likely it became that you'd be stuck for the rest of your life. Being with me wasn't helping you; if anything it was keeping you in the one place you didn't want to be. I don't know if cheating on me was what made you realise that or if some part of you already knew it and needed an excuse to end things, but it doesn't really matter. Once those realisations hit you there's no way to avoid them anymore, and trying only does more damage, to you and to everyone around you. I'm pretty sure that's what you were trying to tell me, although I wasn't ready to hear it. And I know that, in your own way, you did love me. It just wasn't enough to make you happy, but it *was* enough to make you see what needed fixing. Knowing what I know now, I suppose that was the point.

*

At the end of May, despite my emotional crisis – or maybe because of it – Lizzie announced that it was time for another party. My presence was demanded, of course, and since I couldn't avoid it I hoped I could just get into the spirit of it, and not spend all night being reminded of how you and I first met. I was dreading the thought of someone mistakenly asking me how things were going between us; it never occurred to me that you'd actually turn up.

I was walking up the stairs with a couple of bags of groceries – Lizzie had decided at the last minute that there weren't enough crisps and dips to go around – when I heard someone calling my name, and without thinking, I turned.

And there you were.

Alex and Nick were behind you on the stairs, and they both looked like they'd rather be anywhere else in the world than stuck in the middle of whatever was about to happen.

My throat instantly grew tight and I forced myself to breathe. It had been over a month, but it still hurt as much as the very first day.

'Hi,' you said, smiling softly.

I made myself nod back. 'Hi.'

The other guys seemed to reach an unspoken agreement, and they both squeezed past us and disappeared up the staircase into the safety of the apartment.

You waited until they'd gone before you spoke again. 'How are you?' Your tone was gentle – tentative.

I nodded stiffly. 'I'm fine. You?'

You were still smiling up at me, but your eyes had turned sad. 'I'm good, babe.'

My mouth twitched at the corner and I berated myself for even that tiny betrayal, clearing my throat angrily and forcing the tears back down. You didn't deserve them… even thinking that was painful.

You climbed up the stairs towards me, slowly, like you were approaching a wild animal. You reached me and I thought you were going to say something else, but instead you took my face in your hands and planted the gentlest of kisses on my lips.

I froze, wanting more than anything to kiss you back but refusing to let myself feel even the slightest twinge of warmth towards you. I knew that if I let my guard down, even for a second, all the hurt would come pouring out and you'd see how much I still loved you. I couldn't stand the thought of you knowing how pathetic I was.

You let go of me and stood back, maybe expecting me to say something.

I cleared my throat again and looked up the stairs. 'Shall we?'

I didn't wait for an answer, I just turned and walked up the last few steps as though nothing had happened. I'm sorry if that hurt you – actually, scratch that, I *know* it hurt you, maybe even more than it hurt me – but it was all just too much for me to process.

Everyone looked worried when they saw you follow me in, like they were waiting for one of us to explode or something, but I made sure I didn't get stuck on my own with you again and everyone seemed to forget after a while. I was a bit pissed off with Alex and Nick for bringing you along, but I reasoned that you'd all been friends with Lizzie long before I came into the picture, and it wasn't really fair of me to expect you to stay away forever.

A few hours into the party I was feeling more at ease – or at least more in control of myself – and I managed to look at you a couple of times without feeling like I was going to break down in tears. Once I caught you looking back and I tried to smile, but the effort of keeping my face composed was enough of a struggle and I don't think it looked like I was smiling at all.

It got to 1 a.m. and I decided to call it a night. I was just about to slip away when Lizzie's friend Mikey came lurching over to me, his arms outstretched to envelop me in a bear hug.

'Hey, sweetheart!' he slurred at me. 'How you holding up?'

'I'm fine, thanks, Mikey.' I hugged him back and smiled up at him fondly. 'Think I'm gonna hit the hay though, it's past my bedtime.'

He laughed and took a deep glug of beer from the bottle in his hand. 'Naw, you're still just a kid really, huh? You know what though?' He beckoned me closer, as though he was about to tell me a secret. 'I think you're very… mature.'

'Thanks,' I said, stepping back a bit. He was clearly heading towards loved-up mode and I was reluctant to get sucked into a long, drawn-out ramble about how awesome everyone was. I just wanted to go to bed and be left alone.

'Yep. The way you handled that whole thing with Liz, I think you're a class act.'

I frowned at him. 'What thing?'

'You know…' He waved his hand vaguely in your direction and my stomach twisted into a knot.

'No,' I said. 'Why don't you tell me.'

'You know, at New Year's? Back when you guys were together? The thing with Liz and… Shit.' He tried to focus on my face. Even in that state, he realised he'd screwed up – big time!

'Lizzie?' I croaked, my face on fire. 'He slept with *Lizzie*?'

'Shit, Aph, I'm sorry! I thought you knew! Shit, I'm such an idiot!'

I shoved past him and made for the front door, grabbing my coat and shoulder bag from their hooks on the wall. My whole body was as taut as an over-tightened guitar string, ready to snap under the slightest pressure; unfortunately, Lizzie had to go and tighten it just a little bit more.

'Aphyyyy! Where are you going, girl?'

'Fuck you, Liz!' I whirled on her, taking an angry step towards the sofa, the coat in my hand flailing out into the air with the force of my movement. 'And you!' I jabbed my finger at you across the living room, which had suddenly become devoid of all sound apart from the thrum of music from the stereo. 'Were you *ever* going to tell me?'

Your face was white and still, as though you were in shock.

'Aphy, listen,' Lizzie began, looking from me to you and back again, 'it was just—'

'Shut. Up,' I snapped at her, my lip curling in a snarl. 'Don't tell me it was a mistake, that's bullshit.'

'It's not her fault,' you murmured. 'Please, babe, just calm down.'

'Do NOT call me that!' I yelled, not caring if I sounded like a maniac. 'Don't ever call me that again! I'm not your *babe*.' I turned back to Lizzie, 'And I'm not your *friend*. How could you do this to me, and then just carry on like nothing happened?'

'Aph, please—' Lizzie tried again.

'Shut up!' I was glaring at you, even though I was talking to her. I struggled to find words cutting enough to inflict even a fraction of the hurt I was feeling, but they stubbornly refused to come out.

You looked right back at me, your eyes pleading with me to understand. It only made me more angry.

'Actually, you know what?' A bitter laugh rattled from my throat. 'Do whatever you want, I'm going.'

'Aph!' Lizzie called, but I didn't look at her; I couldn't look at her.

I slammed the door as hard as I could and stormed down the stairs and out onto the street, raising my hand for a taxi. I didn't know where

I was going but I wanted to get as far away as possible and as fast as I possibly could.

The driver dropped me at a hotel – a cheap place that looked out over the Hudson. I closed the door to my room and slumped against it for a while, swimming in grief, unable to think of anything beyond those last terrible moments at the apartment: all those people with their stunned, embarrassed faces, all the yelling and crying and stupid, selfish excuses…

I rushed over to the bed and threw myself down on it, painful sobs heaving from my chest and tearing at my throat. It was the worst I'd ever felt, even worse than when you'd told me we were over. Now I had lost the two people who mattered the most to me in the world, and as much as I hated you, what hurt more than anything was that I still loved you – both of you. My heart was tearing itself in two.

I'd never felt so desolate in all my life. They say the first heartbreak is the worst, but I think every heartbreak is crushing when you're in the middle of it, and at that point I didn't even remember that it wasn't the first time I'd lost someone, and I certainly wasn't in any state to realise that it would pass. After having to leave Hearthfire and uproot my entire existence, maybe I should have been more prepared to let people go; I knew that was the deal, right from the beginning. But I was still so young and new to the world. I bruised easily, and that night had left me black and blue.

I had absolutely no idea what to do. I was physically and emotionally exhausted, but I knew I wouldn't be able to sleep. I sat up and dug around in my bag until I found my Discman, slipped the headphones over my ears and pressed play, hoping the music would drown out my tortured thoughts. I let myself out onto the balcony and took a few deep breaths of the cool night air, then leaned on the railings and spaced out for a while, half-listening to the music and gazing down at the many-coloured patches of light that floated on the surface of the river far below.

Suddenly my attention snapped back to the present as I heard the opening bars of one of my favourite songs: 'Nothing Compares 2 U' by Sinéad O'Connor, and I knew it was a Song like the others that had come before. All the pain and sadness came flooding in like a relentless wave of heartbreak. I'd really lost you. It wasn't just a bad dream, it was all true.

The chorus kicked in and fresh tears started in my eyes. It hurt so much I felt like I might pass out from the pain. But then it ebbed again with the music, and I let Sinéad's voice lull me. She understood how I was feeling. She felt it too. Somewhere out there, someone was trying to tell me that I wasn't alone.

I stayed in New York for another few days, but I knew my time there was over. I didn't go back to work, and I didn't go back to the apartment; I couldn't face Lizzie. I wanted to remember all the happy, fun times we'd had together, not make things even more painful for both of us.

I decided to go to one last open mic night before I left: a farewell to the city that had taught me to sing.

I walked into the small, dimly lit bar, got a drink and sat down at a table near the stage, scanning the faces around me to see if Alex's was among them. I wondered if maybe he'd stopped coming, and felt bad that I might have been the cause of that.

I watched with vague interest as a couple of guys finished setting up the sound equipment. It was nothing flashy, just a small PA system, some microphones, a drum kit and a keyboard. The place was filling up and a few musicians began tinkering around, playing little bits of jazz and blues. I knew some of them, and a couple of people asked if I'd be singing. It was nice to feel like I belonged, even if only for a little while.

I slouched wearily in my seat, absorbing the music and letting my mind wander. I was sad to be leaving, but also relieved. I wanted a fresh start, a new beginning.

Time for another chapter.

Sometime around 11 p.m. there was a break between performers, and one of the old jazz guys came over to ask why I hadn't sung anything yet.

I smiled at him and shrugged. 'Lost my guitarist.'

'Well, that was careless of you.' His eyes twinkled and he gestured for me to follow him over to the rickety upright piano at the side of the stage. He held a songbook out to me. 'Know any of those, sweetheart?'

I flicked through it, and a few pages in I found a song I knew: 'Kissing You' by Des'ree.

He nodded in approval, then pointed to the stage and took a seat at the piano.

I'd never stood on the stage on my own before – I'd always had Alex beside me – and I suddenly felt horribly nervous. I lifted the microphone from its cradle, mostly just to have something to hold onto, and stared out across the room, which had suddenly grown quiet. The pianist looked at me and I gave him a nod, inhaling slowly to steady my nerves. The opening chords rang out into the expectant hush that had settled, so I cleared my throat, took a deep breath, and began.

I closed my eyes under the glare of the lights, feeling the music ring through my body in a way it never had before. I was less nervous with my eyes shut; I could pretend it was just me and the pianist, practising in an empty room like I used to do with Alex.

And even though it was my own voice I could hear, I felt a strange detachment from it, like something else was singing through me and I was just a channel for the feelings that were pouring out of me into the world. I felt the sweet, poignant pain of the words and the deep, soul-wrenching longing that led the melody through its tender highs and desolate lows, and I let it speak for me the way my own clumsy words never could.

There were moments when my sorrow threatened to rise up and engulf me, but I managed to keep my voice steady, even though my heart felt like it was being crushed inside my chest. I focused purely on the Song, letting everything else wash away, and after a while I began to feel stronger, like the music was feeding my body, making me stand straighter and breathe easier.

The music moved into an instrumental and I paused, opening my eyes. I realised I had tears on my face and I wiped them away, too sad to be embarrassed. I looked up through the lights, squinting against the glare, and almost choked when I saw your face at the back of the room. I blinked, doubting my own vision, but then I noticed Alex standing beside you and he nodded; in that second I knew it was really you. You were really there, listening to my singing this one last time.

The instrumental ended and I filled my lungs to sing the final part, my eyes locked on yours. I let the pain pour out of me. I didn't attempt to hide it. You'd hurt me and given me this terrible burden to bear, but I couldn't hate you, and I knew that there was a part of you that was hurting too, at least as much as I was. I sang to you and you looked at me, and we were the only two people in the world. I think you smiled a little, the way you used to smile when you thought I wasn't looking – the secret smile of your hidden heart, that was too fragile and afraid to let me in.

I knew you'd be gone by the time I left the stage, but it was OK. We'd said our goodbyes. I left New York the next day and I never saw you again, but I know now that that was the way it had to be.

Perhaps I'd approach things differently, if I had to do it over again, but probably not. I was exactly the way you needed me to be at that moment in your life. That naïve little girl got into your head far more than any cynical, worldly woman could have. I hope, somehow, that girl helped you get where you needed to go. And most of all I hope that, wherever you are now, you've finally let someone in.

Wanderer

I stepped off the ferry onto the pier in Thong Sala and stood still for a moment, taking in the sights and sounds so I could get my bearings. The smell of saltwater and diesel mingled with the brighter scents of lemongrass, coriander and chilli that wafted from the mobile food trucks further along the pier. I was surrounded by the bustle of fellow tourists and busy locals – some on motorbikes – making their way to and from the ferries. The sky was pale blue with a smattering of hazy cloud, and the coastline was marked out by a thin strip of white sand that separated the water from the patchy treeline. Between and above the trees I could make out a few sun-bleached buildings – the outskirts of the town – and beyond it all were the blue-green mountains, rising in knobby humps in the far distance.

I followed the flow of people, past the seating areas with their blue sloping roofs and the covered pick-up trucks that served as taxis, ready to whisk groups of passengers off to various places around the island. It was my second week in Thailand, and I'd spent the last few days taking in the wonders of Bangkok and figuring out whether to head south to explore the islands or north to the mountains and temples of Chiang Mai. Sand and sea had won out, for now, and I'd decided to begin my island-hopping adventures with a trip to Koh Phangan: a paradise of beaches, palm trees and lush tropical jungle, renowned for its full-moon beach raves and abundance of tourist activities. I had nowhere to be and all the time in the world to get there, and I felt like taking it easy for a while – slowing down and soaking up some sun before traipsing up and down mountains.

I made my way into the town, passing cafés and seafood restaurants, diving schools and bars, and checked into the first place I could find that looked decent: a bright little guesthouse with a communal living room and shared bathrooms. It was late afternoon and I was sleepy from the journey, so I had a nap on my bed, which was surprisingly comfortable, and took a leisurely shower before slipping into the only dress I owned at the time and heading out to see what Thong Sala had to offer in the way of food. I was famished!

My hair had grown long in the years since I'd left New York, so I twisted it up into a knot as I wandered through the town, enjoying the sensation of the evening breeze cooling my neck and whispering around my bare legs. I watched the people around me, all absorbed in their own affairs: street vendors at work over great sizzling pans, couples holding hands and sharing confidences, backpackers strolling and pointing and laughing together. I envied them all, a little. I might never know what it was like to be one of them, to have families and homes to go back to – to belong somewhere. Still, there was something comforting about being a tourist among other tourists; somehow being in close proximity to them made me feel less alone.

I'd had a wild few years travelling around Europe, going to parties and festivals and swapping tales of adventure with people from a thousand different places. Through all my journeying, I had never forgotten my purpose; I was always aware of the Path leading me on, like a distant call just beyond my hearing that buzzed and hummed through my bones. Somewhere out there was the person

I needed to find, I just had to trust my inner compass to point me in the right direction.

The smells of frying spices and cooked meat grew stronger the further I went, and my mouth started watering in anticipation. I found an empty table outside one of the restaurants, and watched the sky darken to a deep royal blue as the light leached out of the world, to be replaced by the hanging lamps and bar signs that lined the street like strings of fairy lights.

My dinner was green curry and jasmine rice – which was fast becoming my favourite dish – and I gobbled it up, my tongue tingling with the heat of the succulent shallots and chillies and the distinctive citrus tang of kaffir lime leaves. I stayed for a cocktail afterwards, waiting for my stomach to deflate a little, watching the faces of the people around me relax and grow soft with repletion.

It was still early in the evening and I decided a walk would be a pleasant way to finish off my day – maybe down to the beach to catch the final dying rays of the sun. I asked the waiter to point me in the right direction and set off down the narrow street. The darkness lent the buildings an ethereal quality that was absent in the day, and transformed the shopfronts full of tourist tat into alluring treasure troves. The patches of dusty waste ground, streams of power cables and jagged smudges of graffiti were softened – blurred away into insignificance – and the smell of motorcycle fumes and hot tarmac was overlaid by the fruity, tropical perfume of frangipani.

After about ten minutes I spotted a dense clump of palm trees looming up at the end of the street, and a narrow dirt path leading between them to a large, lit building. As I got closer I could hear music spilling out into the night, accompanied by the sound of raised voices and laughter from inside. I hesitated, wondering whether to investigate further or continue on down to the beach. I almost chose the former but I was prevented by a sudden pulling sensation, like someone had tugged on a rope that was attached to my insides. The feeling was vaguely familiar: an irresistible craving mixed with a hint of vertigo and a splash of anticipation. Despite only having experienced it twice before I recognised it immediately, and I felt a little thrill as I wondered where the Path was leading me this time.

I skirted the building and made my way down to the beach, guided by that inner pull, my sandals sinking into the sand which still held a remnant of the day's warmth. The noise from the bar gradually faded to silence at my back, and I stood for a while listening to the waves as they broke along the shore, the white froth just visible in the faint light. The sun had disappeared, leaving only a pale band of yellow sky across the horizon. I tipped my head back to feel the breeze as it played over my skin, and in the quiet I became aware of another sound: the soft thrumming of a guitar. I turned my head towards it and saw the glow of a small fire further along the sand. As I approached the music resolved into a sweet, rippling melody – nothing I recognised, but beautiful, and skilfully played.

A voice rang out in the darkness, mellow and true, and although I couldn't understand the words they stirred something inside me – something mournful and bittersweet, but also warm with hope. And then I saw you, and I knew it was you who had brought me to this place. The rope in my belly grew taut, anchoring me to the spot.

I waited, watching you, not wanting to interrupt the lovely flow of notes that caressed my ears and my heart with their soft sadness. You were long-limbed and lean, with olive skin and straight black hair that hung loose around your shoulders. You looked completely at ease, leaning back against a low rock that jutted up from the sand, the body of the guitar resting on your thigh as your fingers picked out the tune.

The song finished and I clapped quietly, drawing nearer to the fire and to you. You started, looking a little sheepish, and almost got to your feet but then sank back down in a self-conscious heap.

'Hi,' I said, coming to a stop a few feet away from you. 'That was beautiful.'

'Oh, thank you.' You seemed unsettled by my presence and I wondered if you'd rather be left alone, but then you glanced up and offered a warm smile. 'Do you want to sit down?' Your speaking voice was as musical as your singing one, with the blunted consonants and drawn-out vowels of India. It appeared I had encountered another lone wanderer; the question was, did you like it that way, or were you – as I was – hungry for some company?

'Is that OK? Would you mind?' I couldn't imagine what I would do if you said you'd rather I leave, but you shook your head and gestured for me to take a seat by the fire.

Your eyes tracked my movements as I drew closer and settled onto the sand, but when I looked back at you they darted away quickly, like you didn't want me to catch you watching me. Up close, I could see that the irises were a bright golden-amber colour; they shone like glowing embers in the firelight, almost luminous in their brilliance.

You lifted the guitar from your lap, like you were going to set it aside, but I held up my hand. 'Please, don't stop because of me. I'd love to hear more.'

You hesitated, and your golden eyes flickered in my direction, twice, three times. After a moment you settled back against the rock and laid your fingers on the strings once more, and I closed my eyes as you began to play another song – happier this time, with a lively staccato rhythm.

You finished off with a rapid, tuneless strumming of the strings, and I clapped in response, letting out a whoop of appreciation. You didn't begin another one but kept hold of the guitar, relaxing around it and clenching your fingers to stretch them out.

'You're really good!' I said, leaning back on my hands.

You smiled shyly and half-shook your head, shrugging. 'I enjoy it but it's not really my... You want to play?'

'Oh, no, I'm a terrible guitarist,' I laughed, watching the flames as they licked around the gnarled chunks of driftwood. 'Definitely more of a singer. I had a friend in New York and...' I trailed off. I didn't know exactly where I'd been going with that sentence.

'You're from America?' You studied me with interest, your glance taking in the details of my appearance in quick, inquisitive sweeps.

'No, I lived there for a while, but... I'm not from anywhere, really. I've travelled around a lot. You?'

'India... Delhi. But I want to travel more. You're very lucky; it must be so exciting to go to different places all the time.'

I shrugged. 'It has its moments. Meeting interesting people is probably my favourite thing about it.'

You caught my eye and held it, and I felt as though something passed between us: a glimpse of each other's worlds. But then you looked away, like you were afraid of showing me too much. I could relate to that; some things aren't meant for sharing.

'I don't know, people can be complicated,' you said, frowning as your gaze settled back on the flames. I wondered where your thoughts were taking you. There was definitely something behind that comment.

'That's true.' I edged a little closer and settled onto my side, digging my fingers into the sand and wiggling them around to feel the grains shift between them. 'But that's what makes them so fascinating. Everyone has a story.'

'Hmm. Some are more interesting than others. My story's pretty boring, so far anyway.' You were looking down at your guitar, still frowning. Your stillness was absorbing, and I got the sense that all the activity was happening on the inside, beneath the surface.

'Have you been here long?' I asked. 'In Thailand, I mean.'

'No. About two weeks.'

'Oh. I got here last week – well, Bangkok. This is my first day here.'

You nodded, the frown lines disappearing as you looked back at me. 'It's beautiful, isn't it? A real paradise.'

We shared a smile and the warmth of the fire travelled down into my chest. I watched the long strands of your hair stirring gently in the breeze that blew up from the water.

'I haven't seen much of it so far,' I said. 'I'm planning on exploring more tomorrow.'

'How long are you staying?'

'In Thailand? I don't know yet. You?'

'At least a couple of months, I hope. But… it depends how quickly I run out of money.' As soon as you said the last part you clamped your lips together, as though you regretted it. I pretended not to notice.

'Yeah, I suppose that's always what decides it.' I tried to sound like I knew what I was talking about, but that was one thing I never really had to consider. 'You could always do some busking?' I pointed to the guitar, eliciting a look of amusement and another head shake.

'No, I couldn't do that.'

Is he blushing?

'I don't see why not. Honestly, you're really good.'

Now you were definitely blushing. It suited you.

'You're just being kind.'

'Oh, no, I'm not a kind person,' I said, pulling a serious face. 'I'm actually really mean, I just like musicians.'

A dimple twitched on your cheek as you threw me a questioning look, and my heart gave a little flutter before settling back down. That made me want to tease you even more, just to see that dimple again.

'Well, that's OK with me,' you said, surprising me. Were you flirting? It was hard to tell. 'Although I'm not really a musician. Not a proper one anyway.' You looked up at me and away again, clearing your throat. 'I don't think you're mean, though. You're too… I don't know. Too nice.' You gave a shrug, and I guessed that hadn't been the first word that came into your mind.

I laughed, raising an eyebrow. '*Nice*?'

'Well, no, not nice… genuine. You seem like a genuine person.'

'So I'm *not* nice?'

You let out a chuckle and rubbed your hand down over your face. 'No, I didn't mean that. You are nice, but genuine is a better word.'

'Hmm.' I eyed you, delighting in your embarrassment: it was refreshing not to be the shy one for a change. 'Well, it sounds more interesting than nice. But I don't know if it's true.' You met my gaze again, and this time I was the one to look away first. 'I mean, I try to be—'

'No, you don't *try* to be genuine. You just are, or you're not. And you are.'

'We only just met. What makes you so sure?' I meant to sound like I was joking but you didn't laugh; your face was still and serious, like you were waiting for me to say something more.

You blinked a few times, and your dimple gave a brief twitch as you smiled. 'I don't know. Sometimes I just get a feeling about people. Not always.'

'Are you ever wrong?'

You grinned, raking your hair back from your face. 'Of course. But not about you, I think.' You shook a finger loosely in my direction. 'You're… you stand out, somehow.'

I laughed away the comment but a shiver passed through me as the words left your lips, and I wondered if you were just playing or whether you really could see the thing that set me apart from other people. It didn't sound like a line – although the best lines never do – and I wasn't even convinced you meant it as a compliment; it had come across more as a neutral observation, although I was pleased that, for whatever reason, you seemed to be as intrigued by me as I was by you. That had to be a good thing, surely.

I was quiet for a few moments, patting the sand flat in front of me and beginning to trace a pattern with my fingertip. 'So, if you're not a musician, what do you do?'

'I'm an artist,' you answered quickly. 'Well, I want to be. At the moment I'm working for my father. I just finished university.' As you spoke you went back to staring at the guitar, and the frown lines appeared again on your forehead.

'Oh, wow. Like a painter?'

'Well, I paint sometimes but I really love drawing, especially in pastels. It feels more… I don't know the word. Like, connected, you know? You use your hands to blend the colours and you're constantly in contact with the paper. Up close and personal.' You gestured excitedly as you spoke, and there was an urgency in your voice that changed it completely.

I nodded. I didn't know the word you were looking for either, but I could sense your meaning and how passionate you were about it. The feeling that you were the reason I'd been drawn here grew stronger as

I listened; you came alive when you talked about art, and the heat in your eyes easily outshone the fire.

'What kind of stuff do you draw?' I asked, entranced.

'People, places – there is so much about India that no one ever sees. Not the tourist stuff… real life. Real people.'

You turned away, reaching for something behind you, and when you turned back you had a large drawing pad in your hand.

'There aren't many in this one, but you get the idea.'

I took the pad from you and opened the first page, my mouth dropping open in wonder as my eyes travelled across the startlingly colourful street scene, viewed from a window above. Every person seemed alive with purpose, even though each one was no larger than my thumb. The longer I looked, the more likely it seemed that the picture would suddenly spring to life in my hands, and I was sure that I could hear the chatter of voices murmuring from the page.

'This is amazing!'

'That's what I see every day from my window – a million people passing by, all with their own stories. And the buildings are so interesting; they don't make any sense, but to me they're… beautiful.'

Your face took on a serene expression and I found myself mesmerised, unable to look away. *I've seen that look before…*

'You love it there.'

'I do.' You smiled softly, and it was tinged with the same sadness that I'd heard in your song.

'I'd love to go one day.'

'You should!' Your eyes blazed and I knew I was right: you were in love. Was it with the place itself, or was there someone back home who made your face light up that way? 'There's nowhere like it in the world. I mean, not that I've seen… but I think it's true.'

I nodded. 'It must be wonderful, to have a home you really love.'

'It is,' you agreed. 'Have you ever had anywhere like that?'

The question made my heart stop for a moment, and my eyes prickled with tears although I had no idea why. Images of Hearthfire flashed through my head – of green grass and blue skies, faces that had been lost to me forever, and a sense of something… nourishing. A purity of happiness that I hadn't felt since, and perhaps would never feel again. It had been such a long time since I'd thought about it, the memories weren't as clear as they'd once been; they were fractured, fragmented, like pieces of a broken mirror. Would I lose them altogether one day? How long would it be until they were erased completely? I was shocked by the thought, and by the powerful tide of grief that swept over me and held me in its grip, but then I realised you were studying me, and the understanding in your eyes plucked me free of it and set me back on solid ground. There was something about you that calmed me, and that made me even more certain that we weren't meeting by chance.

I swallowed hard. 'Yes. Once. When I was a child. It was… magical.'

You nodded. 'Yes. Magical. That's a good word for it.'

I breathed steadily through my nose, waiting for the ache in my chest to subside. I didn't know why it had affected me like that; I'd talked about my childhood home before but had never experienced such a profound sense of loss at the thought. It was disconcerting to know it had been there inside me the whole time, without my even having been aware of it.

'Why did you leave?' you asked. You didn't seem quite so shy anymore; the veil had lifted from your eyes.

'I didn't have a choice. I was only young.' My voice felt like it was trembling, but it sounded steady enough.

'Have you thought about going back?'

I shook my head. 'I can't. I mean… it wouldn't be the same anymore. I'm not the same. There is no going back, really, is there?'

You thought about that for a minute before answering. 'No. I don't think so. And going forward can be painful. But the universe has a plan, even if you can't see it.'

Again, that certainty. *How can you be so sure?* I felt like I was in a better position than most to make that kind of statement, and I wasn't sure of anything of the sort.

'You really believe that?'

'Yes, I do. I know it. It's hard, but you have to trust in Fate. You can't fight it.'

You'd lost something too; you were grieving as I was. Not for your home, but something just as precious. Something that couldn't be replaced.

I flicked to the next page of the drawing pad. Again, the image was alive with a vivid energy, although the subject matter was more troubling: a lone child walking through a slum, his little bare feet sending ripples across a shallow pool of water that flooded the makeshift street. My gut reaction was to feel sad and a little outraged on his behalf, but he didn't look unhappy; he looked like any other child going for a walk somewhere familiar. Somehow that made me feel worse about it. And then I had to ask myself whether I had the right to feel that way or whether I was judging something I couldn't begin to understand.

I let out a long breath, unsure how I should respond. The skill that had gone into capturing the details was incredible, and there was definitely a tragic beauty to it, even though *beautiful* would not have been a word I would ever choose to describe the image. It made me uncomfortable for some reason I couldn't name.

'You don't like that one?' you asked.

'No, it's... I think you're really talented, I just...'

'Some things are hard to look at, but that's what makes them important.' You were smiling a little, but there was nothing humorous about your expression. 'And just because they're hard to see, that doesn't mean they're not beautiful.'

I stared at you. *How did you know that's what I was thinking?*

There was something unnerving about the way you studied me back, like you could see right down into my hidden core. I looked down at the pad in my hands and turned to the next picture. This one was clearly of a different location – not this beach, but one very similar. There were no people this time though, just open sky and glittering water. It was gorgeously serene, and yet... it didn't have the vitality of the first two. There was something lacking, something that didn't quite connect. The next one was the same: a mountain scene, rendered in stunning detail but soulless, somehow. It was strange that such magnificent landscape should pale in comparison to the squalor of a Delhi slum, but it did. At least through your eyes.

I glanced at the first two images again, trying to figure out what was different. I noticed that between the slum picture and the beach, there was a gap where a few pages had been torn out. I stroked my fingertip down the shredded remains of whatever had occupied that space and threw you a questioning look, but you were absorbed in the fire again.

After the mountain picture the pages were blank, so I folded the pad closed and passed it back to you. I wanted to ask you about the torn-out pages, but before I could find the words you began to play the guitar again, so I held my tongue and listened to the music, watching the flames dance on your face and feeling my muscles relax one by one. It was so soothing, with the firelight and the sound of the waves in the background, that my eyelids began to grow heavy, and I pushed myself upright so that I wouldn't nod off to sleep.

We stayed on the beach for hours, talking, singing songs and laughing softly together. It reminded me of another time – a more innocent time – and I almost convinced myself that I was back at Hearthfire, until the firewood ran out and the chill of morning reawakened me to where I really was. We left the smoking pit of ashes and walked together along the beach, up past the bar which was now eerily silent and still, and out onto the road that led back into town.

Everything was so quiet after the buzz of the previous night, it seemed we were the only two people in the world. The scent of frangipani hung heavily in the air, and a few faint stars were peeking out from the lightening sky, along with the slim, silver curve of the crescent moon. I was aware of the pregnant space between us: a warm, sweet vibration in the air that lapped against my skin. I wanted to reach out and take your hand and feel your fingers slide between mine, but I resisted. I wondered if you were imagining the same thing.

We came to a crossroads and I began to walk straight across it, but you had veered off to the left before noticing that I wasn't following. We stopped and looked at each other, realising it was time to part ways. I retraced my steps and came to a stop in front of you. What was I supposed to do now? I couldn't just let you go, not after such a lovely night, but what excuse did I have to keep you? It wasn't as if I could say what I wanted to say: that I felt connected to you in a way I couldn't explain, that you'd given me a sense of home after years of wandering alone, that my Path had led me to you and that we were destined to meet for some reason I wasn't privy to, and that in spite of the fact that we'd only known each other for a few hours I was sure something was supposed to happen between us because that was the whole point of me coming here. I mean, talk about oversharing.

'Are you up there?' I gestured past you, trying not to feel too disappointed as you nodded in response. 'Oh. I'm this way.' I pointed behind me, slightly mollified by the look of regret on your face.

You were clearly as reluctant to part as I was, but neither of us could seem to stop it happening. My head was fuzzy with tiredness and I couldn't think of anything to say. My chest felt heavy, the throb of our connection drawing me towards you but hindered by my hesitating flesh.

At a loss, I reverted to my default setting and held out my hand. 'It was great to meet you.'

'And you. It was… fun talking to you.'

'Yeah. I had a really good time.'

You let go a second after I did, looking like you wanted to say something more, but the silence lengthened and nothing seemed to be forthcoming.

Come on, think of something!

'Are you staying?' you asked, just as I was about to give up and turn away.

Relief rushed through me like a wave. 'Yeah, I'll be here for a while. There's so much to see – I've heard the full moon parties in Haad Rin are pretty wild, but that's not for another couple of weeks.'

You raised an eyebrow and I wondered if I'd said something wrong. 'Really? I thought they sounded a bit…'

'What?'

You shrugged, adjusting the strap of your backpack with your free hand.

I crossed my arms and poked at the dusty tarmac with the tip of my sandal. 'Not your cup of tea?' I looked up and found you grinning. Your dimple was showing and I had an urge to reach out and stroke it. 'What's funny?'

'Nothing, it's just… cup of tea.' You chuckled, like that had really tickled you. 'That sounds funny to me.'

We stood looking at each other. *Would it be weird to ask you if we could see each other again?*

You rocked on the balls of your feet and clasped the guitar against your stomach with both arms, resting your cheek on the neck. You were tall, standing up, and although you were slender your shoulders were broader than they had looked from the side. Your hair fell almost to your waist, and shone softly silver-blue in the predawn light.

'I'm probably going to stay a couple more days and then go – maybe Saturday.'

I nodded. 'That sounds like a good plan.'

'Yeah…' You blew the air out through your lips and let your gaze wander around the perimeter of the crossroads.

A pick-up rumbled past, carrying passengers towards the pier. As though that had been a signal, two motorbikes appeared from different directions, and a woman materialised from the road opposite us and made her way across, passing us with a shy nod of greeting.

'Well, enjoy the rest of your trip,' you said, twisting your body in the direction you were heading.

'Thanks. You too.' We both lingered, the air between us pulsing like a heartbeat, but finally I managed to persuade my feet to move, and I raised a hand in farewell before continuing on my way back to the guesthouse. I should have found something else to say – wasn't I supposed to be better equipped to handle these sorts of situations?

No Song, I remember thinking. *There was music, but I never heard a Song. Does that mean I was wrong?*

When I got back to my room I crawled gratefully into bed and slept for hours, not stirring until the sounds from the street outside woke me as morning turned into afternoon. I was groggy from sleep – or maybe lack of it – so I took a shower to wake myself up and decided to go for a wander.

I found my way to the pier, bought some lunch from one of the roadside stalls and went for a stroll along the beach, which wasn't the widest or prettiest I'd ever seen, but still gave a spectacular view of the turquoise waters. It was November and the tourist season was just starting to pick up, with clumps of people lolling in the sun outside the various bars and hotels that were tucked back along the shore, which I hadn't even noticed in the dark the night before. Out on the water were a number of slender little boats, like upturned leaves bobbing on the tide, and the looming ferries that came and went with unhurried regularity.

I flopped down on the sand between two seating areas, resting my elbows on my knees and taking a swig from my water bottle. The air was warm and heavy, and I found myself daydreaming as my gaze rested on the gently lapping waves. I thought about all the places I'd been in the years since I'd left Hearthfire, and was struck by what you'd said about how lucky I was to have done so much travelling, but also by the fact that I'd somehow ceased to think of it that way. I didn't know when that had happened. I loved getting out and seeing the world after being shut away from it for so long, it was just… there was no one to share it with. Not a friend or a family member or anyone.

Despite the heat of the day my skin turned cold at the thought, and I rubbed my arms in irritation. It was pointless, and selfish, dwelling on what I didn't have when so many people had so much less. Better to think about what I did have: the things I got to experience and the people I encountered along the way. I thought about your amazing drawings and your blushes and your dimple, and the delightful discomfort of our combined awkwardness. That feeling was what made it all worth it; I could still share some parts of my life with people I loved – even if they were just passing moments – in ways that no one else would ever be able to do. I wouldn't trade that for anything, and maybe, when the right person came along…

I stayed to watch the sunset, which began around six and was easily the most stunning display I'd ever seen, the lurid orange sun setting the sky aflame and the sea along with it. The clouds hung russet-red, gold and purple against the backdrop, and the boats became black silhouettes as they headed back to shore. I stood up and began to make my way along the beach, looking for somewhere to eat. Almost everyone was heading indoors, and I imagined the best eateries would be filling up fast.

I found myself back outside the beach bar I'd noticed the night before and climbed the few shallow steps to the terrace, which glowed with light from the lamps that hung down from its bare wooden beams. A few tables were already occupied, some by couples and others by clusters of young people, chatting over bottles of wine or interesting-looking cocktails.

There was a small table in one corner, to the side of the main doorway into the bar, so I quickly claimed it and ordered a drink, perusing the menu while I waited. The night air was warm and fragrant, and I was lulled by the low hum of chatter all around me. I was half-expecting to see you, but my food came and went and there was no sign of you, and I wondered if I had imagined the whole thing. Had I dreamed you up as an antidote to my solitude?

I glanced around at all the people at the other tables, overhearing snatches of their conversation: sights seen on a hike, a massage planned for the morning, how cheap the trains were on the mainland, the elephant sanctuary and how awful it was to learn about how they'd been treated before they were rescued. It all became a cacophony that vibrated against my ears, and I was swamped by a sudden longing to be part of one of those conversations – any of them – just to be with someone else instead of on my own.

Where are you? I thought, scouring the place for any sign of you. *Surely that can't have been it, otherwise what was the point of coming here?*

Thinking about you was enough to stop the whirling in my head; I remembered how calm I'd felt, observing your stillness, breathing in and out to the same rhythm as we sang together. I thought about your slow smile and hesitant humour, your golden eyes that could sift through the outer layers and find beauty in the most unexpected places. You and I had a destiny to fulfil, I was certain of it. You'd said it yourself: the universe always has a plan.

So, what do I do about it? I puzzled, frowning at the dark waters out beyond the glare of the lights. I could wander around hoping to bump into you, but there was no guarantee it would work. I wracked my brain, trying to glean some clue from what you'd said about your plans. Then I remembered that you'd mentioned you were leaving on Saturday. Three days from now. And since the ferry was the only way to get to and from the island… it wasn't exactly a plan, but it was the only idea I had.

*

I slept badly on Friday night. I lay awake thinking of you in the darkness of my room, listening to the motorbikes zooming past outside, and the muffled bumps and rustlings of the other guests. I'd been keeping my eyes peeled for you everywhere I went, at the beaches I'd explored and the night market, the various bars and restaurants, but to no avail. The pier was my only hope.

I got up early in the morning, worn out and grouchy. After packing my things and settling my bill I made straight for the ferry, stopping only to purchase a breakfast of *pa tong go* and hot, sweetened soy milk from one of the stalls at the roadside. I savoured the fatty, deep-fried pieces of dough as I scanned the faces around me; even at that hour the streets thronged with people of all nationalities, ages and backgrounds.

I was just finishing my meal when I spotted you, perched on the railing partway along the pier. Your hair was tied in a loose loop at the nape of your neck, and you were dressed in a T-shirt and cargo shorts, with the guitar slung across your back and your backpack on the floor at your feet. I licked the delicious warm grease off my fingers and made my way towards you, trying to figure out what I was going to say that wouldn't make me sound like a crazy stalker.

You hopped down off the rail as you noticed me approach, and I was heartened by the expression of pleased surprise that lit up your face.

'Hello,' you said. 'Leaving already?'

'Hi. Yeah, I… How are you?' I smiled, so relieved to see you that I leaned in to give you a hug before I realised what I was doing. You received it awkwardly, patting my shoulder, but it was too late to take it back. Up close I could smell your aftershave – a blend of cardamom, sandalwood and nutmeg – and I longed to stay in that moment, breathing you in, but I didn't want to make things any weirder. 'Did you see everything you wanted to see?'

'I think so. All the important stuff anyway.' Your gaze dropped almost imperceptibly down the length of my body and back, so quick it was like the flash of a camera. 'How are you?'

'Good, thanks,' I answered, tucking my hair up into a knot to cool my sweating neck. 'Ready for the next adventure.' I peered at the signs around us, trying to figure out my next move and whether I should come clean about why I was here. 'Are you waiting for the ferry?'

'No. I was waiting for you.'

My head snapped back towards you. The line was delivered so casually that I wondered if I'd heard you right. 'Me?'

You shrugged. 'Sort of. I thought maybe you'd come. I mean, I didn't, but… I hoped you would.'

I didn't know what to say to that. I was delighted to hear it, of course, but I hadn't been prepared for you to just come out with it so bluntly. 'How long have you been here?'

You gave another shrug, which seemed to be your default response to questions you didn't want to answer. That made me think it must have been a while. The first ferries began leaving at around 5 a.m., but surely you couldn't have been here that long?

'I wanted to show you something,' you said, opening your backpack and pulling out the drawing pad. You glanced up at me anxiously before leafing through the pages and holding it out to me. 'I probably should have asked you first, but… well… take a look.'

The page was a blur of colours – red, yellow, deep indigo – and as I made sense of the shapes I let out a gasp of genuine astonishment, taking the pad by the edges and studying the picture intently.

'It's… it's…' I couldn't seem to find the words.

After another few moments of silence we both spoke on the same breath.

'Amazing,' I finished.

'You,' you said simply. 'I hope you like it.'

'Like it?' I was still staring, overwhelmed by the detail.

It was a portrait – *my* portrait – and it must have been the way I'd looked to you while we sat by the fire on the beach, because I could read the feeling you'd captured in my eyes as clearly as words on a page: it was the moment I'd realised how much I missed Hearthfire. The devastating love for something that no longer existed was written all over my face. It hurt to see my own pain and longing mirrored back at me, but I couldn't look away. The picture had the same living, breathing energy as the street scenes you'd drawn, and the patches of light and shadow seemed to flicker across the planes of my face, shifting with the bright tongues of flame that occupied one corner of the page.

'Do you mind?' you asked softly. 'It's just, I saw that expression and I *had* to draw it. I haven't been able to draw like that since… well, for a long time. But after I saw you I felt this crazy burst of energy and… I don't know how else to explain it.'

You stopped, like a wind-up toy when the motor runs down, and nervously rubbed the back of your neck. When I didn't speak you started to fidget, chewing on a fingernail. I knew you wanted me to say something, but what I was feeling in that moment was beyond words.

'Have I upset you?'

I let out a long sigh that turned into a chuckle, and your shoulders visibly relaxed. 'No, not at all. I just… I wasn't expecting…'

My legs suddenly felt a little unsteady, and I handed back the drawing pad and slumped against the railing, letting the top rail take some of the weight of my backpack. I hadn't been wrong after all – I knew I hadn't been wrong: whatever it was I was feeling, you were obviously feeling it too. I didn't know what that meant, but it was something. And now that you were here, maybe I'd have the chance to find out.

'So,' I said, watching as the breeze teased a few long strands of hair out from your ponytail, 'have you decided where to go next?' We were so close I could count the long lashes framing your eyes, and see the steady movement of your chest as you breathed in and out.

'No,' you answered, your accent giving the word a blunted sound. 'I still don't know.'

I sensed a Moment coming on – that funny, disjointed feeling like the world was tilting slightly off-balance. I cleared my throat, grateful for the railing propping me up and the sea breeze lifting the heat from my flushed cheeks. The caps of the waves seemed to sparkle with promise, and not a single cloud marred the perfect blue of the sky.

'Well, there's loads to see on the mainland. Or there are the other islands – Koh Phi Phi, Phuket—'

'Where are you going?'

'Um… I was thinking of heading to Koh Samui maybe, and then—'

'OK,' you said. It had the ring of a decision made. And there was that insanely cute dimple again.

'OK?' My heart gave a joyous little skip, and my stomach was so full of butterflies I thought I might take off.

'I'll go with you.' This time neither of us looked away, and the world around us faded into nothingness.

I grinned, watching the echoing smile spread across your face. 'I'd really like that.'

'Could I…' You looked down at the picture again, your thumb stroking the edge of the page. 'Only, I think I could do more like this – I mean more of you. I've been so stuck lately; nothing's been coming out the way I want it to. But something about you… inspires me or something.' You laughed, embarrassed. 'That sounds so stupid, I know. But… would you mind?'

You were watching me with those beautiful amber eyes, and they were just as bright and candid as they'd been during our talk on the beach. It was all I could do not to just stare at you.

I swallowed, tearing my gaze away from yours. 'No.'

'No?'

'I mean, I wouldn't mind.'

'Really?' You were almost twitching with excitement.

I wanted so much to reach out and touch you, but I restrained myself. 'Really. I'd like the company anyway, and if that helps you out too then great. We'll be wanderers together.'

'Yes,' you said, nodding happily. 'Let's go and wander the wonders.'

I broke into a giggle, and that was that.

*

In the weeks that followed we did everything together, and the sights and sounds and smells were infinitely more fascinating now that I could experience them with you. After years of travelling alone it was thrilling to wake up each day knowing I had someone to share the journey with, especially someone who took as much pleasure in it as I did. You had a thirst for adventure that matched my thirst for company, and your constant presence was like a cheery fire blazing in my heart, warming me from the inside.

We sought out remote beaches that could only be found by trekking through the jungle – endless stretches of pristine white sand, and water so clear we could see the fish darting along the ocean floor many feet below our paddling limbs. We shovelled plateful after plateful of delicious street food into our watering mouths, exclaiming over the flavours and laughing as we burned our tongues in our haste. We visited breathtaking temples that stunned us into awed silence, exchanging looks of wonder before examining each minutely detailed painting and statue, and we went kayaking around the unearthly caves and lagoons of Phang Nga Bay, with its towering limestone cliffs jutting up out of the water.

Most evenings, after we'd eaten our fill and found somewhere quiet to relax, you got out your drawing pad and made sketches of the scenery and the people around us while I practised playing on your guitar. You taught me some basic chords and showed me how to strum properly, and it didn't take long before I stopped sounding terrible and started sounding reasonably OK.

You'd often ask if you could draw me, and I'd find a comfortable position and sit still for a while, letting my thoughts wander off to distant places and people, none of whom I would ever see again. I felt less sad about that when I was with you; knowing that you saw the sadness made it less acute, and I felt that with every picture of me you drew, a little more of it seeped out of me and sank into the paper. And you had such a brilliant eye for the details of an expression or a pose, it was as if you could take everything that was going on inside my head and lay it bare. You were fascinated by the tiniest shift of muscle that announced a corresponding shift on the inside, and no matter what I was feeling you filled the page with that emotion, so that my thoughts were practically written across the paper.

I laughed at how intense you could be sometimes, and you laughed at how difficult I found it to hold still. You said I was the twitchiest subject you'd ever had, in a voice that was half-despairing and half-delighted.

I have no idea how many images of me you composed during that time, but I know it was a very large number. I hope that you still keep a few of them nearby – maybe in your swanky, purpose-built studio in some expensive neighbourhood – and look at them every once in a while, and remember.

My favourite was a full-body portrait that you drew one evening as we rested on the beach after a swim. I was leaning back on my hands in the sand, wearing a loose white top over my bikini, and I'd found a lily – probably discarded from some wedding flowers – and tucked it behind my ear. As we lapsed into silence, you suddenly reached into your bag and grabbed your pad, and told me to stay exactly where I was. I smiled to myself as I kept my eyes fixed on a patch of sand just beside my outstretched legs. All I could think about was your eyes on me and your fingers smudging and blending the colours over my replica body on the page. I flushed as I imagined you touching my actual skin that way, turning that feverish energy to something less artistic but equally worthwhile.

It took you a little while but the finished result was breathtaking; you really were immensely talented. The colours were beautifully rich and warm, and together they created the overall impression of a soft, peachy glow. The background of pale sand was tinted pinkish-brown by the sunset, and the lily in my hair looked so real and fragile you could stir the petals with a breath. You'd given my lips a more reddish tint than they naturally had, but the colour worked with the hints of pink to highlight the slight flush of my cheeks, giving the picture a feeling of subtle allure. I looked like I was daring the viewer to guess what I was thinking. I looked like I was in love.

You beamed at my reaction and shrugged as though you couldn't explain how the picture had come out that way.

'I think you might be my muse,' you said, with that adorable blush I found completely irresistible.

I smiled happily and looked back at the drawing again. 'I think you might be right.'

It was a blissful existence, paradise on Earth, apart from one excruciating detail: nothing more had happened between us. We had a connection – an understanding that ran deeper than any I'd ever known – and I was sure you felt it too, but so far neither of us had found the courage to act on it. The sadness we both carried inside us faded away when we were together, as though each of us plugged up the cracks in the other's heart and made it whole again. Maybe we were afraid of spoiling that.

As the days drifted by I found myself growing increasingly frustrated. One night we were walking through the market in Phuket, caught up in a discussion about what makes 'real' art. We were surrounded by a rich kaleidoscope of fabrics, jewellery, ornaments and pictures, carved soaps, woven baskets and other souvenirs, and the air was redolent of burning incense, heavily scented flowers and, of course, cooking food.

I stopped and held out my hands. 'But there has to be some kind of standard, surely? Otherwise what's the point in learning how to do it properly?' I was grinning, enjoying the argument and eager to know what your comeback would be.

'Yes, but what I'm saying is that art's about more than technique. It's about feeling – emotion. It doesn't matter what anyone else thinks or tells you to think; it speaks to you or it doesn't, that's what's important. A mother whose child draws a picture for her to put on the fridge will love that picture more than any million-dollar collector's piece.'

Then, to my complete surprise, you took hold of my hands and held them against your chest, and I was suddenly unable to remember what we were even talking about, never mind the point I'd been trying to make.

'It's about what it says to you in *here*. No matter how well an artist captures an image, if there's no feeling in it then it's not really *art*, it's just pretension. Like the pictures I drew when I got here; they were meaningless. Until I met you, and then...'

The sound of the market melted away, and I was filled with a strange sensation, a pleasurable discomfort, that burrowed deep into my tissues and nestled somewhere in the centre of my being – a sweet, keening ache.

I gazed up at you, as speechless as I'd been in the most magnificent temple we'd visited, and the whole of my awareness was fixated on the firmness of your chest under my palms, your fingers pressing against mine, the fragrance of your skin and the smile that slowly shrank on your lips. I felt sure you were about to kiss me; the pulling sensation inside my belly was vibrating like a steel guitar string. All you had to do was lean forward a little and...

You dropped my hands as suddenly as you'd seized them and stepped away, looking anywhere but directly at me.

'I'm sorry,' you said. 'I didn't mean to do that.'

'It's OK.' I took a deep breath and pushed my hair back from my face. 'I've actually been thinking—'

'We should go back to the hotel. I mean, I think I need to get some sleep. I'm tired.'

'Oh.' I nodded, my fingers itching to reach out and touch you again. 'Is there... Do you want to talk about anything?'

'No, I just...' You finally met my gaze and seemed relieved at whatever you saw there, giving me a sheepish smile. 'I got carried away, sorry.'

I wanted to say, *Yes, I want you to get carried away!* Surely you knew how I felt about you? With all the time you spent looking at me, studying me, committing my expressions to paper, you couldn't possibly have missed what was staring you in the face... could you? So if you knew and were refusing to do anything about it, then what did that mean?

We went back to our hotel, to our separate rooms, and I spent another night staring at the ceiling, wondering why the Keeper of Love was destined to be alone.

Another time we were sitting in the garden of the hostel we were staying in, mesmerised by the flickering citronella candles that sat on the glass-topped table in front of us. You'd been playing guitar and I'd been listening to you sing, not understanding the words but feeling their meaning anyway.

I realised that you'd stopped playing – I wasn't sure how long ago – and I glanced across to find you watching me, your elbow on the arm of your chair and your face leaning against your hand. Your eyes held the candlelight, gleaming like polished gemstones, and contained so much feeling that they seemed about to brim over with it and flood the world. I didn't move, I just looked back at you. We must have stayed that way for several minutes, and in that time my heart beat softly and steadily, with never a flicker. You made me feel utterly calm. And then you took my hand and held it gently, turning your face back to the flames. I watched you a moment longer and then did the same.

Something was coming. I didn't know what it was, but I knew it would be soon. I couldn't play this waiting game much longer. And where the hell was my Song?

*

It all came to a head one night in Pattaya; we were in a beer garden at a bar just off Walking Street – a place so crammed with neon lights it was like being stuck inside a giant carnival ride, with music blaring from every venue and go-go dancers strutting around in impossibly tall heels and impossibly tiny shorts. You hadn't been all that eager to come, but after hearing about it from a group of young backpackers I'd wanted to experience it at least once, and it was so different from anywhere else we'd been in Thailand that I was curious to see what you'd make of it once we were there.

I could tell you were uncomfortable with all the noise and mayhem, so I'd compromised and found us a table in a quieter spot with a balcony overlooking the bay, the dark water shot through with long tongues of light from the resorts and clubs on the beach, and the coast outlined in tiny bright specks from faraway buildings. We watched the people prancing around on the sand below as we chatted about everything and nothing. Part of me wished I could go down and join them – I'd been bitten by the party bug on my way through the vibrant, clamorous crowd – but not if it meant leaving you behind, and you clearly didn't share my enthusiasm for plunging into the madness.

The beer garden was more sedate, although still packed with people and loud enough that we had to raise our voices to be heard. We were sitting opposite each other, leaning our elbows on the wall of the balcony, and I was admiring the shape of you as the outside lamps gilded your hair in fiery gold.

On a whim, I asked you about the missing pages that had been torn out of your drawing pad, and immediately realised that my question had touched a nerve. But rather than backing off I decided to push further this time.

'Is that a sensitive subject?'

You shrugged: your default answer. But I was suddenly certain that those missing drawings were all part of the same puzzle – the reason you were suppressing your feelings for me – and that if I didn't get the truth out of you tonight then I never would, and our time would slip away while we danced around the subject. I couldn't let that happen.

'OK, I can't do this anymore. Every time I ask you anything remotely personal, you just change the subject. What's that about?' The words came out more abruptly than I meant them to, but my head was all muddled by my feelings and I couldn't think of another way to say it.

You clenched your jaw and your fingers tightened around your beer bottle. I felt guilty for making you uncomfortable, but I wasn't going to be put off. I needed to know if you felt the same way I did. I was sure you must, after all the moments we'd shared, but I couldn't do anything about it unless you told me what was bothering you.

I leaned my elbows on the table and slid my hand towards you. 'I'm not trying to upset you. I just want to understand. Please, you have no idea how insane you're making me.'

You shifted in your chair. My outburst had clearly unnerved you, but now that I'd started I couldn't seem to stop.

'You must know I like you. Not just as a friend, as someone I want to *be* with. And I think you like me that way too. Am I wrong?' My heart was pounding like a kick drum in my chest. If I was wrong about this then I might have just lost the only real friend I'd had for years, but I wasn't – I *wasn't*. I couldn't be. I'd stake my whole life as a Keeper on it.

You looked like you wanted to shrink into your chair, and your eyes were fixed on my hand, which was still resting on the table in front of you. Your silence stretched on and on, and I began to question whether I'd actually said those words out loud or if I was stuck inside a dream, confessing my feelings over and over in a closed loop.

I stared at you, willing you to say something – anything – but you didn't move a muscle, and eventually I huffed in exasperation and sat back in my chair, taking a deep gulp of my mojito.

Great, I thought, studying the clump of mint leaves and chunks of lime at the bottom of my glass. *Now he's not even speaking to you. Way to manage that situation!*

'You're not wrong.'

Your voice was so quiet I couldn't be sure you'd really spoken, but I answered anyway. 'Then what's the problem?'

You regarded me a moment longer then heaved a sigh and sat back, toying with a paper napkin on the table.

'The problem?' you repeated.

I nodded, crossing my arms as I waited.

'OK.' You took a deep breath, and I hoped that whatever was about to come out of your mouth was worth all the weeks of painful anticipation. 'There was… a girl.'

You looked at me like that was supposed to explain everything.

I looked right back at you, baffled.

'We grew up together,' you continued, 'and… when we got older, we… we were supposed to get married. I loved her.' You picked at the label on your bottle and I watched you silently. It seemed that whatever was eating away at you was trying to get out. 'We planned the wedding, everything was perfect, and then… then she said she wanted to move away. For good.'

'You mean leave Delhi?' I asked.

'No, India.' You looked up at me, your eyes hot with indignation.

'Wow.' I digested that for a moment. 'So, she just broke the whole thing off?'

'No… ' You sighed, rubbing your face with your hands. 'She wanted us to go together, after the wedding.'

'Ohhh.' I let the word ring out into the silence.

'I love India,' you murmured quietly, frowning as you resumed your label-picking efforts. 'It's my home. She thought I'd want to go too – somewhere more… exciting.'

I frowned in sympathy. 'So you let her go?'

'Yep. She left. And I haven't been able to draw since. Not like I could before. Until…'

It made sense now – the longing for something lost that could never be recovered. To have to choose between the person you'd loved your whole life and the place where you belonged, in your bones…

I waited a while, trying to wrap my head around it all. There was still something that didn't add up.

'You must have been devastated,' I said, trying to get you to meet my gaze. 'But that still doesn't really answer my question: what's stopping you now? Are you still in love with her? I mean I'd completely understand, that must have been—'

'No.' You swallowed nervously and hunched into yourself, like you were preparing to announce some awful secret. Your gaze glanced off mine, a stone skimming the water, and you cleared your throat, your scowl deepening.

'She was…' you began, then coughed again and squared your shoulders, '…the only one I ever… you know.'

'Ohhhh,' I said again, leaning my cheek on my hand.

I pondered that for a moment then realised you were studying me nervously, like you were waiting for me to laugh at you. Instead, I reached across the table again and placed my hand over yours.

'You know,' I said, gently running my thumb across the bumps of your knuckles, 'there's an easy way to fix that.'

The lights from the surrounding lamps were reflected in your eyes, which were now regarding me with an intensity that made my body pulse with excitement.

'Come on,' I said, standing up. 'That's enough talking. Let's go somewhere we can dance.'

Your face fell but I just laughed and hauled you to your feet. I strode out of the bar, pulling you along by the hand, and a wall of light and sound hit me as I skipped out into the street. There were people everywhere, swarming and weaving between each other, laughing and shouting and dancing under the flickering neon lights. My blood was singing from the electricity in the air, and the Path summoned me on, imperious as a queen.

I'd been looking at this all wrong, thinking I needed to wait for you to take the lead and tell me what you wanted, but it turned out you'd been waiting for me. You didn't need a gentle, timid girl to follow you around like a shadow, you needed me to take charge and show you what *I* wanted: to tease out your wild side and make you tear off the mask of polite reticence so you could just… *be*. Wholly yourself. Without worrying if that was enough or if some part of you wouldn't measure up. It was time to stop waiting and take control – to become who I was destined to be.

We plunged into the chaos and I didn't look back once. My feet were leading the way and I went where they took me. Outside one of the clubs I felt that tug again, and I veered towards it and in through the luminous pink doorway. As if the universe had been waiting for some cue, the second we stepped inside the Song started playing. I knew it right away. It was Jimi Hendrix: 'Voodoo Child'. There was no mistaking that guitar riff. I smiled to myself as I squeezed through the crowd; finally I had a glimpse of the way forward, and the future was enticing.

The room was narrow but long, with mirrored walls that multiplied the faces and bodies, reflecting the lights that flashed and spun over our heads in yellow, pink and red. A canopy of wheeling stars darted across the ceiling like a shoal of luminescent fish, first one way, then the other, and the air stank of sweat and desire, all fermenting in alcohol. Women in leather bikinis and fishnet body stockings stood atop podiums spaced along the walls, winking and blowing kisses at the people surrounding them. Everyone was moving to the beat, some thrusting their fists into the air, others holding glowsticks in their upraised hands. The whole room shook as the drums kicked in, and the pulsing in my body skipped in time like an extra heartbeat, while the sea of bodies heaved and surged around us.

I could feel the link between us tightening, the rope being pulled taut. I knew I'd been drawn to you for a reason and that I hadn't been mistaken in thinking you were the one I was supposed to find. I wasn't a little girl anymore, I was the Keeper of Love, and everything in my being was telling me that if I really wanted you I was going to have to show you how I felt, in no uncertain terms.

I turned and pulled you after me with both hands, leading you right into the depths of the churning mass until we were surrounded by people and sound. You were shaking your head like you still thought you could get out of it, but I shook mine harder and gave you a provocative glare.

The music poured into and through me, shaking my bones and rumbling in my core, rippling along my arms and down my spine. I couldn't resist it, even if I'd wanted to, and I gave myself over to it completely, offering myself up to the Path, the universe, and whatever forces were at work inside me – I was their instrument and they could do with me what they willed.

I began to dance, my hands high above my head, the current of energy spilling out of me in tantalising waves. You looked a little awkward, glancing around as though you thought everyone was watching, but I wasn't concerned with what the rest of the world was doing, and soon you seemed to forget about them too as you focused all your attention on me. We were so close I could taste your scent on my tongue, and my mouth began to water as I thought about your lips pressing against mine. The air filled with vapour – a dry, chemical taste – and the floor pounded with the bass and the stamping of feet, loud and exhilarating as thunder.

I sensed rather than saw the space growing around us, the bumps and jolts of other people's limbs receding into a caress of warm air, as though we were caught in the vortex of a storm and I was a lightning rod – a conduit for pure force. My arms snaked out either side of me as my body responded to something beyond my control; I could feel the power of my nature working through me and flowing into you, shifting something inside you until you stopped resisting and fell under its spell. A burst of heat burned deliciously at the centre of my chest, crackling and jumping with ever-increasing intensity, and the music kept coursing through me until it seemed to have become a being in its own right.

This was what it meant then, to be consumed by the Path; in that moment nothing remained of the girl I had once been, there was only Aphrodite in all her raw, unbridled potency.

I grasped your hands and laid them against my hips, which snaked and twisted like a coil of flame, flickering. I closed my eyes, the bass beat pounding through me from the floor, from the air, from the blood pumping in my arteries, from the answering echo in my body. I was vital and vibrant, a force of nature, a primal being of energy focused on a single purpose: love. The buzzing in my chest cranked up a notch and I felt electrified, fizzing with glorious life and desire. My senses were amplified and I could smell the heat radiating from you; you were in the grip of the current, as I was – we were two opposite poles, magnetising the air.

I opened my eyes and found you watching me, transfixed. A lot of other people were watching too by then, gazing hungrily without understanding what had drawn them, but it didn't matter. None of them mattered. It was just you and me.

You took a deep breath as if trying to bring yourself around from some kind of trance, and I moved closer still, our bodies a scant inch apart but not quite touching. A charge flashed through the space between us and I grinned, sliding my palms over your wrists and knitting my fingers through yours.

The Song broke into a chaos of drums and furious guitar, and the fire rose up inside me, rushing through my veins like liquid flame and radiating out to the people around us. I wasn't dancing anymore. We stood facing each other, static crackling around us as if the very air was about to burst into flame. I couldn't see anything but you. My ears were filled with a rushing sound and my body hummed like a live wire.

And then, at last, you kissed me, suddenly and forcefully as though you didn't want to stop and think about it. I wrapped my arms around your neck and you crushed me against you, until it seemed the entire length of my body was touching yours. You tasted how I imagined –

warm and musky – and when you stopped for a second and studied my face with a feverish need, I knew there was no going back.

You must have felt the same, because the next moment you took my hand and turned to leave the dancefloor without a word. You led me through the crowd which parted reflexively before us, and there were more than a few avid glances cast in our direction. It was thrilling and somewhat frightening to realise how much my longing for you had affected the people around us. I could see it in their eyes – a fervour bordering on hysteria – and I quickly turned away to avoid making it worse. You were like a whole different person, your steps fast and purposeful, and I wondered fleetingly if I had unleashed something in you that would be more than I had bargained for.

We got outside and the fresh air hit me, cooling the sweat on my skin and making it tingle. You started heading in the direction of the hostel we were staying in, but suddenly I knew I couldn't wait any longer; I needed to dispel the power that was surging through me before it became too much for me to bear. I tugged at your hand, pulling you back towards the beach road, looking for a way through. I wasn't aware of my feet hitting the pavement, or the people around us, or anything; all my energy was focused on keeping myself in check for long enough to get away from the crowds.

I spotted a narrow alleyway down one side of a bar. Someone had left a gate open and I darted through, past a dark doorway and along the paved path that sloped sharply downwards until it met the sand. We emerged onto the beach – a shadowed spot that sat between a jetty and the tall wooden pilings of a large balcony. It was a sliver of sand, quiet apart from the sighing of the waves, the sounds from the street muted by the buildings and the music that was playing in the restaurant above.

Out across the water I could see the lights shimmering, and the moon rode high in the sky, a beautiful silver sickle. I looked at you and laughed, breathless from the speed of our march, and slowly walked backwards between two of the pilings, my eyes never leaving yours.

As soon as we were concealed by the gloom your grip tightened on my hand and you came to a stop. I was grinning as your greedy lips met mine, and the sudden rush of adrenaline made my head spin. I relished the taste and smell of you, breathing you in, buried my fingers in your hair and pulled you closer, gasping as your hands worked their way inside my dress, sending ripples of pleasure through me that grew more intense by the second.

I felt the cold, smooth wood of a post at my back and I crushed you against me, tearing at your clothes so I could touch the skin beneath. We were frantic in our eagerness, desperate almost; your mouth was on my neck, and I dug my nails into your back as the roaring flames sucked the air from my lungs. The fire was rising up inside me again and I was struggling to master it, determined not let it consume me and forget to savour the moment; you were too delicious to wolf down all in one go. I'd been waiting so long for you, I didn't want to miss a single chance to luxuriate in the feeling of being in your arms at last.

'Shhh, slow down, it's OK.' I reached up and ran my fingertip over your lips. 'It's just you and me, there's no rush. Let's just… enjoy this.'

You paused, panting for a few seconds, then bent down to kiss me again, slowly and deeply, and I felt a shift in your body like you were rooted more firmly to the ground. Your hands moved over me with greater certainty, no longer hurried and nervous but with a sweet reverence, and my skin glowed warmly everywhere you touched. The self-conscious boy in you had been scoured away by the fire, just as the hesitant girl had been scoured away in me. We were becoming something else – something more than ourselves – or perhaps simply awakening parts of each other that had been lying dormant all along.

You took hold of me gently and lifted me up, pinning me to the post, and I had to bite down on your shoulder to stop myself crying out as our bodies finally fused together. Your rhythm synced with mine and we moved slowly, prolonging every second of motion to its fullest. You pressed your face into my hair and your fingers clung to my back as we swayed, our lungs matching breath for breath and our hearts thudding together through the skin, flesh and bone that held them apart. If it were possible for two people to meld together utterly I think we would have done, and in the last, rapturous movement, with reality fragmenting around us, we became one; just for a heartbeat, we were truly one being in perfect equilibrium.

And then it was over.

You stood still for a while, your head bowed against my chest, before carefully letting me down. I leaned against the post as I fought to regain my breath, and then your forehead met mine and we stood in silence, not wanting to break the spell. I couldn't believe something so brief could have touched me so profoundly.

I laughed, giddy with euphoria now that the fire had subsided.

'What's funny?' you asked.

'I'm just so glad that finally happened, it was driving me mad. And,' I slid my fingers between yours and squeezed them, 'it was really beautiful. No one's ever made me feel like that before.'

You laughed, still breathless, and stood up straighter. 'You don't have to say that. I'm not... I haven't—'

'I mean it. We're good together, you and me.'

You watched me quietly, then took my face in your hands and kissed me.

'We are,' you said, still holding me. 'You make me feel… different. New.'

'New. I like that.' We grinned at each other again, delighting in the moment, before straightening out our clothing and sneaking back up the alley to make our way to the hostel.

Our travelling became even more of an adventure after that. Our conversations had the clarity of air after a thunderstorm, without all the unspoken feelings and insecurities cluttering them up.

After leaving Pattaya we continued our journey north, taking the train from Bangkok up to the historic ruins of Phra Nakhon Si Ayutthaya, then on to the giant Buddha in Sukhothai before reaching the mountains. The incredible countryside flashed past us – rice fields and rivers, villages and monasteries – and the rumble of the train was a constant, comforting drone in the background.

There was one afternoon, as we lounged in the glass-clear water of a hot spring near Pai, surrounded on all sides by the brilliant green foliage of overhanging trees and the babble of little waterfalls, when you asked me, outright, what I liked about you. From someone else I might have taken it as a disingenuous question, but from you it seemed like it came from a place of sincere curiosity, so I kept the teasing to a minimum… Obviously I had to tease you a little bit.

'Hmm,' I murmured, pondering your many delightful attributes. 'Well, you have beautiful hands.' I reached across and knitted my fingers through yours, turning your hand over to examine the graceful shapes and tracing the lines on your palm with my thumb. 'And… I love the way you smile with your eyes. And you have the cutest dimple when you laugh, I like that too.'

You proved me right before leaning over and giving me a soft kiss that tasted of ginger and garlic from the food you'd eaten earlier. You were so different to the wary wanderer I had met a few short weeks ago, and I was deeply glad I had stuck around to let the magic do its work.

'Let's see, what else?… You see the beauty in everything, even things that seem ugly to everyone else. You see into the heart of things. It's a real gift.' I wiggled my toes just beneath the surface of the pool, sending ripples flowing out across the water.

You drifted away from the side, turning to face me and cocking your head. 'I see you.'

I chuckled, flicking water droplets at you. 'And?'

'You have a secret.' You weren't playing anymore.

I stopped smiling. 'What do you mean?'

You shrugged, stroking my outstretched foot just beneath the water. 'Just… I know… there's something you're not telling me. Something you don't tell anyone.'

I drew myself upright, feeling unnerved. I knew you had a different way of looking at the world, but how much did you really see during all those hours you spent studying me? I reached out and touched your arm to make you look at me.

'It's OK. I get it.' You took my hand in both of yours and steadily met my gaze.

'Get what?' I wrapped my arms around your shoulders, inordinately afraid that something was about to change between us that couldn't be changed back.

'You.'

I searched your face for clarification but couldn't find any. 'What do you mean you *get* me? What's this about? Are you OK?' I laid my hand on your cheek and you turned to plant a kiss in the centre of my palm.

'I'm fine. I'm better than fine, I'm inspired…'

'But?'

'You'll never show me all of yourself. And I won't ask you to.'

I couldn't think how to respond. What was I supposed to say? I couldn't tell you the truth – you'd think I'd lost my mind – but I didn't want to lie to you. You deserved better than that.

It still made me dizzy thinking about the glut of power that had risen up in me that night in Pattaya. I'd had no idea that it could happen that way, and I didn't think it would be wise to try and summon it again, even if I could. I wasn't convinced it was something I had a say in, and I had no idea where it might lead to if I lost control. It was a frightening thought, but I was also fascinated by it, in the same way other people are fascinated by the experience of peering out over a cliff without holding onto anything. It had been the most intense rush I'd ever known, but even so, I wasn't in a hurry to repeat it.

'It's alright,' you finally murmured, 'really. I just… I know you're not like other people. You have… a destiny.'

The Path. That agonising, glorious road of light and shadow. It had led me to you – to this place and this life, and I loved you with all of my being, with every fibre and every cell – but wouldn't it also lead me away again? What we had was real, the most real and perfect love I'd ever felt, so if it couldn't be forever, then what did that mean? My purpose was to find a love that could take root and bloom, scattering its seeds to the winds so that its essence would be spread to every corner of the world. That was what I was made for. That was my reason for existing. So if true, lasting love was an unattainable fantasy, then what did that say about *me*?

You smiled with that wistful look you had sometimes, shining your golden light onto my face, and I huddled against you, eager to be rid of the creeping feeling that was slithering across my skin.

'You know what you make me think of?' you asked quietly, your chin resting on the top of my head.

'What?' I prompted, mumbling into your chest.

'*The Birth of Venus*. The Botticelli. Have you ever seen that painting?'

I nodded. I was vaguely familiar with it: the nude figure of Venus standing upright on a seashell, flanked by figures on either side who gazed upon her face.

'She has this *look*,' you continued. 'I don't know, it's supposed to be this serene innocence, like she's completely pure and untainted.'

'That doesn't really sound like me,' I joked, trying to lighten the mood, even though I didn't feel light at all.

'But I don't think that's it,' you carried on, refusing to be diverted.

'No?' I tilted my head back, breathing in the smell of your neck.

'I always thought she looked more… resigned and… distant. Lonely maybe.'

I swallowed hard. *Is that really what you think of when you look at me?*

'She's there on her pedestal for everyone to admire, but she's removed from it all, you know? Like she's sick of being on display, so she shuts herself off because she has to keep that last, tiny piece of herself hidden away. It's the piece no one's allowed to see because then she'd have nothing left for herself; she'd be empty… I always thought that made that painting really sad.'

You were speaking more to yourself than to me by then, but the words buried themselves in my heart like molten knives.

You took a deep breath, and I think in that moment you must have realised you were meant to be explaining why I reminded you of that painting. You tensed, like you were afraid of my reaction, but I reached up and stroked your face, keeping mine pressed against your neck and clamping my eyes shut so the tears wouldn't fall.

The thought was terrifying: that I'd find myself back on the lonely, rambling Path, with no one and nothing to call my own. The memory of that feeling gathered in the pit of my stomach like a cold, hard stone.

I don't want it, I thought. *I don't want it, I don't want it. I can't do it anymore.*

You bent to kiss me, and the warmth of your love chased away the chill that had crept into my bones. You were here, now, with me, real and present and adoring. I drew back and gazed up at you, forcing the panic down and away, wondering at the miracle of your eyes, so beautiful and so keenly perceptive that they even saw down into the impossible core of my hidden self.

How is it you can see what no one else ever has?

I wanted so much to ask you, but I couldn't risk you finding out the real truth, not all of it. I suppose I was afraid that for all your perceptiveness you wouldn't actually believe it anyway.

'You have a beautiful soul,' I said instead. 'You see things for what they are, not what they seem to be.'

I studied you – the rich black curtain of your hair and the relaxed set of your shoulders, the water glinting off your skin and the curve of your eyebrows – and was flooded with a deep, aching love for you that seemed too immense to bear. You were everything; your mind was as beautiful as your body, and I wanted nothing more than to stay in this place with you and never have to leave.

'I don't think you realise how rare that is,' I said, partly to myself, wondering if I would ever feel this way about anyone again.

We didn't say any more after that. We just lay in the warm water, watching the current flow past us and the emerald leaves flutter in the breeze. I hoped that you knew I meant what I'd said. It seemed important for you to know that I saw you too – saw you for who you were, as clearly as you saw me – and that it was enough. You were more than enough to please anyone.

Sometime in January we were eating lunch at the sole restaurant of a tiny village outside Chiang Mai, resting after a few days of exploring the nearby mountains. Our table was a tiled plank of wood that stood on roughly hewn posts, and we sat on plain, handmade stools that had been worn smooth with use. The view was of misty, tree-covered mountains that rolled away like waves into the distance, and a sky so brilliantly blue it made my eyes ache. The restaurant served one dish per day, and we were tucking into our delicious bowls of noodles and curry broth with immense relish. That was probably the best bowl of food I've ever had in my life.

I could tell something was on your mind, but I suppose the fear of being parted from you prevented me from asking what was wrong. I was too much of a coward to confront the inevitable truth: our destinies weren't meant to intertwine forever, only to overlap for a while – to flow together like the confluence of two rivers and then separate again.

'I've been thinking it'll be time for me to go home soon,' you said quietly, leaning your leg against mine.

I swallowed back my sudden panic and managed to reply calmly. 'Yeah, I guess… I hadn't really thought about it.' *And I don't have a home to go back to anyway.*

The idea of being alone again loomed up around me like the walls of a prison. How would I go on without you? Together, we were adventurers exploring the world; on my own I was just… lost. A leaf on the wind. But I had to face the fact that this was the inevitable conclusion. The time had come to be honest with myself: what we had was never meant to last forever. For you, it was a holiday romance, nothing more. And for me… it was another stopping place along the Path, a warm, sweet place to rest my head and stay long enough to create something beautiful and unique – something that would bring a little more love into the world. And then move on. Always.

'Oh,' you said. It was a weighty word for only two letters.

'How soon?'

You shrugged uncomfortably. I wanted to take you in my arms, to keep you near me and not let go, but that wouldn't have been fair to either of us.

'I understand,' I told you, because I meant it and because I wanted you to know it was OK, 'I really do. You have your work to get back to, and I…'

'And you?' you asked, taking my hand. 'What are you going to do, after this?'

'I have a world to explore.' I smiled and leaned my head on your shoulder, gazing out across the flawless landscape. The world looked enormous from where I sat, and I knew I should be excited, but—

'Will you miss me?' you asked in the end, the plaintiveness of the question making my heart twist in my chest.

I answered you soundlessly, with a blurred kiss that filled my world for a moment and then left me utterly empty. I rose and stood between your legs, cradling your head as though I might be able to hide you from the world before it could drag you away, but I knew I couldn't fight it.

'I wish you could come with me,' you mumbled. Your breath warmed the skin in the middle of my chest, like an extra heart, beating.

'I wish I could too.' The words came out in a harsh whisper, and I stepped back from you, looking down at your beloved face.

'Why don't you?' you asked, gripping my hands. 'You said you wanted to visit one day, why not now?'

I freed one hand and combed your hair back from your face, hoping my fingertips would remember the texture after we had parted. 'Would you come with me, if I said the same thing to you?'

I could hardly bear to utter the words, and I don't know why I said them since any answer you gave would only add to the pain, but I wanted to hear it anyway. And yes, maybe I wanted you to say you couldn't possibly live without me, that you would rather die than be parted from me, and that you wouldn't go home unless I agreed to go with you and stay by your side forever and ever.

You didn't though, of course. You knew better than that. You shook your head slowly, and in that moment I think we both accepted that our time was almost at an end.

'I have my own destiny, remember?' I whispered, my lips grazing your forehead.

You were silent for a while, but then you fixed me with that warm, unwavering gaze, drew my face down to yours and kissed me until I thought I'd melt. When you pulled away you looked at me for a long time, your thumb following the curve of my cheekbone as you stared into my eyes.

I wished I *could* go home with you – or that you'd come travelling with me, and belong to me the way you had once belonged to that other girl you'd loved – but it would never have worked. My Path didn't lead that way; you weren't the one I was looking for, the one I would find at the end of my journey, and I wasn't the one you were looking for either. Trying to force something that wasn't meant to be would have broken both our hearts, and we'd have ended up even worse off than before. Instead, we mended each other, for a while. We found love, however fleeting, and it healed our hurts and made us stronger. We were two wandering souls who found each other – two nomads who found somewhere that felt like home.

We lingered a little while longer in Thailand. There were a few more places to see before we headed back to Bangkok and went our separate ways. You were my lover for that time, but more than that, my friend.

At our final goodbye in the teeming departure terminal of Bangkok International, you held me so tightly it seemed you wouldn't let go. But you did. And then you looked at me in your open, uncomplicated way and said, 'I loved you.'

'I know. I loved you too.'

You stepped back and smiled that slow half-smile, with the adorable dimple I had grown so accustomed to.

We stood watching each other, seeing right down into the core of our beings. I wanted to stay that way forever, and at the same time I wanted to run as fast as I could to escape the unbearable sadness.

Out of nowhere, I suddenly remembered a song I'd begun to learn on the guitar a couple of weeks before, and I decided I wanted to hear it. More than that, I wanted *you* to hear it with me.

I know this has to happen, I thought, to whatever forces might be listening, *but I'm going to have this one, small thing. This time I'm choosing the Song.*

'Just a minute,' I said, digging my MP3 player out of my bag. 'Can I play you something?'

You nodded, taking a deep breath like you were bracing yourself, and I handed you one of the earbuds, stuffing the other one into my ear as I cycled through the tracks. I didn't know why it mattered so much that I shared this with you, but it did. Perhaps it was just that it would allow us to have one more moment together – to stave off the inevitable for just a few minutes longer.

I found the one I wanted and pressed play, reaching out to take your hand and drawing you towards me. Around us people hurried past, but their existence hardly registered; there was only you and me, in our reality. Only that perfect space between our bodies. The Song rang out in my ear and I ran my fingers up your arms, tracing the shape of you until I reached your shoulders. I could see that you were struggling to hold back tears and I kissed you gently, not to stop them falling but to tell you it was alright. Your arms encircled me and I let the music roll over me. It was 'Hallelujah' by Jeff Buckley. It said everything I wanted to say.

Thank you, I thought, feeling the melody take root in my soul. It was a part of me now, a part of our story that I would never forget.

I hugged you closer, resting my forehead against yours and rocking gently to the music. You let out a long, sad sigh and your mouth twitched downwards at the corners, marred by a bitterness that it hurt me to see.

'Shhh,' I whispered, reaching up to touch your lips with my fingers. 'It's OK. We'll be OK.'

You relaxed against me and we stood there together, swaying gently in the tides of pain that washed through our bodies and stripped away the soft, protective layer of love that had kept us safe and warm for those few precious weeks. It seemed like we'd belonged to each other for far longer than that, but I had begun to think that maybe love is not something you can measure in terms of minutes or days or years; a lifetime of feeling had passed between us: pleasure and pain, joy and bitterness and truth.

The memory of our Song stayed with you too, I know, because years after that day you produced a painting of two lovers standing in a pool of golden light, arms encircling each other and foreheads touching in an expression of shared grief. Sorrow was etched into every brush stroke, but there was sweetness too. A perfect, frozen moment, existing outside the normal rules of time and space. Two souls breathing as one.

I kissed you and stepped back as the final notes of the Song died away.

I love you. I spoke the words to you with my eyes, knowing you would hear.

You smiled – a tiny, sad smile – and passed the earbud back to me. *I love you too. My Aphrodite. My muse.*

I kissed your fingers, inhaling the scent of your skin one last time, and then before I could do something stupid I walked away towards my departure gate. I could feel your eyes on me until I rounded the first corner in the corridor, then I let the tears fall, safely unseen.

I thought about what would happen when you got home – about all the drawings and paintings you'd create that I'd never get to see. I thought about all the love you had to come, all the passion and sweetness and joy, and probably sorrow too, although as an artist maybe that was just a necessary evil on the quest to find your truth.

I hope you found someone who realised, as I did, how precious and rare you are. I'm certain you must have. The universe is far too full of love to have overlooked someone as worthy of it as you.

As I sat in the departure lounge waiting for the boarding call, desperately trying not to break down and sob, I heard it. Another Song. I wasn't expecting to get another one now, after we had already parted, but it came to me anyway: an unlooked-for antidote to my loneliness. Into the soundless void in the centre of my being poured the liquid, tumbling notes, and even though the words made my eyes brim over again with tears, I felt comforted by them.

You understand, I thought, to whatever being or beings were behind that gentle solace. *You're always there when I need you.*

It was 'Iris' by the Goo Goo Dolls. It was exactly what I needed to hear.

I closed my eyes and listened, a familiar tune but one without any special meaning until that moment. I cranked up the volume and sat back, letting the sound fill the hollow place inside as the tears drained out of me.

Just you and me again, I guess.

The music didn't answer, but it was already telling me what it had to say.

Fighter

I've been dreading this part of my story. I guess I'll just have to give it the bungee jump treatment: *Don't think, just go.*

I was in Las Vegas. I'd been there for about four days, riding the seductive undercurrent of excess that seemed to run through every inch of that crazy place. The night we met, I was on the prowl. For over three years I'd been alone, distracting myself with every possible thrill and amusement so I didn't have to think about the crushing futility of a life spent building sandcastles only to see them washed away by the tide. I'd been travelling for so long the places and people were all starting to look the same – landscapes and faces blurring into a featureless jumble in my mind, with nothing to tell them apart. What had once seemed like a wonderful adventure was becoming an endless trudge through the wilderness. I could disappear off the face of the Earth and no one would miss me or even notice I was gone. I hadn't exactly been avoiding the Path, but I wasn't really following it either. I was pushing my limits, rebelling against the forces that dictated who I should be and where I should go. Vegas was just another stop on the way. Or so I thought.

That night I could sense the tension in the air, or maybe it was coming from somewhere inside me, and the feeling intensified as the evening wore on. My mind wasn't focused on love or on my purpose as a Keeper; I was acting on impulse – raw instinct.

I had chosen to wear a bright red halter-neck dress with a low-cut neckline and a skirt that flirted around my thighs, catching the breeze as I strode through the balmy night air. It was fun to reacquaint myself with the experience of strutting along the pavement in a good pair of Mary Jane platforms, a jaunty bounce in my step as I made my way from one lively venue to another.

Sometime after midnight I wandered into a dive bar a little way off the Strip, so unobtrusive I would have walked straight past if not for the irresistible pull I felt as I approached the door. I just knew, from that old familiar feeling, that inside there was someone I needed to meet. I resisted for a moment, toying with the idea of ignoring what my gut was telling me and deliberately thwarting my nature, the Path, whatever plans the universe had and anything else that tried to control me. I was tired of being pushed and pulled between happiness and loneliness; at least if I was on my own I didn't have to deal with the crushing sense of loss that ripped me apart every time I had to move on. But as the pulling intensified, searing through me with white-hot urgency, I knew the fun and games were over and it was time to bow to the inevitable. I hoped that whatever happened this time, it would be less painful than what had gone before; I couldn't cope with another tragic ending. This one had to be all or nothing.

I have to say, first impressions weren't hopeful: muted lighting and melancholy music, people muttering in dark corners. There was something disquieting about the atmosphere, like the loaded silence when you walk in on an argument, which was pretty weird considering how dead the place was. The other bars were getting rowdier as the night went on, but a subdued unease seemed to pervade the entire room, and as I approached the bar I saw a few people hurriedly finish their drinks and leave.

I figured I might as well get a drink and see what happened; if I was meant to be here then something would materialise. I slid onto a stool and leaned my elbows on the counter, scanning the tired-looking chalkboard menu for inspiration. Only one other person was at the bar, a few feet away on the stool to my right, and when I glanced across I saw that my sole drinking companion was slouched over in a man-shaped heap, contemplating something in the bottom of a whiskey glass.

It was you.

Like the bar, first impressions weren't great. In a flick of my eyes I took in the baggy jeans and faded red hoodie with the arms cut off, the tatty baseball cap pulled low over your face… but as I looked closer I noticed details that piqued my interest, particularly when I examined the arm that was curled protectively around your empty glass. It had tattoos covering the copper-brown skin from shoulder to wrist, and was – for lack of a more eloquent description – ripped. I mean… damn.

I let my vision blur, trying to see beneath the surface and figure out what was underneath: to see with my heart instead of just my eyes. You worked out a lot, that much was obvious, but you weren't enough of a health nut to abstain from drinking. You were alone, so… maybe you weren't from around here? Either that or you weren't very popular. Your body language was defensive – dejected even. Your head was propped on your hand and you hadn't moved since I'd arrived. That kind of stillness usually meant there was more going on inside: physical activity suspended in favour of mental strain. Or maybe you were just really, really drunk.

I caught the attention of the bartender and asked for a margarita. As he made it his eyes kept darting towards you, as though he was expecting you to do something unpleasant at any moment. I took the drink from him, wondering how I was going to get any answers from someone who didn't even seem to be aware of my existence, and whether I even wanted answers anyway. Was it you? No one else stood out to me. And as I watched you I felt the tiniest prickle of sweetness stir in my chest. It was the first time I'd felt anything at all for quite a while – enough to remind me that there was more to being Aphrodite than getting my heart broken; there was also the part that came before that, and the hope for… something beautiful. Maybe. I didn't particularly want to hope again; it hurt too much to have it taken away. But still…

You straightened up and held out your glass, waggling it to indicate you wanted a refill. You looked across at me and I could see straightaway that you were drunk. Like, alone-in-a-bar-in-Vegas drunk. It took a second longer for me to notice that your right eye was swollen shut, with a nasty lump of puffy flesh surrounding it that had been hidden under the shadow of your cap. I must have looked disturbed at the sight, because you smirked and let out a small snort of derision before turning away again.

'What?' I asked, irritated by your reaction.

'Huh?' you replied, trying to focus on my face again, without much success.

'I was just wondering what's funny.' I cocked my head at you. I hadn't made my mind up about you yet, and if you were going to be rude then I was out of here. Probably.

'Oh.' You looked away and watched the barman filling your glass from the bottle, although by the look on his face it was against his better judgement.

That was all the answer I got.

Seriously? This is what I have to work with?

Your whiskey appeared in front of you and you took a sullen swallow. I watched, debating the wisdom of continuing down this road… It really was a *very* attractive arm. And there was that prickle again, uncomfortable but also strangely pleasant.

'What happened to you?' I tried another tack, thinking that maybe sympathy would prompt a more communicative response.

I was kind of right.

'What the fuck do you think?'

I sipped my drink and carried on staring at you, feeling defiant. 'I don't know. You fell down some stairs? Walked into a door?'

A touch of disbelief coloured your expression, and I thought perhaps I could detect the beginnings of amusement.

'Something like that,' you mumbled.

'I should see the other guy, right?'

The humour vanished without a trace. 'Is that supposed to be funny?'

'What is your problem?' I snapped back, my composure crumbling.

The barman was glaring at me but I couldn't see why. As far as I was concerned I'd made a perfectly innocent comment, you were the one being obnoxious.

'My problem?' You scowled and then winced as the movement creased the skin around your eye. 'Listen, I'm not interested, OK? Whatever you're selling, take it somewhere else. Hookers ain't my thing.'

I was actually struck dumb, not a common occurrence I'll admit but that one got me. My face was burning with indignation and I realised I was gripping the edge of the bar to keep my hands from shaking.

'What's the matter? Did I say something to offend you?'

A cold fury washed through me and I found my voice again. 'Did you actually just call me a *whore*? Who the hell do you think you are?'

'Riiight,' you said, swivelling round to face me. 'You're just a woman out drinking, all by yourself, and you happened to walk into this shithole, and then you decided to stick around so you could talk to *me*.' The sarcasm was so thick I could have spread it on toast.

'That's exactly what happened,' I retorted, glaring back at you and refusing to be cowed. 'Although the last part was clearly a big, fat waste of time.'

You were regarding me with a kind of confused scepticism.

'Bullshit,' you said.

'Nope,' I shot back.

You almost looked disappointed, which seemed strange considering a moment ago you'd been telling me to get lost. You turned away from me and took another mouthful of whiskey.

I twisted around to face the bar again and tried to figure out what to do. Despite your surliness I couldn't shake the feeling that something was about to happen, and I'd learned to trust those feelings; they had never led me astray, although never before had I been so drawn to anyone I found so... annoying!

A new song started playing on the jukebox at the far end of the room, but it didn't seem to be telling me anything. I waited for something to change but you maintained your silence, clearly doing your best to ignore me. I decided it was time to take the hint and leave you alone. Maybe it was just bad timing or something; maybe I'd been wrong after all and that little twitch was just... indigestion.

I set my glass down and stood up, nodding my thanks to the barman and sliding my bag onto my shoulder.

'Well, nice meeting you,' I muttered, with more than a trace of sarcasm.

Just then the track changed and I heard the soft sound of a piano. I turned my face to the jukebox, convinced suddenly that this was something I needed to hear. The voice that began to sing was gentle, but the words sent chills up my spine. It was one of the saddest, most beautiful songs I've ever heard: 'Glitter In the Air' by Pink. I'd never noticed the breathtaking blend of sweetness and pain in her voice until I heard that Song; it was a message I couldn't mistake.

Don't walk away, it seemed to say. *You're needed here, more than you've ever been needed before.*

I stood listening to it, hypnotised by the achingly poignant melody as it filled my ears and filtered through my body. Just as the verse led into the refrain I felt the touch of warm skin on my forearm, and I turned back around, astonished to find that it was your hand. Did you feel it too, the magic of that Song? Did it make you stop and lose yourself for a moment like it did me?

'Hey, I'm sorry, OK?' you mumbled. 'I'm not the best company right now.'

I snorted. 'No shit.'

Your lips curved into a rueful smile. You let go of my arm and sat back a little, studying me.

And then I saw it: the pained expression had nothing to do with your injuries. There was something else behind it, something I hadn't noticed before. You looked back down at your whiskey, avoiding my gaze. I can honestly say I've never seen anyone look so heartbroken in my life.

I slumped back down on my seat, struck by a feeling of sympathy so intense it made my chest hurt. I'd never felt so compelled to obey a Song before; it wasn't just prompting me to act, it was demanding it, and somehow I knew that ignoring it would mean missing out on one of the most profound experiences of my life.

'You want another drink?' you asked, staring fixedly at your glass. Somehow it seemed like you expected rejection, like you assumed you were setting yourself up for a fall.

'Yeah. I do,' I answered quietly.

You glanced up, wary, waiting for the punchline. When it didn't come you waved the barman over to refill my glass.

'So, why *did* you come here?' you asked, studying me more closely as I sat watching you back. 'You trying to get murdered or something?'

I laughed. Beneath that prickly shell there was a playful humour, I could feel it.

'I don't know.' I shrugged. 'I just… felt like it was the right place.'

'For what?'

'Interesting people.'

'Humph.' You sounded dubious, but you seemed to accept that explanation. After a moment's pause, you spoke again, 'What's your name?'

'Aphrodite.'

'Huh?' You raised your eyebrow in surprise.

'Aph-ro-di-te.' I smiled. It wasn't the first time I'd had that reaction, and I was pretty sure it wouldn't be the last.

'Oh. That's cool. Happy to meet you, Aphrodite.'

'Thanks. Aph is fine… So, are you going to clear up the big mystery?'

You shrugged. 'Maybe.'

I could see a different light in your eye now. I wasn't sure what it was but it changed your face completely. There was something endearing about that twinkle of yours, even with half your face mushed into a pulp.

I took a sip of my newly replenished drink.

'Have you ever been to a fight?' you asked, sneaking a glance at me from under your cap.

'A fight? Like… a boxing match?'

'MMA,' you said, snorting with amusement. 'I'll take that as a no.'

'Oh. No. I don't know what that means.'

'Mixed martial arts.'

You took a swallow of whiskey, the muscles of your arm bunching as you raised the glass to your mouth. It wasn't so much that they were *big*, just… *dense*. Your physique made perfect sense now that I knew you pummelled people for a living – or, well, got pummelled by the looks of it – and I thought about how fit you must be, with all that working out and training and… whatever else fighters did when they weren't fighting. I made a bet with myself that you were pretty energetic when you wanted to be. The thought made my insides tingle.

'So is that it? You're a professional fighter?'

'Yep.' You let the 'p' pop out as if the question annoyed you, but I didn't feel like your irritation was directed at me.

'And you had a fight tonight?'

'Uh-huh.'

'So what happened?'

Your face clouded again. 'What do you think?'

There was no mistaking it: beneath the sharp snap of sarcasm, you were devastated.

'You lost?' I prompted, my tone conciliatory.

'Yeah.' You cleared your throat and sniffed loudly. 'That's kinda my thing. That's what losers do, right?'

I looked at you for a while, caught between an urge to comfort you and a desire to give you a sharp slap.

'Hey.' I poked you gently on the arm. 'It must take some guts to do that for a living.'

'It's about all I'm good for,' you said, staring down into your glass with that dejected look again.

I edged a little closer. 'I'm sure that's not true.'

'You are, huh?' You clenched your jaw and shook your head a little. When you looked back up at me I noticed for the first time how incredibly dark your eyes were, the open one appearing almost black in the reflected light from the neon around the bar. I've heard people talk about being lost in the depths of someone's eyes, but until that moment I'd never experienced it myself. 'You sound pretty sure about that, for someone who just met me.'

'Well, that's kind of *my* thing.' I moved even closer, feeling a whisper of electricity pass between us as my right arm and thigh came to rest against yours. 'So, what do you do when you're not getting beaten up for a living?'

'Well, I get drunk,' you held up your glass as evidence, 'hang around in shitholes, and insult beautiful women.' You dropped your gaze, like you were too shy to observe my reaction to the last part. 'And then sometimes,' you leaned in close as though confiding a secret, still not looking at me, 'I go and get beat up for fun.'

'Really?' I laughed. You did have a sense of humour after all. 'Well, that sounds... depressing.'

'I know, right?' You straightened up and held out your glass again for the barman. You sure did drink fast. 'Hey, amigo, I'll take another one of those.'

The barman swallowed nervously and braced his arms against the counter.

'Sorry, man, I don't think—'

'I said, I'll have another.' You glared at him.

'Look, I don't want any trouble.' He was sweating under the lights. I couldn't help but feel sorry for him.

'No?' you snapped. 'Then fill me up.'

'I'm sorry but I think you've had enough.' He shrugged apologetically.

You got to your feet, looking a lot scarier than when you'd been sitting down. You were just shy of six feet tall but you seemed far larger with your imposing build, especially when you were puffed up with anger.

'I don't give a shit what you think,' you snarled, pointing your finger across the bar. 'I'll stop when I wanna stop, and right now I wanna drink.' You glowered at him for a moment and then dropped your hand and sank onto your stool again, but it had moved when you'd stood up and you slipped, losing your balance and grabbing hold of the counter.

'Hey!' I took hold of your shoulders, steadying you. 'Come on, why don't we go? You look like you could use a lie-down.'

You peered up at me and grinned broadly, a surprisingly boyish expression considering how morose you were being. A shiver chased across my skin from the nape of my neck right down to the small of my back, as my mind conjured up an image of the way you must look without the injuries marring your features – maybe not the most stereotypically good-looking guy, but there was something fierce about you that seemed to render such notions completely inconsequential.

'You wanna come lie down with me?'

I pouted, amused that you were trying to flirt even though you were probably close to passing out. 'How about I just keep you company instead?'

'Sure,' you said, heaving yourself upright and laying your arm across my shoulders. 'That doesn't sound as much fun, but I'll take it.'

I couldn't help but notice the look of relief on the bartender's face, and I suppressed a smile, sliding my bag onto my shoulder and taking a firmer grip of your waist. 'OK, come on. Can you walk?'

'Sure I can walk, what kind of question is that?'

'Just checking. You're too heavy to carry.'

'I don't need carrying,' you said, but you leaned on me all the same as we shuffled out of the door and onto the street.

'Your place or mine?' I asked, looking up and down the road. It wasn't far to my hotel and I didn't know how long I could hold you up like this.

'You got booze at your place?'

'Of course,' I replied, as if it was a silly question.

You considered for a long moment and shrugged. 'OK. Your place it is.'

I nodded and turned left, hoping I could remember the way; I wasn't exactly sober either. I could feel the muscles in your back bunching and relaxing with the movement of your body, and I could detect the faint scent of your skin: a mingling of sweat and deodorant, and something else that reminded me of childhood somehow… a slightly antiseptic smell. I liked it.

As we walked into the hotel lobby I noticed furtive glances being directed our way from the few people who were around, and their chatter stopped abruptly as we approached the reception desk so I could retrieve my room key. I don't know what they thought was going on but I was sure they must have seen worse, so I ignored their stares and concentrated on not tripping over your feet as they wove their way to the lift. We stepped inside, and as soon as the doors closed I looked up at you and grinned.

'So that's what you look like in the light,' I said, making a show of examining your face.

'Yeah… Bet you wish it was dark still, huh.'

'No. I like being able to see people when I'm talking to them.'

You returned my gaze and I started to feel mesmerised, losing myself in the gleaming depths of your eye, so dark it was almost black.

When we got to my room I threw open the door and flicked on the light, before helping you over to the giant, plush sofa in the centre of the lounge area. I'd gone for luxury on this occasion, and had booked myself a large suite with all the trimmings. The place was decorated in shades of plum and grey, with soft, tactile fabrics, gleaming wooden furniture and glowing up-lights spaced along the walls. There was a reception room, a separate dining area and a bedroom off to the right, with a raised floor that stood a foot or so higher than the rest of the suite.

I caught you sneaking a peek at the huge, sumptuous bed and smirked to myself as I crossed the room and opened the door to the minibar. I grabbed you a beer and poured myself a rum and Coke, before making my way back over to you. After I handed you the bottle we watched each other for a moment. There was something endearingly open and unguarded about your stare, a vulnerability that completely contradicted what I'd imagined a fighter to be like.

I sat down beside you, kicking off my shoes and curling my legs under me. When I'd finished arranging my skirt I looked up to find you studying me.

'What did you say your name was again?'

'Aphrodite.' I laughed, amused that you'd forgotten already.

'Aphrodite,' you repeated. 'What a name!'

'What's wrong with my name?'

'No! Nothing, I just meant…' You saw the corner of my mouth twitch and you relaxed again. 'You're funny. You should be a comedian.'

'Yeah, well… maybe I am. It's better than being mistaken for a hooker.'

You cringed and I smiled maliciously.

'Hey, I'm sorry, OK, I didn't mean—'

'It's fine. You're drunk so I'll forgive you.'

'I am pretty drunk.' You went to rub your face but stopped the moment you touched the swelling, hissing softly and prodding the spot gingerly. 'So, what *do* you do?' you asked, sitting back and letting your head flop against the sofa.

'What do I *do*?… Guess.'

'Hmm,' you mused, closing your eye. 'Are you… a showgirl?'

'Nope.'

'How about… a card dealer?' Your voice was low and drowsy, and your body had sunk deeper into the cushions.

'Wrong again,' I said, dropping my voice to a murmur. 'I'll give you a hint: it's got nothing to do with casinos or cabaret shows.'

'Right… I don't know, I give up.' You opened your eye a crack.

I glanced across the room to where my guitar stood propped up against the wall in the corner. I had bought it just after leaving Thailand and it had travelled everywhere with me since: my one constant companion. It was the only way I'd managed to claw myself out of the desperate sadness that had descended; I'd spent hours and days and weeks practising on it, and now it felt like an extension of my own body – a detachable limb that was as vital as the heart beating inside my chest.

'I'm a singer,' I said. 'And I play guitar.'

'Really? Huh.' The last sound came out almost as a whisper, and I gently took the beer bottle out of your hand and put it down on the coffee table.

You didn't stir as I stood up and retrieved a blanket from the bed, and you were already snoring softly when I lifted your feet onto the sofa and pulled off your shoes. I studied you for a minute, watching as your face relaxed into slumber, and I was touched by how innocent you looked – almost angelic.

*

The next morning was probably one of the strangest of my life. I got up and had a shower, trying to be quiet so I wouldn't wake you. When I came back out of the bathroom in my thick, fluffy robe you were sitting upright on the sofa, stretching your arms and yawning expansively. I gave you a little wave as I caught your eye, and was rewarded with a huge, spontaneous smile. You were about to say something but then your phone started ringing and you picked it up, giving me a glance of apology before taking the call. It seemed like the rest had done you good, and I smiled at the thought of having a chance to get to know you when you weren't all sullen and slurring into a whiskey glass. Hopefully sober-you had better manners.

Right then I heard a knock at the door.

Room service! Good timing.

Never to this day have I had any breakfast like a Vegas hotel breakfast. There were pancakes with bacon and syrup, fresh fruit salad and thick, creamy yoghurt, fried sausages and onions, two kinds of eggs, grilled tomatoes, hash browns, French toast and garlic mushrooms, plus fresh orange juice and coffee, of course.

The waiter parked the service trolley next to the dining table, and I nodded my thanks and dug a tip out of my bag before he left, noticing his bemused glance in your direction. I loaded up a plate with a selection of tasty morsels and carried it over to the coffee table so I could sit and eat in comfort on the sofa. I took a sip of orange juice and nestled back against the cushions, chewing on a sausage and flicking through the newspaper that had been left, neatly folded, next to the plates on the trolley.

You finished your phone call and picked up the other sausage from the plate, slumping back to chew on it in silence. I watched you for a minute, waiting for some comment. Your face had taken on that dark expression again, and I guessed that whoever you'd been speaking to hadn't had anything positive to say. You'd removed your cap, and I noticed that you had a small gash running up from your forehead into your hairline.

'Sooo…' I started, not really knowing what I was planning to say next. 'Um, how's the head this morning?'

You snorted in response and reached for a slice of toast. 'Be better if I didn't have to deal with condescending assholes telling me how much of an idiot I am.'

'No. Doesn't sound like the best cure for a hangover. There's a whole load of food over there, by the way. Just in case you feel like getting some of your own.'

I was only teasing, but you threw the half-eaten piece of toast down on the table, sprang to your feet and stalked towards the bedroom, then changed your mind and strode back towards me, your face drawn in anger.

'You know what? I'm so sick of this shit.'

'Hey, I was just playing. It's OK, you don't have to—'

'OK? What exactly is OK about it? I lost, again, and now everyone thinks I'm a joke. And they're totally right!'

What had I got myself into? Last night I'd been too impulsive to think about the consequences of arguing back at you; today was different: I didn't have the energy for another confrontation and I was sober enough to feel daunted by how strong you were. I still wanted to help you – it seemed like you needed someone on your side – but I didn't want to put myself in a dangerous situation, and right now you seemed like the most dangerous person I'd ever been alone in a room with.

'Fuck!' You slammed your fists down on the back of the sofa, and I felt the impact through the frame. 'Why the hell can't they just leave me alone for five minutes?'

You started pacing, getting more and more worked up as you went along. 'I suck! I know it! I don't need some douchebag telling me over and over again. And this is the guy who's supposed to have my back.' You came to a standstill, your hands clenching and unclenching at your sides. 'I mean, how much of a loser do you have to be?'

'You're not a loser,' I murmured quietly, wishing I could rewind the last few minutes and keep my mouth shut about the stupid toast.

'I *am* a goddam loser!' you screamed, storming towards the bathroom.

'Why would you say that about yourself?' I called after you, shocked and saddened at how much rage there was inside you. I didn't want to provoke you, but somehow I was certain that there was more to your outburst than simple loss of temper. I remembered the forlornness I'd seen in you the night before; something inside you was crying out for someone to cut you some slack – to let you breathe for just five minutes. Maybe it was foolish or even arrogant of me to think I could make a difference when I was practically a stranger to you, but that Song had been impossible to ignore. I could have walked away and left you right then and there, but there was something we needed from each other and every fibre of my being was screaming at me to wait – just wait. You were lonely in the same way I was lonely; maybe, together, we could find a way not to be lonely anymore.

'Why do you care?' You turned back just as you reached the bathroom door. 'You don't even know me.'

'No,' I answered, standing up and crossing my arms. 'But I know what it's like to be all alone. Nobody deserves that.'

I could see the crushing pain in your face, and your left cheek was wet with tears. I couldn't help myself anymore; I strode across the carpet and wrapped my arms around your shoulders, squeezing you tightly and pressing my cheek against yours.

'Get off me,' you groaned. 'I don't need your pity.' But you made no attempt to push me away.

'Shut up,' I said. I wasn't letting go, regardless of what you had to say about it.

You sank down to the floor and I knelt beside you, keeping you firmly pressed against me. We sat like that for a while, and eventually you encircled me with your arms, sobbing like a lost child and trembling uncontrollably.

I guess maybe some people would have thought it pretty pathetic: a full-grown man – and a cage fighter at that – crumpled on the floor and crying, but the tears you cried had nothing to do with sorrow, or pain or even rage; it was loneliness that made you weep your heart out into my hair, a loneliness that I was all too familiar with and could understand maybe better than anybody.

Never before or since have I met anyone who was so strong and so vulnerable at the same time. You needed me more than I'd ever been needed before, just like the music told me when I almost walked away.

We clung to each other as I waited for you to calm down. I could tell it must have been a long time since anyone had just let you vent like that. At last your breathing evened out and your arms began to loosen, relaxing enough that I could sit back a little and look at your face. You refused to meet my gaze for a minute, as though you were embarrassed at what you had shown me. I reached up and brushed the tears from your cheek, waiting for you to speak.

You finally looked at me and I gave you an encouraging smile, just a little one.

'I'm sorry,' you croaked.

I shook my head. 'Don't be sorry,' I murmured. 'Don't ever be sorry.'

I saw you trying to figure me out, like you were waiting for some catch. Then tentatively, as though I might vanish if you moved too fast, you leaned forward and pressed your lips to mine, and I tasted the salt of your tears as they mingled with the sweetness of your mouth. It wasn't an amorous kiss – more an expression of a gratitude that went beyond words – and I was surprised by the tenderness of it after everything that had just happened.

You pulled away after a moment, looking down at the floor, and I could have sworn you were blushing as you dusted your fingertips across the carpet in a nervous gesture.

Your phone rang again and you swore, leaping up from the floor and dashing to the sofa to dig it out from among the cushions. I heaved a sigh and decided to get dressed while you were talking. If there was going to be another explosion I didn't want to be in the vicinity this time.

When I emerged from the bathroom you were standing with your arms crossed, gazing out of the window, lost in thought. You noticed me and cleared your throat, dropping your hands to your sides. 'I um… I have to get back to LA.'

'Oh.' I grabbed my hairbrush from the nightstand and ran it through my hair, wondering what that meant for me. 'What's in LA?'

'Home.' You shrugged, toying with your phone. You inhaled deeply and gave a dispirited sigh.

'I've never been to LA,' I said, tossing the hairbrush down on the bed.

'No?' You met my gaze properly for the first time since you'd kissed me. 'There's room if you wanna come along for the ride?' You tried to make it sound like you were playing around, but you didn't fool me.

I pretended to think about it, sitting on the edge of the bed and leaning back on my hands. 'Hmm... OK.'

I would have paid to have a picture of the look on your face.

'What?'

'I'll come with you. Or were you joking?'

'No! Well, I mean... Really? You'd just... pack up and go?'

I nodded, enjoying your incredulity, and gave the room an indifferent inspection. 'I've seen enough of this place. You're the most interesting thing to happen to me since I got here.'

I couldn't fathom the look you gave me then; it was as though hope and disbelief were warring inside your head.

'Why do I feel like you were expecting that to happen?' you said, sitting down on the mattress beside me.

I smiled enigmatically. 'I don't know. Why do *you* think you feel like that?'

'You're... different, you know that?'

'Yup,' I answered, in a matter-of-fact tone. 'You're pretty unconventional yourself. I guess we go together.'

Your grin was so wide and so sweet that I was tempted to kiss you again, but I decided against it. Jumping into something with you seemed like a bad idea, given how emotional you were right now and how volatile you could be when the tide turned. I'd wait and get to know you better first.

'Seriously?' you asked again, tilting your head. 'You're not kidding?'

'I've never been more serious in my life.' I looked at the clock. 'What time do we need to leave?'

'Like, five minutes ago.'

I looked around the room and sighed. 'Lucky I travel light.'

*

We arrived at your hotel thirty-five minutes later. As we approached the entrance I noticed a stern-looking guy in long shorts and a sports vest walking towards us from the corner of the building. He had black hair and piercing blue eyes, which were fixed on you like a predator tracking its prey.

He tapped his watch and shook his head. 'What the hell took you so long?'

'Sorry, I was…' You glanced at me and faltered.

He looked at me like he was only just registering my presence, and his expression became even more disapproving.

'Hi,' he said, giving me a cursory inspection before his eyes flicked back to you.

'Um, Matt, this is Aphrodite. Matt's my head coach and… I guess, my best buddy,' you finished sheepishly.

'Nice to meet you.' I held out my hand but Matt was too busy scowling at you to notice.

'What going on, man?' he snapped.

You grinned winningly. 'She's coming with us.'

Matt seemed to be on the verge of punching you in the face, but after a second of staring blue murder at you he just nodded curtly and waved us towards the side of the building. 'Fine, just… come on, we were waiting for you.'

You turned to wink at me before trailing after him. I sensed that you and he were the kind of friends who were either standing back-to-back facing down the world or at each other's throats.

Behind the hotel was a car park, in which a small grey bus sat waiting with its engine running. Matt sprang up the steps and you looked back at me before heaving yourself inside. As soon as I climbed aboard I found myself being scrutinised by six pairs of eyes – eyes that happened to belong to some of the toughest-looking men I'd ever seen in my life. None of them said a word as you squeezed down the aisle towards the back and plonked into an empty seat. After dropping my rucksack on the seat behind you and carefully wedging my guitar case into the footwell, I slid in next to you. You threw me a brief smile before crossing your arms and turning to stare out of the window.

As the bus began to move into traffic, I kept catching glances being thrown in our direction over the low-backed seats. After we'd been on the road for maybe five minutes or so – heading down Tropicana Avenue – one of the guys came back up the bus and sat in the aisle seat across from us. He was at least six-foot-four and solidly built, with neatly trimmed dark hair and a large-featured face.

'So, I guess you had *some* luck last night,' he quipped in a deep, resonant voice that carried a clear Southern twang, grinning broadly and throwing me a wink, even though his comment was directed at you.

I heard stifled snickering from further down the bus and I knew it would be OK.

I flashed you a mischievous look before answering, 'Luck had nothing to do with it. He won me over with his eloquent conversation and subtle charm.' I winked back at him.

He howled with laughter and slapped his leg. 'Oh man, she's got an even smarter mouth than you do!'

You stared at me in wordless surprise for a moment before breaking into a chuckle. 'She'll fit right in with you assholes then.'

'She sure will. I'm Joe.' He held out his hand and I shook it, gripping firmly so he wouldn't think I was intimidated.

'Hey, Joe, nice to meet you.'

'What did you say your name was?' he asked, leaning his elbows on the seat-backs either side of him.

'I didn't, but it's Aphrodite.'

'Say what now?'

'You can just call me Aph. I know you meatheads aren't so good with the speaky-speaky.'

Joe burst out laughing again and bent forward into the aisle to shout down the bus, 'Hey, Matt, I think we finally found a bigger smartass than you!'

I followed the direction of his gaze and received cheerful nods of greeting from the other guys. Apart from Matt, who kept his face stubbornly facing the front.

'Ah, ignore him,' Joe muttered, waving dismissively. 'He's got his panties in a bunch today.'

The rest of the trip went by in a flash as I listened to the cheerful bickering going back and forth between you all. It was obvious you spent a lot of time together, and I was glad to see your mood lift in response to the friendly mockery.

I watched the scenery race by: hazy, arid stretches of desert, pale and shimmering in the heat beneath an achingly blue sky; and yellow-grey mountains like colossal, ruined fortresses poking up from the plains. After what seemed like an eternity of sand and scrubby bushes, we moved into the stippled greens and browns of the Cajon Pass with its soaring, cloud-garlanded peaks. As I gazed out at the immense panorama I wondered how on Earth I'd ended up here, on a random road trip with a bunch of rowdy cage fighters on my way to Los Angeles, with nothing more than a vague gut instinct that I was supposed to find a way to help you turn your life around. As whims go, it was a pretty drastic move. But then, like most of the best things that had ever happened to me, I hadn't really had much of a choice.

You weren't like anyone I'd ever met before, and I couldn't begin to guess where it would all lead. But every time I thought about that one, frozen moment when I'd almost walked away and left you at the bar, a fist closed in my chest and my eyes began to ache with tears. That Song – it was the most tantalising, bittersweet thing I'd ever heard in my life. What did it mean? Was the sweetness what was to come and the bitterness what you needed to leave behind? Or was the sweetness inside you beneath the bitter exterior? Or… what if it was all to come? How could that much pain go hand in hand with love?

I just had to trust… if I could find it in me to do that again. I couldn't love someone incompletely, it just wasn't in my nature. So if this was going to happen, I would have to give you all of it – all of me. It was a big ask. Not that you were really the one doing the asking. But maybe, if anything about that Song was a sign, you'd be worth it. I wouldn't know until I tried.

'Hey, when we get there, do you need someplace to crash?' you asked, with about an hour of the journey left to go.

'Oh. Yeah, I mean… I could stay in a hotel.' I hadn't actually thought about the logistics of it all. I hadn't really thought about much of anything, I was just winging it and hoping I wasn't making a huge mistake.

'I've got plenty of room, if you want? Not that… I don't want you to think…' You were looking down at your hands, and again I was touched by how shy you were underneath all that bravado.

'No, that would be great. If you don't mind.' I didn't feel like doing any more thinking today. I could at least stay at your place for one night, and then maybe find somewhere else tomorrow if things got weird.

'Sure, no problem.' You looked up at me, relieved. Then your face suddenly fell and your cheeks darkened further. 'Umm, it's kind of a dump right now. I mean… I wasn't really expecting… y'know. Company.'

'I'm sure I'll survive,' I said, thinking about some of the more questionable places where I'd laid my head and wondering whether your idea of a dump was any worse than what I was picturing. How bad could it be?

The chatter began to die down in the final hour or so, after we turned off Interstate 15 towards Pasadena. A little further on I had my first view of the city, and my jaw actually dropped as I realised quite how enormous it was: a sprawling, sun-bleached forest of buildings, pylons and cell-phone towers, streaming with traffic like a great, urban anthill. I saw you studying me, amused by my expression of wonder, but you didn't say anything and I continued to marvel in silence as we headed down the freeway to Santa Monica.

It was around 8 p.m. when we arrived at our destination: a long white building on a street off Ocean Park Boulevard, with a small, faded sign above the door and large windows either side of the entrance. It turned out to be a lot bigger than it looked from the outside, and contained a large, fenced-off area of blue and black grappling mats, a long row of punchbags on the opposite wall, a separate space for cardio and weight-training, and a full-sized boxing ring, right at the back of the room.

There were a few men and one woman rolling around on the mats as we came in, and a couple of people were working at the punchbags, hammering the padding with low, guttural grunts. As soon as we walked in everyone stopped what they were doing and came over to offer congratulations and commiserations to you and the other guys who'd been fighting the night before. Your temper had definitely evened out since that morning, and you accepted their sympathy with quiet gratitude.

As I followed you down the length of the room taking in the atmosphere, I noticed the two long rows of posters and framed pictures lining the walls on either side, just below the ceiling. There were quite a few with you in, some advertising fights and a couple that looked like enlarged magazine covers, with you squaring off against other fighters. It was nice to see what you looked like without the cuts and bruises: softer than I'd imagined – younger maybe, like you hadn't quite grown into yourself yet. Free of the blemishes, your face was surprisingly… sweet, even with the fierce expression.

There was one I particularly liked, where the photographer had managed to catch you looking slightly cocky, as if you could beat anybody and winning was a sure thing. There was something else about you in that picture… something in your eyes – a candidness, like you were offering your heart up to the world. It was the same thing that had made me take a chance on coming with you, even though your behaviour so far hadn't exactly been commendable.

After a while we left the gym and you drove us back to your place in your battered blue Chevy. I had a major shock when we pulled up on the driveway: the house wasn't what I'd expected at all. I mean… it was big. And expensive-looking – a two-storey Mediterranean-style place with cream-coloured walls, red roof tiles and large arched windows. A few random palm trees stuck up around the edges of the small square of grass in the front, and alongside the brick-paved driveway stood a double garage that jutted forwards from the rest of the house.

'This is a *dump*?' I asked, staring up at the building.

'Um. Well, no, but… wait until you see the inside.' You gave me an apprehensive look and killed the engine. 'Things have been kinda crazy lately, so…' You shrugged in lieu of further explanation.

I climbed out of the car and grabbed my bag and guitar off the back seat, then followed you up the steps to the front door, which stood inside a small inset porch. When we got inside you flipped on the light switch and I gaped in astonishment. The entrance hall alone was bigger than some of the places I'd lived in, with a travertine tile floor and a staircase that swept up in a curve of walnut-coloured wood to the floor above. I tilted my head back to look at the ceiling, which was cut away at the top giving the staircase extra height, and from which was suspended an ornate cast-iron chandelier that matched the bannisters.

'Wow,' I breathed, letting my bag drop to the floor.

You spared the room a brief glance. 'You get used to it.'

I threw you a puzzled look but you had already turned away, and I followed as you strode across the tiles towards a wide square doorway, our footsteps ringing softly across the silent space.

As we stepped through, my nostrils were assailed by a musty odour, and I paused for a second, willing myself not to wrinkle my nose. The kitchen was like one of those dream homes I'd seen on TV, but the whole place was a mess, with plates, mugs, utensils and empty food packaging strewn across the counters. A large, complicated-looking blender was surrounded by the peelings from various fruits and vegetables, the jug turning rancid from the decaying matter inside. I took a tentative breath and let it out again, reluctant to get any closer to the source of the smell.

You opened the fridge, ignoring the clutter, and pulled out a large carton of apple juice, swallowing several mouthfuls before turning back to meet my gaze.

'Told you it was a dump,' you said, clearing your throat and covering your mouth to burp. 'Sorry it's so nasty in here.'

'It's OK. It's not me who has to clean it,' I said, taking a step towards you and letting my gaze wander across the tiled countertops and dull chrome appliances.

You chuckled, taking a few more gulps before replacing the carton in the fridge and closing the door. 'You hungry?'

'Oh my God, I'm starving,' I said, clasping my stomach and leaning gingerly against a clean-ish bit of worktop.

You thought for a moment, frowning at the chaos surrounding us. 'Pizza?'

I nodded enthusiastically, and we made our way out of the kitchen and further along the hallway to the living room, which smelled better but still carried a lingering scent of stale air. You heaved a sigh of relief as you dropped onto the sofa, shedding your jacket and throwing your shoes onto the floor.

I studied the room as you called for pizza. It was fairly large, and one wall was floor-to-ceiling windows with sliding French doors in the centre of it. A number of family pictures were dotted around – you, an older man who I assumed was your dad, and a young woman who bore a definite resemblance to you at a certain angle: your sister, I guessed. There was one picture of two small, grinning children on their own, and another with all of you together, along with another man about your sister's age. I couldn't see anyone who might be your mother, which I thought a little strange considering how many photos there were. Was that deliberate? It probably wouldn't be polite to ask.

The living room appeared to double as a laundry basket, with clothes strewn on the furniture and stray socks littering the floor. The cabinet below the TV was piled high with video games and DVDs, and it took me a while to notice that there was a small iPod station poking up behind them, which presumably was attached to the two tall tower speakers that stood on the floor either side.

You finished on the phone and sat back with another heavy sigh. We were silent for a moment. So much had changed in such a short space of time: one minute I'd been strutting along the Strip, knocking back cocktails and flirting shamelessly, and the next I was sitting in a swanky LA pad belonging to a cage fighter, whom I'd only met the night before in a Las Vegas dive bar. I mean, you couldn't make that stuff up. I wondered if anything like this ever happened to normal people, or whether it was just a Keeper thing. Somehow, I couldn't imagine that many people would be willing to follow a complete stranger – especially an imposing, volatile stranger – to a different city for no other reason than a gut feeling prompted by a song on a jukebox. When had that become normal to me?

I let my head rest on the sofa cushion, staring up at the ceiling. 'I think this is the nicest house I've ever been in. Apart from all the mess, I mean. No offence.'

'Really? You kinda seem like you'd be…'

I glanced at you again to find you studying me. 'What?'

You shrugged. 'I don't know. Used to the high life.'

I snorted, my thoughts racing back over the last few years, conjuring images of freezing cold tents on barren mountainsides, roach-infested hostels and earthen-floored huts in remote villages. You were right, it had been the high life, but not the way you meant it.

'Don't let the fancy hotel fool you,' I said, tucking my hands behind my head to form a pillow. 'I can rough it with the best of them.'

'Well,' you replied, looking around the room, 'that's great, because right now I think roughing it's about the best I have to offer. Damn… when did this place get so dirty?'

I shrugged, admiring the tattoos that ran down your arm in an intricate sleeve of interlocking designs. 'It's only dirt,' I said absently. 'There are way worse things.'

We smiled at each other, like we were both thinking how glad we were to be sitting there together. Some things don't need to be spoken out loud to be understood.

Your smile grew wistful. 'How'd you get to be so cool?'

'Me?' I shrugged again. 'I don't know. I guess I've just seen enough of the world to know what's important. Messy houses come pretty low on the list.'

You turned towards me and propped your head on your fist. 'So what comes at the top?'

'People you love,' I said, catching your eye and holding it.

I know some people would have laughed that comment away, or maybe felt awkward at the implications considering how little we knew each other, but it was never like that for us, even from the very beginning. Even then I felt that we were going to change each other in ways we couldn't possibly foresee, and I think maybe you felt it too.

After the pizza arrived and we'd eaten, you showed me upstairs where there were three spare rooms to choose from. I was glad to see they had been spared the abuse of the downstairs rooms.

'Do you have a lot of houseguests?' I asked, leaning on the doorframe of the one I had decided looked the most comfortable.

'No. I sorta... got this place on a whim,' you said, rubbing the back of your neck and giving an embarrassed wince. 'I er... I got ahead of myself a little, when I hit the big leagues. Thought I was going straight to the top so I figured... why not?'

'This was an impulse buy?' I chuckled in disbelief. 'That's crazy.'

'Yeah, well. I wanted somewhere big enough to make a real home, you know? Settle down, have a bunch of kids. I know, it's dumb but… that was the idea.'

'I don't think it's dumb,' I said, feeling a stir of tenderness for you that made me want to reach out and stroke your face. You were trying to act like it didn't matter to you all that much, but the way your voice softened when you talked about how you'd envisioned your life told me it was a dream you still longed for – maybe something you had always longed for.

You had the next few days off to recover, and on the first one you drove me down to the beachfront so I could spend the day relaxing and soaking up the sun while you got the house back to a habitable state. I did offer to help but you flatly refused.

'It's cool, I'm a big boy,' you said, waving away any argument. 'I didn't ask you here so you could come and be my mommy.' You were laughing but there was an edge to your voice when you said the word *mommy*, and I wondered again about the absence of your mother from the pictures. Had she died? If she had there'd be photos of her, right? I wasn't sure how people dealt with losing their parents. I'd never known mine, or if I had I couldn't remember.

I started off my morning with a stroll along Venice Beach, watching the surfers and wakeboarders negotiating the waves. The shore was crowded with people, walking, running, sunbathing and working out at the open-air gym, and occasionally I caught a whiff of marijuana smoke carried on the breeze, mingling with the scents of sea, warm sand and frying meat from the restaurants.

The boardwalk was a dazzling jumble of clothing stores, tattoo parlours, coffee houses, food markets, skate shops and spiritualist caves full of sparkling crystals and incense smoke. Music rang out all around, from buskers on the street playing drums and guitars, and from portable speakers that had been set up by street performers doing acrobatics, BMX tricks, beat-boxing and a host of other entertaining things that had me grinning in delight.

There were so many people my eyes couldn't track them all, and it seemed like every one of them had a completely different style and attitude to the next, from dreadlocked hippies to modestly dressed couples with children, skaters in tight jeans and hoodies, pierced and tattooed rockers, elderly couples eating ice-creams and everything in between. The whole world was out basking in the California sunshine, and as I threaded my way between them there was a lightness in my step that I hadn't felt in years.

When I got back to the house in the late afternoon it had been transformed – the surfaces sparkling, the floors spotless, and not a hint of the staleness that had saturated the air the day before. You cooked us paella for dinner on the giant gas hob and chatted to me across the breakfast bar, my stomach gurgling as the savoury-sweet scent of chicken, shrimp, garlic, saffron and paprika blended into a single mouth-watering concoction.

We ate at the dining table, which was off to one side of the kitchen, and I asked you how you'd become a fighter and what that was like.

'My dad got me into jiu jitsu when I was a kid. I had kind of a temper.' You caught my eye and grinned. '*Have* kind of a temper. But it used to be way worse. It was like I finally found something I was good at, you know? The discipline was great for me. I don't know what would've happened if I hadn't started training. And then I found out about MMA and it sounded fun so I gave it a try.'

I nodded, my mouth too full of food to reply. You were an amazing cook; it was the best paella I'd ever tasted and I couldn't gulp it down fast enough.

'How about you? Didn't you say you were a musician?'

I chewed faster and swallowed, taking a sip of water before answering. 'Yeah, that's right. I'm surprised you remembered, you were out cold.'

'Are you any good?' There was a cheeky glint in your eye and I cocked my head, fixing you with a challenging look.

'You'll have to decide for yourself,' I said, swallowing some more water. A burp rose up from my stomach and came out a lot louder than I expected, and I covered my mouth, giggling as you shook your head and laughed.

'Was that the pre-show?'

'Yep. Did you like it?'

'It was beautiful,' you said. 'Music to my ears.'

I liked seeing you laugh. Even with your swollen eye you looked so much younger and cuter with a big grin on your face. I tucked my hair behind my ear and reloaded my fork, glancing at you from beneath my lashes as we carried on talking companionably.

I stayed over again, since you seemed to like having me there and I was enjoying your company. On the second day you took me hiking in Tuna Canyon: a stunning wilderness of whispering grasses, sagebrush and gritty trails that led up to a high vantage point, which looked out over the magnificent expanse of Santa Monica Bay. The whole of the city was laid out beneath our feet, disappearing into the distance under a white veil. I let out a long, slow breath as I peered across the vista below, and when I looked back at you, you were smiling softly, watching my reaction to the view.

'Welcome to California,' you said, pulling the cap off your water bottle and taking a deep swig. Your chest rose and fell gently as you rested from the climb, and I took the opportunity to admire you while your head was tilted back. My heart was thumping anyway from the walk up the trail, but it thumped a little harder as I watched you. This version of you was a total shift from the drunk guy I'd met wallowing in his own shame at the bar, and that prickle of excitement expanded into a fizzing crackle in my belly as you winked at me before turning to carry on along the path.

At the end of the third day – which we'd spent lazing on the decking in the freshly mown back garden and cooling our feet in the pool, which was still too dirty to swim in – you asked me if I could play you something on the guitar. I retrieved it from my room and took it out to the garden, resuming my place on the rattan sunlounger. I gave the strings a quick tuning while I thought about what to play, running my fingers over the fretboard, looking for inspiration.

I remembered a song I'd written a year or so ago, on another lazy summer day spent lounging around in good company. I tested out the chord shapes to remind myself of the sequence, and started playing. It wasn't a Song, but it suited the moment with its jazzy, summery melody, and it definitely suited my mood at the time. It was called 'Heartbeat of the World'.

As soon as you heard my voice you turned your head, pulling your shades down with one finger and watching me intently. I glanced at you, smiling a little around the words, then stared out at the sun-scorched grass as I let the music do its thing. Songs change their meaning every time they come out, and by then I'd stopped trying to bend them to my will and learned to let them roam free.

When I finished you were silent for a second, before letting out a long breath and nodding in astonishment.

'Wow,' you said.

'Thanks.' I smiled, flushing under your gaze. 'Glad you liked it.' I adjusted one of the tuning pegs – the string had stretched and needed replacing – and fiddled with another melody I'd been working on.

'How long have you been playing?' you asked, watching my fingers as they moved.

'A few years.'

'You're really good.'

I shrugged. 'I do OK.'

You sat up and swung your feet to the floor, facing me. 'I always wanted to learn but I'm tone deaf. Plus my hands are all messed up,' you said, holding them up for my inspection.

I reached out and took hold of one, making a show of examining it. Your knuckles were scarred in places and the skin was hard and compact, but there was nothing wrong with them as far as I could see. The fingers were long and firm; they curled in towards the palm as I ran my thumb across it.

'They look fine to me. Look at mine.' I held my left hand up so you could see the calluses on my fingertips. 'I'll never be a hand-model now.'

You grasped them lightly, your eyes flickering over my face, and slowly drew them towards you to press them against your lips.

The sounds of birdsong and the soft lapping of the pool were muted as I stared across at you. We waited, neither of us moving.

And then something sweet and delicate bloomed in my chest, and I leaned towards you, my hand sliding across your cheek as our lips met. The sensation of your mouth moving against mine was exquisitely enjoyable, and I breathed in the scent of your skin, savoury-sweet and a little bit sweaty from a day spent basking in the sun.

I paused, laying my guitar down flat on my lounger, and kissed you again. You took both of my hands and drew me towards you, shifting over on the cushion to make room. Once more I was surprised by your gentleness as your arms tightened around me, undeniably strong but careful, protective. Your lips drank me in with a growing thirst, and my body responded as I sucked in air through my nose. I pushed myself up and straddled you, your hands firm around my thighs, and I felt my pulse racing in my throat as you planted kisses along my collarbone. I pulled your top off over your head and discovered a beautiful Japanese dragon tattooed across your chest, along with more scrapes and bruises that were still healing from your fight. I crooned in sympathy but you pulled my face to yours and kissed away my concern, loosening the ties at the nape of my neck and sliding the zip of my dress down my back.

You always refused to accept pity from anyone, especially at the times when you were hurting the most. It was as if the sympathy stung more than your injuries, and the second you sensed that someone felt sorry for you, you had to prove to them that nothing could hurt you – that you were superhuman.

I could have believed it too, as you lifted and turned me over with effortless ease. I kicked off my sandals, wrapping my legs around your waist and pulling your body against mine. I enjoyed the weight of you on top of me, my chest and stomach squashed against yours and our ribs pressing into each other. Your hands explored my body, moving with inquisitive slowness as though you wanted to learn every detail. I groaned softly as your lips worked their way down my stomach, claiming every inch of my flesh until you pushed my skirt up around my hips and buried your face between my thighs.

We made love slowly and deeply, my whole body tingling so much it almost hurt. I felt like I couldn't get close enough to you, like I wanted to melt into you and be absorbed.

Sometime later, as we lay panting and bathed in sweat – your face pressed to my neck and our limbs wrapped around each other – I marvelled at how much energy you had, considering you were still so battered and sore. It shouldn't have been surprising I suppose given how much training you did, but I didn't understand that then and I hadn't expected it to make such a difference to *that* kind of exercise.

A swelling flood of happiness surged through my body, piercingly sharp in its intensity. We breathed in and out together, perfectly in unison, and I was sure that nothing had ever felt so right as being in this moment with you. I squeezed you tighter, a tear springing to my eye as the joy of having you next to me brimmed over from inside. This time would be different – I knew it; I felt it in the core of my being. This time I had found the person I would be with forever, who I would build a life with and love to the end of my days. We'd only just met and everything was happening so fast, but somehow you had already claimed a huge piece of my heart, and I didn't think I'd survive if I had to give it away.

That night I stayed in your room, and the following morning you said I could move my stuff in there too if I wanted. I asked if you'd rather I stayed in a hotel or found a holiday rental, but you shook your head and pulled me into a hug.

'Stay as long as you want,' you said, planting a kiss on my temple. 'It's good having you here. This place has been way too quiet lately.'

We were lying on your bed watching the light filter through the curtains, stroking each other's hands and curling our feet together. The turquoise walls made it feel like an underwater cave, and the mirrored closet doors cast reflections on the surfaces, which shimmered as the curtains stirred in the breeze.

'Are you sure?' I asked, tilting my head back to look at you. 'It's OK, if you need your space. I know how cranky you get when people won't leave you alone.'

You let out a snort and flexed your fingers between mine, closing them around my hand. 'You're not people. You're…'

'What?' I smiled up at you.

'You're *my* person.' Your eyes searched my face to see how I would respond, flickering with anxiety for a second. The bruised one was starting to heal up, and I could see the iris now, gleaming like polished onyx.

'Does that mean you're my boyfriend?' I said in a childish voice, giggling as you scrunched up your face.

'That's so lame,' you answered, your stomach twitching as you laughed. 'The whole boyfriend-girlfriend thing. Bleugh.'

'So… what then? My lover?' I let the word ring out. 'My soulmate?' I was teasing but you smiled softly at that one.

'How about… your man?'

'My man,' I repeated, staring up at the ceiling and watching the light flickering. 'OK. That sounds good to me.'

'Yeah?'

I turned back to you and nodded, my gaze dropping to your lips, and you kissed me and slipped your arm up across my back, your fingers stroking the nape of my neck.

I loved that you wanted me to know you were mine, and that it mattered to you that I was yours and no one else's. You were so hesitant to push me for anything, probably because you were scared about what I would say, but you weren't the kind of person to love by halves: you were all-in or all-out, just like me. It felt so good to share that with you – not to have to hold back or worry about seeming too eager in my affections.

After that conversation you stopped being so cautious and showed me exactly how important I was to you, and how determined you were to keep me around. We plunged headlong into each other, and this time I was determined to stick around too. I was the one who was chosen to embody love for my generation, so I got to decide where that love would germinate and manifest. Nothing would induce me to uproot myself again, not the Path, not a Song, not the whole wide world.

*

You returned to training and the next few weeks were a revelation as I watched you settle back into your normal routine, which seemed completely insane to me at the time. Every morning you got up at 6 a.m. and went for a run, which took you around an hour, give or take. When you got home you showered and changed, and got all your food ready for the day, which took almost another hour. Then, six days a week, you'd head off to the gym and spend the mornings and afternoons with the fight team and coaches, working on technique, sparring and doing weight training and cardio. Three or four nights a week you taught classes, which meant you got home late. The only days you had off completely were Sundays, and even then you still got up early to go for a run.

I decided I should find something to occupy myself, so I started writing some new songs and tweaking the older ones, arranging them into a set so I could start going out and doing gigs. I didn't feel right about living in your house without contributing anything, especially after I realised how much it was costing you. Besides, I wanted to get out and explore LA, which I found endlessly diverting with its quirky cafés and larger-than-life characters, so after a few weeks – when I felt confident enough that what I'd written was passable – I started going to open mic nights, playing on the boardwalk and Santa Monica Pier, and catching the metro across to Hollywood Boulevard to play cover songs for the tourists. It was really good practice, not just for my guitar-playing but for dealing with people too. Some of the other buskers were quite territorial and not always thrilled to see someone new in 'their spot', but I went out of my way to make friends with them anyway, and before long I was starting to recognise a few faces and receive warmer welcomes when I turned up with my guitar.

I didn't make a lot of money at first; I didn't have an amp or a microphone, so I was often drowned out by the noise of the crowds and the other players who were better organised with their equipment. On the plus side, being quiet meant no one heard my mistakes, and by the time I'd saved up for an amp and a mic I was polished enough not to worry about that so much.

It was really fun, catching people's eyes as they walked by, sharing smiles with strangers and watching the tourists get excited over stars on the Walk of Fame. Sometimes there'd be a hushed murmur that would thrill through the crowd as a movie star or famous musician was spotted doing something really ordinary, like getting a coffee or shopping for clothes, and once I got a fifty-dollar bill from a pretty, smiling woman with big sunglasses who one of the other performers told me afterwards was Katy Perry, but I still don't know if that was true.

*

About two months after I arrived you had a call to say you were booked for another fight, just before Thanksgiving. It was over a month away, which I thought sounded like plenty of time, but apparently that was considered last-minute as far as you were concerned. Another fighter had dropped out due to an injury and you'd been invited to fill the spot. It was an opportunity you couldn't turn down. Another chance at redemption and a decent chunk of money in your pocket, whatever the outcome.

Your training ramped up another level after that, not just the physical side but the constant discipline of watching what you ate, studying the other guy's previous fights and mentally preparing yourself for what was to come.

*

One evening, a week or so before the fight, we were lying on Venice Beach watching the sky change colour as the sun sank over the water. You reached out and knitted your fingers through mine, and I turned to look at you, wondering what was stewing away in that head of yours; you'd been quiet all day and I was worried about what the pressure would do to your temper. You'd hardly drunk any alcohol at all since I'd started staying with you, which I took as a good sign, but I didn't know if that was because you were happier or just because it would mess with your nutrition.

Your profile was outlined softly in the fading light, your features no longer disfigured by the swelling that had marred them when we met. I sat up and looked down at you, captivated by the golden gleam of the dying sun as it reflected in the black pools of your eyes.

'I can't lose this time,' you said, staring up at the sky. 'One more screw-up and I'm finished.'

'Why do you say that?'

'Because it's the truth. Seriously, if this one doesn't go well, I'm through. The mortgage payments are crazy, my sponsors are pissed off because I keep losing fights, and I'm not going to get another contract if my record doesn't pick up soon. I can't keep doing this to myself. I feel like a loser all the time; I hate it.'

It killed me to hear the resignation in your voice; you lived and breathed fighting, and I worried what would become of you if you gave up doing it professionally.

I watched you in silence. One thing was clear: wallowing in negativity wasn't going to help you win. And you needed a win. It wasn't just about the money or even about ego, it was about… faith – the belief that you could be truly great at something. And I knew you could, I could feel it in my bones.

I climbed on top of you, resting my elbows on the warm sand either side of your head and stroking your freshly shaved scalp. 'Do you *want* to win?'

'What?' You looked almost angry at the question, but you didn't scare me anymore.

'Well, I mean… it's a pretty hard life. Maybe there's a part of you that just wants to quit.'

You looked incensed, as I knew you would. Our eyes were locked together and I could feel your muscles bunch beneath me like lumps of steel.

'I've never quit anything in my life.'

'Then fight,' I said quietly. 'Stop with all this loser bullshit and fight.'

You grabbed my hands suddenly and rolled us over, pinning me to the sand, although your grip was relaxed enough to avoid hurting me.

'Of course I'm gonna fight!'

I shook my head and freed a hand from your grasp, squeezing your bicep as I spoke. 'I don't mean fight with these.' I let go and touched your forehead with one finger. 'I mean fight with this.'

You scowled and pretended to bite at my finger, making me giggle before you kissed me. A warm tingling started to spread through my body, as we lay there bathed in the light of the sunset, with the waves softly sighing along the shoreline.

'How about with this?' you murmured, pressing your hips closer to mine.

I laughed and let my head flop back on the sand. 'I think there's a good reason no one else has thought of that.'

You grinned and I saw the anxiety drain out of you. You had such a beautiful smile; it made you look so much younger and softer, like the twenty-seven-year-old you were rather than an old, tired man with the weight of the world on his shoulders.

Your face turned serious again and you studied me for a moment. 'Are you coming with me?'

'To the fight?'

'Uh-huh.'

'Try keeping me away.'

You looked at me for a few moments before pushing yourself to your feet. You held out your hand to help me up, and before I knew what was happening you had swept me across your shoulders and begun to walk up the beach towards the promenade, heading back to the car. I yelled in mock outrage and kicked my legs, protesting your manhandling of me and laughing at the same time. You refused to set me down until we were off the sand, and stoically suffered the ear-bashing I gave you for taking liberties with my person.

As soon as we got home you proceeded to take even more, and we drifted to sleep amid a tangle of sand-coated sheets.

I couldn't believe the clamour of the crowd as the announcement echoed across the arena that your fight was about to begin. I was seated in the VIP section right next to the cage, three rows from the front. I felt a bass rumble in my chest, but I couldn't tell if the unsettling vibrations were caused by the music from the PA system or my own heartbeat. Several hours had passed since I'd seen you and I felt impotent and anxious, desperate to catch a glimpse of your face so I could reassure myself that you were coping. It was stupid really, you'd fought and survived dozens of times without me, but still…

My breath caught as I saw you approaching the cage down the long walkway off to my right, your face set in a menacing scowl and your eyes focused straight ahead. You looked like a different person. All the bright flickers of emotion that normally played across your features had been absorbed into a mask that was as cold as it was determined. I understood that it was your game face, but I still found it chilling.

Rage bubbled up inside me as I heard the taunts and jibes rising up from the crowd. I shut them out and concentrated on you, willing all my love and pride to cut through their scorn. You entered the cage and the jeering increased, but you didn't acknowledge any of it. You focused on a point across the mat, bouncing lightly on the spot and looking more composed and relaxed than I had ever seen you, except in your deepest sleep. You were here for one thing and one thing only: to win.

The announcer's voice rang out through the enormous speakers and I saw your face on the big screens above the cage, followed by the face of your opponent. You both approached the centre to listen to the referee, and then he sent you back to your corners, checked you were both ready and dropped his hand to signal that the fight could begin.

All I can say with certainty about the next few minutes is that I hardly dared to breathe, the rest was just a blur of adrenaline-fuzz from where I was sitting, punctuated by a few brief moments of lucidity.

You tussled around the mat for a while, neither appearing to have the upper hand, and I was surprised at how slow you both were to close the gap. The klaxon sounded at the end of the first round and I felt my body slump, amazed at how much tension had gathered in my muscles. One down, two to go.

The other guy came after you the moment the next round started, and my stomach lurched as he caught your leg with his foot and dropped you on your back. I thought I was going to be sick as I saw him raining down punches on your torso and face. Then, in the space of a blink, you had managed to get your arm hooked over the back of his neck and had pulled his head down to the mat. He was struggling to free himself but even I could see you weren't letting go, and the roaring of the people around me became so loud I had to clamp my hands over my ears.

Before I knew what was happening the referee had yanked you apart and raised his hand to make a cutting motion. You sprang into the air with a cry of undisguised triumph, leaped to the top of the cage and screamed your defiance at the shocked and raucous crowd.

Your eyes sought me out and you grinned madly, your gumshield poking out from between your lips, kissing your forefingers in salute before dropping back down to the mat. Matt, Joe and the rest of the team were clapping and cheering behind you. They swamped you as you turned to face them, their hands reaching out to pat your shoulders and rub your head.

At last you were allowed out of the cage, and you skipped straight down the steps and circled round towards me. I edged out of my row and met you in the aisle, and you nearly knocked me over as you pulled me against you, lifting me a few inches from the ground and devouring my face. You let go just as suddenly and flashed me the most enormous smile I'd ever seen, before running back to your team to a storm of applause.

There was a party in our hotel room that night, and it was unquestionably the wildest I'd ever been to. All the guys from your team were there, and the atmosphere was like New Year and Christmas and Mardi Gras all rolled into one. Someone had hooked up their phone to a portable speaker, and the music was blasting out at an impressively high volume.

It was so much fun seeing you all clowning around and listening to you trading anecdotes. I had that weightless feeling like the moment of suspension before a big drop on a rollercoaster, when there's nothing but the sound of your own breathing and the wind rushing in your ears. We toasted you with champagne and the bubbles cascaded down into my stomach, fizzing like a waterfall and making my whole body tingle with excitement. We'd done it. *You'd* done it. I was so proud of you, and so elated to see you lit up with relief and joy, your dark eyes blazing with a fierce happiness.

I think Matt was probably the biggest surprise of the whole night; I couldn't believe how relaxed and chatty he was with a few drinks in him. At one point, as I stood watching you get your picture snapped with some of the team, I turned to find him regarding me with a thoughtful expression.

'You two are getting pretty serious, huh?'

'I'd say we've been pretty serious from the start.'

Despite the frostiness of our first interaction, I'd grown to like Matt. He'd stuck by you through all your lowest points, and if he gave you a hard time it was only because that was what you needed sometimes. I wanted him to like me too, and I hoped he could see that I was on your side as much as he was.

'Don't hurt him, Aph,' he murmured, a heartfelt appeal in his eyes. 'I know he looks tough but he's had a rough time. And... he's really into you, you know?'

'I'm really into him too.' I looked back at him steadily, the glow of warmth in my chest pulsing as I thought about how precious you'd become to me. 'I'll make a deal with you: you take care of him out there,' I pointed outside but I meant the cage, 'and I'll take care of him in here.' I placed my hand over my heart and then held it out to him.

He took it solemnly and shook it twice, his face suddenly breaking into a smile. 'Welcome to the winning team.'

I grinned back, glad we'd finally reached an understanding. He loved you, in his way, at least as much as I did, and I knew he meant it about being on the team. Everything in your life affected how you fought, and since I was now a part of that it was important I knew the stakes. He needn't have worried. I knew them all too well.

At one point I found myself out on the balcony – I think maybe I'd wanted some air, I can't remember – and suddenly the sky blazed with colour, and I was filled with giddy excitement as a firework display lit up the night.

You came outside to join me and stood behind me to watch the beautiful bursts of colour as they rose in plumes into the sky, your arms wrapped around my shoulders and your lips pressed to my ear. And in that misty euphoria, when it seemed the celebration would never end and we were king and queen of the whole world, I heard the next Song playing through the speaker inside, and it felt like a little piece of heaven had opened up and swallowed me. It was 'Dog Days Are Over' by Florence and the Machine, and it still makes me smile every time I hear it.

It began softly, the beat steadily building as the vocals rounded out, and I closed my eyes and leaned my head back against your chest. Then suddenly the drums kicked in and I couldn't hold back anymore; I laughingly broke free of your arms and danced around you, the blood singing in my veins and the love sparking between us like a shimmering curtain of light.

The Song was a gift from the gods of music themselves – pure and perfect, ringing with untempered joy. Every word came alive inside my head and every beat of the drums was answered by my heart as I jumped and twisted around, caught up in the surge of jubilation that had possessed my soul.

You weren't dancing but you laughed along with me as I sang the words out to you in our little bubble of bliss. Towards the end of the Song you grabbed me – accidentally sloshing beer down my back – and covered my face with kisses. I wrapped my arms around your neck and kissed you right back, and we grinned secretly together in the midst of our embrace.

We fell into bed that night, too exhausted to do anything but hold each other, drunk on euphoria and giggling like children. You whispered words into my ear that didn't actually register until the next morning, but they were the first thing I remembered when I woke up: *You're my guardian angel.*

*

You had a whole week off after the fight, and we spent the first couple of days doing absolutely nothing. You stuffed your face with hamburgers and barbecue chicken, and we hung out in the garden, occasionally taking a dip in the pool. The weather had cooled to a more tolerable temperature, and the first showers of rain had quenched the dry soil and given the air an earthy smell, rich and deep.

On the third afternoon you left me fiddling with a new song I was working on and disappeared for a few hours. I knew you were up to something but I didn't ask; it was more fun to wait and see. When you came back you had a new tattoo on your ribs – a pair of doves in black and grey, which I exclaimed over in delight. They were beautifully done in the most incredible detail, one flying slightly above the other with their wingtips overlapping. I could see that you were waiting for me to grasp the significance, but when several moments had passed and I'd failed to figure it out, you rolled your eyes and told me they were a symbol of the goddess Aphrodite.

'What?' Tears sprang to my eyes and my throat closed up as I gazed at them with awe.

You gave a shy grin. 'For you.'

I was utterly speechless.

Your smile grew wider and you pulled me close, tucking your finger under my chin.

'My guardian angel.'

I could hear the words you wanted to say – could sense them trembling on your lips, aching to be spoken.

'I love you,' I murmured, a happy tear spilling down my cheek. It was the sweetest thing anyone had ever done for me.

*

At Christmastime you took me to meet your family in San Diego, and although I was mildly terrified by the idea they welcomed me with open arms. The second I met your dad I could see exactly where you'd got that amazing, beaming smile. He opened the door wearing one that was almost identical, and I knew we'd be the best of friends in no time. He was tall and softly spoken, with kind, laughing eyes, and hands so large that mine looked like a child's when he clasped it between his palms.

His house in Emerald Hills was small but bright, with photographs everywhere of you and your sister – from baby pictures to graduation photos and other big events in your lives – and of his grandchildren. Again, I was struck by the absence of your mother; there wasn't a single image of her anywhere. I'd asked you about her but you'd only given the vague answer that she hadn't been around when you were growing up, and I wondered if I'd have the chance to solve the mystery while we were here.

Your sister was visiting too with her husband and their two children, who were both significantly taller than they were in the photos that were adorning the wall of your living room. I had no idea how we were all going to squeeze in with only three little bedrooms to share between us, but your dad seemed confident that we'd manage. It was actually kind of nice, being around people who knew you so well and were so close to each other. I watched you all as you talked and laughed and teased, the warmth emanating from every pore of the house like it was happy to be filled with so much noise and love. The children – who were five and seven – were lively and clever, constantly absorbed in some exuberant game or craft project, and eager to complete chores with competitive zeal.

I saw another side of you while we were there – actually, several more: you were a much-loved son, brother and uncle, and you seemed more at ease in their company than you were anywhere else. You were a hero to your sister's children, and you could hardly be in a room with them for five minutes without one of them being slammed, laughing and squealing, onto the sofa cushions, or all of you falling in a heap of tangled limbs on the floor. Seeing you together, I realised how hard it must have been for you to live apart from them for so long, and I felt a pang of regret for the childhood friends I'd had to leave behind – the only family I'd ever known.

On Christmas Eve I was helping your dad peel potatoes at the table in the kitchen while the rest of you were out fetching groceries, and he mentioned what a terror you'd been as a child and how he was glad you'd started jiu jitsu when you had. I stole a look at him, unsure whether now was the right time to ask about your mother or whether it was too much of a sensitive subject.

'What made him act like that?' I asked, testing the waters.

'Well,' your dad sighed, rubbing his nose with the back of his wrist, 'he didn't have the easiest time, growing up. I was working a lot and he got left with his sister most of the time. Neither of them were too happy about that, let me tell you. And then… the kids at school found out about his mom and started making jokes – no one's as cruel as kids, right? – and he decided to shut 'em up. He never did have the coolest head on his shoulders.'

We shared a smile and he chuckled – a deep, rumbling sound.

'He told me… his mother wasn't really around,' I ventured, concentrating on the potato in my hand.

'No.' He sighed again and stopped peeling, his eyes losing focus as he thought about something. 'He never really knew her. She'd gone before he was old enough to remember her, so…'

'Can I ask what happened? Or is that a rude question?'

'He hasn't told you?'

I shook my head, studying his face. He didn't seem offended, but maybe a little sad. I wasn't sure if that sadness was for you or for himself.

'OK. Well, I guess he wouldn't have. He doesn't much like to talk about it.'

'No. I got that. You don't have to tell me, I'm not trying to pry or anything.'

He let out a low huffing sound, and his shoulders twitched as he smiled. 'It doesn't bother me anymore. Been a lot of years since then.' His gaze swept over my face, like he was debating with himself. 'She left. When he was six months old. He always thought it was about him, but... I guess I should've seen it coming; she wasn't all that happy about being a mom the first time around. That's hindsight for you.'

'Oh.' I frowned. I had so many more questions now but I didn't know whether to ask them. 'Did you hear from her again?' I said, not wanting to push too far.

He shook his head silently and went back to peeling the potato. I worried that I'd upset him, but after a while he looked at me and gave me one of those trademark grins the two of you shared.

'That boy has a fire under his ass,' he said, eyeing me with amusement. 'You keep him on a tight leash, you hear?'

I laughed, dropping my potato in the pot and picking up a fresh one. 'Yes sir,' I said, returning his smile. 'I'll keep his ass exactly where I can see it.'

He chuckled and shook his head again, making a hoo-hoo-hoo sound. 'Damn. He's found himself in a whole new heap of trouble, hasn't he?'

I nodded with mock conviction, smirking. You and I were both in a heap of trouble, with no sign of getting out of it. And I didn't want to get out of it. Ever. Your kind of trouble was exactly what I'd been searching for all those years, even though I hadn't known that until I met you. Everything about you made me light up inside, like propane to a flame, and as long as I had you I'd never know darkness again.

Christmas Day was amazing, especially watching the children's faces light up as they exclaimed over their presents. I had grown quite used to spending the holidays alone, but it was far more fun being able to share them with other people, especially *your* people. In only a few short days they had already made me feel like I was part of the family, and that meant more to me than all the Christmas presents in the world. They were all just so… wholesome. There's no other word for it.

Despite all the excitement I could tell there was something on your mind, and after everyone else had gone to bed I finally found out what it was – the absolute last thing I was expecting it to be!

I had just switched off the reading lamp next to the sofa bed in the living room, and I turned back over to find you staring across at me in the twinkling glow of the Christmas tree lights, with a look of such unguarded adoration that the breath caught in my chest. You leaned over to kiss me before pulling me into a hug and burying your face in my hair.

'I love you,' you whispered, holding me tightly against you.

I pulled away a little and placed my hands around your face, stroking your eyebrows and cheekbones with my thumbs as we gazed at each other across the pillow. 'I love you too.'

'You know I'm gonna take care of you, right?' There was an unfamiliar thickness in your voice that I found almost frightening.

'You do take care of me,' I answered quietly. 'We take care of each other.'

You were struggling to put something into words, and although I could tell it wasn't coming out the way you wanted, I felt exactly what you meant. I felt it with all my heart.

'I mean, you know I'll *always* take care of you. Do you think all this is just for me?'

I didn't need to ask what *all this* was. I knew that every second you spent training and planning and suffering was only worth it to you because it was for something greater than yourself. It was for your family – for us.

'No,' I said simply, but until then I don't think I had fully understood.

'I have one more gift for you, but… I wanted to wait until…' You propped yourself up on one elbow and dug something out from under your pillow, laying it down on the sheet between us – slowly, as if your fingers were reluctant to let it go. It was a small, square box, not gift-wrapped but covered with black velvet, soft and beautiful and terrifying. I couldn't look at you for a moment; I could hardly bring myself to breathe.

'I don't want you to feel like… I mean, I know we haven't been together all that long…'

The world came back into focus and I stared across at you. You were still looking down at the box, like you were afraid to meet my gaze.

'Yes,' I said, laying my hand lightly over yours. I didn't need to see what was inside to give you the answer to that question.

'I haven't even asked you yet,' you said, beaming with relief and a love so radiant it shone out from your face.

'So ask,' I replied, biting my lip as you pushed yourself upright and took both my hands in yours.

'Aphrodite,' you said, taking a deep breath and expelling it through pursed lips. 'Will you be my wife? Will you... marry me?'

We stared at each other, tears slipping from our eyes and shaky laugher bubbling from our throats.

'Do I have to say it again?' I asked, as you lifted the lid of the box and pulled out the ring – a simple, elegant band of gold bearing a single sparkling diamond.

The grin stretched all the way across your face from one ear to the other. 'Yes,' you insisted. 'This is some scary shit! The least you can do is give me a proper answer.'

'Yes,' I said again, bathing in the love that poured from your eyes. 'Yes, yes, yes. I can't think of anything I'd rather do.'

You slid the ring up over my knuckle, and it nestled around my finger like it was happy to have found its place in the world. You leaned towards me slowly, watching my face, and then your lips met mine and we sank into blissful silence.

Your family were ecstatic when we told them the news the next morning. Your sister threw her arms around me and squeezed me until I thought I would pop, and your dad gave me a knowing wink, clapping you on the shoulder and nodding his approval with misty eyes.

We'd been taught, at Hearthfire, that once our purpose was fulfilled we would know it. Our Paths would come to an end and we would continue to live our lives as ordinary people, freed from the burden of manifesting whatever Attribute of human experience we'd been chosen to embody. At the time I'd thought that sounded like an awful way for things to end, but since then I had begun to understand what a blessing it would be: to be human. To live out my life however I wanted, with no obligation to a higher purpose. To be free. If that happened now I could stay with you, forever and ever. I could marry you and have your babies, and we could grow old together and die together without ever needing or wanting anyone else. Wasn't that the point? Wasn't that true love?

But if you were The One, then why hadn't anything changed? Why was I still a Keeper, still Aphrodite? Had I missed some essential instruction that I needed to follow? Would someone come and tell me that my time of service was over, and that it was time for a new Keeper of Love to shoulder the burden? I didn't know. All I knew was that you were all I wanted and all I would ever want, and that was all that mattered… I hoped.

We stayed in San Diego until New Year and then you were back to training again. You had another fight booked in Chicago in March and you were determined to get another win, particularly since this fight was with an old rival you hadn't squared off against in years. This time it was personal.

I went with you again to watch your next fight and you won by technical knockout in the third minute of the final round, although by the time it was finished you looked like you'd been in a car crash. I was just relieved that it was over.

Two days later we were back in LA and everything went crazy. The phone was ringing constantly and you had offers coming out of your ears. Every day there was something new to get excited over, and the next few months passed in a whirl, marked only by a few standout occasions like our birthdays, our one-year anniversary and your next fight. You won again, and we celebrated again, and then autumn arrived with soft, balmy days, and the smell of frying and spices and burnt sulphur. We jogged every morning and ate together every night, and talked about what kind of wedding we would have – where it would be and who we'd invite, and where we'd go on honeymoon. It was blissful.

I had been getting some gigs and improving my guitar-playing, and the tracks I'd posted up online were getting really good feedback. I was feeling more creative than I ever had in my life – the music pouring out of me as a celebration of our love. I wanted to share it with everyone, spread the joy far and wide so the world would ring with happiness. That was my purpose, after all: to be a conduit for love to flow through, and since I had a boundless supply of it I could afford to be generous. This was how I would fulfil my destiny; this was my Path, I was certain of it. I can honestly say it was the closest I'd ever come to being contented. I don't mean happy – I've been happy plenty of times – but settled and stable, like I was really there to stay. It's funny how simple life can be when you have love: black and white, but still full of colour and joy and madness. It seemed like nothing could touch us in our impregnable happiness.

New Year rolled around and we spent it in New York, kissing at midnight in Times Square with thousands of other people, cheering as the fireworks filled the sky with scintillating brilliance and the confetti rained down like a blizzard.

Your manager called two days after we got back; there were rumours that you were going to be offered a title shot. To you that meant a whole lot more than just getting a pay rise, it was a chance to test yourself against the best in the sport: to prove unequivocally, to yourself and everyone else, that you were a champion.

*

We had a party at our house the following Saturday. All the regulars from the gym turned up with their partners, and I spent the night flitting between the kitchen and the garden, eating pizza and drinking, occasionally breaking out the guitar when someone requested a song.

We'd decorated the garden with fairy lights and bamboo torches, and the pool was lit up in shifting colours, fading from red to blue to green to yellow.

The women were all demanding to know when we were going to set a date for the wedding, and Joe's wife Lisa insisted that she'd do my hair and make-up for me as a present from them. I was overwhelmed by suggestions on where to get my dress and who should supply the flowers, and you busted us as we stood around the island in the kitchen making plans for the bachelorette party, which sent us all into a howling gale of laughter as we caught the look of trepidation on your face.

Music was blasting out from the speakers in the living room, cycling through your collection of heavy metal and rock and filtering into the garden through the open glass doors. It seemed to infect everyone with a joyful kind of recklessness: people were bouncing around on the grass, throwing each other in the pool, and playing tag between the trees and around the furniture, with the rule that every time someone got tagged they had to take a gulp of the noxious concoction in the jug on the outdoor table.

As the night wore on everyone seemed to grow more and more raucous, and after a vase got broken in the hallway I shooed everyone outside where they couldn't do as much damage. No one was deliberately being destructive, but the atmosphere had gone from being a relaxed gathering to a full-on house party, and I doubted anyone would stick around to help clean up the mess after.

At one point you and Joe decided to have a wrestling match in the living room, and the whole gang gathered around to watch, standing or crouching in the doorway to the garden and perching on the back of the sofa, egging you on and calling out suggestions like they were cornering you in a fight. You were both drunk and looked more like circus clowns than hardened athletes. A picture frame got smashed when you caught it with your foot after dropping an elbow off the sofa, and Joe ended up knocking beer all over the cupboard under the TV when he caught you in a guillotine choke and fell back against it.

I was laughing and cheering along with everyone else, revelling in the feeling of being at home among friends, when the house phone began to ring. I looked at my watch and realised it was 2 a.m.

Who could be calling at this time of night?

I edged around the room towards the hallway, skirting the two of you as you grappled on the floor and motioning for someone to turn the music down. The phone was on a stand just outside the living-room door, and I was still laughing at your antics as I held it to my ear.

My stomach dropped as I heard the voice on the other end of the line. It was your dad. I listened to what he had to tell you and felt the blood draining from my face.

'Babe?' I croaked, my mouth suddenly devoid of moisture.

You didn't hear.

'Babe!'

'Yeah?' Your voice was muffled by the carpet as Joe sat on your back, clamping your arm behind you.

I must have looked scared because as soon as he saw my face he let go of you, and you sat back on your heels, your expression growing sober as you studied me more closely.

'It's your dad,' I said. 'He's… there's—'

You leaped up and grabbed the phone off me, and your eyes clouded over as your father's words sunk in.

Everyone sat in total silence while you spoke. I could see Matt and
Joe looking at me questioningly, but I couldn't tear my gaze away from
you. You had your game face on.

'When did it happen?' you muttered into the phone, leaning back
against the wall, your eyes burning a hole in the tile floor. 'Was anyone
there with her?'

You shook your head at whatever he said in response. I couldn't tell
if you were about to break down or explode. As it turns out, you did
neither. After asking a few more questions you quietly said goodbye
and hung up the phone.

'Hey man, what happened?' Joe called through the doorway.

You didn't answer him, and for a second I thought you were about
to storm out, but then you shrugged, shook your head as if dispelling
it from your mind, and pushed yourself away from the wall in your
loose, easy way, looking like you didn't have a care in the world.

'Who wants another drink?' you called back over your shoulder as
you headed to the kitchen. 'And somebody put some goddam music on!'

Everyone was looking at me but I was too confused to try and
offer an explanation, my pulse throbbing in my throat and my skin
turning cold all over. I followed you to the kitchen, sure that I'd find
you in tears or in a rage or… *something!* But no. You were perfectly
calm, standing in front of the island where we'd amassed all the
alcohol, looking through the bottles like you were browsing in the
supermarket.

'Hey,' I said softly as I approached. I wanted to reach out and put
my hands around your shoulders, but there was an ominous stillness
surrounding you and it made me afraid to get too close. I hadn't seen
you this way since that first morning in Vegas, when you'd gone from
sitting quietly on the sofa to erupting in a blaze of fury. 'Are you OK?'

You looked over at me, and if I hadn't known better I would have thought you were just being drunk and silly, your dark eyes sparkling as you raised your eyebrows. A chill chased across my shoulders and down my back, and I hugged myself against it, feeling increasingly concerned. Why were you being so weird? Did you really not care or was something else going on?

'Sure. Why wouldn't I be?'

'*Why?* Because… your mother… Talk to me,' I said, edging a little closer. My hand was twitching to offer you some comfort, but the heavy dread that had stolen through my limbs kept it clamped against my arm. 'Don't you care?' The words came out in a croak, and I swallowed against the dryness in my mouth.

Something dangerous flashed across your face. 'Why should I?'

You grabbed a couple of whiskey bottles and strode back out of the kitchen, leaving me leaning against the counter in shock. I heard a collective groan from the living room and I knew what was happening before I even got back in there. I stood in the doorway and watched you pouring shots for everyone then toasting the room before downing yours in one swallow.

You cranked the music up until the walls shook with the noise, and started jumping around with the bottle in your hand, shouting along with the words.

The clammy coldness crept through my entire body as I watched you pour everyone another large measure of whiskey, then down yours and pour yourself a third. Then the bottle was empty.

You didn't let up. Partway through the second bottle the other guys were starting to reel, but you were like a mad thing, spinning in a one-man mosh pit as the music pounded through the house, making my head throb as my eardrums protested at the volume.

'It's too hot in here!' you shouted over the noise. 'I'm going outside, you guys coming?'

You almost fell face first onto the decking as the glass door slid away under your hand. You stumbled onto the grass, threw your head back and howled at the sky, the others following you more cautiously and laughing at their own drunkenness. You bellowed in protest as Joe tried to grab the bottle, and took off around the garden, cackling and shouting unintelligibly as you wove between the trees, stopping every once in a while to take another swig before dashing off again.

I'd never seen you this drunk before. You'd mostly been sober since the night we met – minus a few evenings when we'd been celebrating – and even on that night you'd still been marginally aware of what was going on around you. But this was just… madness. It seemed like you'd lost your mind. Beer and wine didn't do this to you, only whiskey. Why had I picked up whiskey? I should have remembered how crazy it made you, but that had been such a long time ago. We were happy now. *You* were happy now. I'd thought you'd left all that behind you but I guess I was wrong.

You ran out of steam and collapsed onto the bench on the far side of the lawn, still drinking. Matt was standing beside me on the decking with his hands tucked under his armpits, watching you. He noticed the look on my face and shook his head at me.

'What?' I snapped.

'Don't be the voice of reason, Aph,' he muttered, tipping his head towards mine. 'He won't want to hear it.'

I turned to glare at him but he was already walking away, towards the garden chairs at the other end of the platform. My attitude softened as I saw him position one of the chairs and sit back to observe you. He was obviously concerned too, but he was keeping his distance. Maybe he was right. Maybe it was best to let you drink yourself into a coma and pick up the pieces in the morning… but I just couldn't do it. It felt… *wrong*.

I stepped down off the decking and walked over to you, the soft grass cushioning my bare feet. I sat down on the bench beside you, hugging myself tightly as I tried to figure out how to stop you careening off down this path again – how to save you from yourself before you did some damage you wouldn't recover from.

'Heeeeey!' You held your arms wide, grinning. 'Look who's here!'

I sat watching you quietly but you wouldn't look me in the eye. Matt was at least partly right, you didn't want to hear sense, but this wasn't the time for indecision.

'Babe,' I said softly.

'Yes, my little pumpkin pie.' You were slurring so much I could hardly understand you, and your eyes were unable to focus as you stared out across the lawn.

'You need to stop.'

'Why?' You raised your voice to a yell. 'We're just having some fun, right, guys?'

You were answered by half-hearted cheering and I knew I was on my own.

'Have a drink, baby. Here, there's still like… half a bottle left.'

'I don't want a drink.' I pushed the bottle away from my face. 'And you don't need any more either.'

'Really? Well, that's funny coz I'm having more now.' You raised it to your lips and took a deep swig.

'You don't have to do this,' I continued firmly, trying to keep the worry out of my voice.

'Whatcha talkin' about? Just havin' some fun.'

'We both know fun has nothing to do with it.'

'We do? Oh. I must've missed that part.'

'Please—'

'Oh, shhhh! You're killing my buzz.'

'And you're killing yourself!' I shouted, losing my cool in the rush of fear I felt and the flash of anger that followed it. 'Can't you see that? Or is that the point?'

'Stop being such a bitch!' you screamed back, struggling to your feet and waving the bottle in my face. 'If I wanna drink I'll fucking drink!'

I grabbed the bottle and shoved it away, spilling whiskey on your arm and all over the grass.

'Hey! That's expensive shit!'

'I don't care!' I shouted, standing up to face you. 'I'll tip the whole damn thing away if I have to.'

You glared at me and then started to laugh, the stink of raw spirit filling the air. 'You're such a badass.'

'This isn't a joke!'

'No? Well, HA, HA, HA!' you yelled in my face. 'Seems pretty funny to me!'

Hot tears began to spill down my cheeks as I realised you weren't going to stop.

This wasn't what I wanted. The person I'd fallen in love with was sweet and gentle and brave, not this mean, obnoxious drunk standing in front of me. Why, when everything was going so perfectly, did life have to come and ruin it all with such a cruel blow?

'Why are you doing this to yourself?' I wailed.

You paused for a moment, noticing my tears. 'Why the hell shouldn't I?'

'Because you're better than this,' I answered, reaching out to touch your arm. I couldn't let you go down this road, not again. I'd thought the success would allow you to leave it behind, once and for all, but this wasn't about winning or losing, this was about dealing with life in all its terrifying unpredictability. If you were going to be my husband – the final stop on my Path – you needed to get over this crap. I knew you had demons and I'd never judged you for that, but you had to start thinking about how your actions affected other people – affected me. We were a team. It wasn't just about you anymore, and you needed to take responsibility.

'Bullshit!' you snapped, shrugging me off. You threw the bottle to the ground and it landed with a dull thud. 'This is me. This is what I do.'

'It doesn't have to be.'

'How would you know?' Your voice rose in volume again, and you raised your hands like you were calling me out. 'You don't even know me. You're just a goddam gold-digging whore!'

Something snapped inside me, and before I even knew what I was doing I had hit you. Right in the face. Not an open-handed slap, a full-on, closed-fisted punch square on the nose, and I only realised what had happened when I saw the blood spurting down over your lips.

'Did you just…?' You raised your hands to your nose and they came away slick and shiny. White-hot fury blazed in your eyes, before you marched across the lawn and put your fist through the half-open glass door, letting out a blood-curdling roar and stalking back into the house.

I raised my hands to my mouth and felt the world come to a standstill. *Oh my God, oh my God, oh my God. What have I done?*

Everyone else had stopped to watch and I just stood and stared at the broken glass in horror. Matt came to stand beside me and I thought he might say *I told you so*, but he just put his arms around my shoulders and pulled me against him, stroking my head as I sobbed against his chest. After a while my tears subsided and I stood back from him, wiping my face with the back of my hands.

'It was a good punch.' Matt smiled slightly, lifting my hand for inspection. 'I'd get some ice on that if you want to use it anytime soon.'

His dry humour cut through my self-pity and I realised my hand was actually hurting quite a lot… although not as much as my heart hurt, knowing what I'd done to you.

'I'd better go and see if he's OK,' I said, clearing my throat and feeling utterly ashamed of myself. 'Can you, umm… I think the party's over.' I didn't even want to look anyone else in the eye.

Matt nodded and I gave him a small smile of gratitude, before crossing the lawn and stepping carefully into the living room over the mess of broken glass. Bile rose in my throat as I saw the trail of bloodstains across the carpet. It wasn't enough to make me think you'd hit an artery, but it was an awful lot…

I followed the broken chain of dark red splotches, across the hall, up the stairs, along the corridor to our bedroom. I peeked through the door but the light was off and my eyes couldn't pierce the shadows. I stepped over the threshold and flicked the light switch. You weren't on the bed. I took another two steps into the room and looked past the bed to the bathroom door, which was ajar, although the light hadn't been switched on in there either. But then I heard a congested sniff and a spitting sound.

I found you slouched on the step next to the bath, a bloody towel pressed to your nose and your head resting against the wall tiles. There were gashes in your forearm from the shattered glass, and blood dripped down to your elbow and soaked into your jeans every time you moved.

'Oh, babe,' I whispered miserably. 'I'm so sorry.'

You lowered the towel and sniffed again, twisting to spit more blood into the bath before looking me in the eye. In the mellow light that shone through from the bedroom I could see that the drunken haze had lifted. You looked calm and sober, but something still wasn't right.

'You hit me,' you said. 'In the face.'

I bit my lips and nodded silently, willing myself not to cry.

'I knew you were a badass.'

Relief rushed out of me in a sob and I dashed across the room, almost falling on you in my desperation to feel your arms around me. I buried my face in your neck and clung to you, saying, 'I'm sorry, I'm sorry, I'm sorry' over and over again, until you shushed me and stroked my hair with your battered, bloody hand.

'Hey, it's OK,' you murmured. 'I'm sorry I said... what I said to you. I was being an asshole.'

'Yeah. You were. But that's no excuse. I didn't hit you the last time you called me that, and that was before I even—'

I stopped short as your chest rumbled with a chuckle, and sat back to look at you, wiping my nose on my sleeve. 'What?'

'Is that the story we're going to tell our kids? Well, kids, when Mommy and Daddy met, Daddy called Mommy a hooker and Mommy thought, "Hmm, this guy's husband material!"'

I let out a honk of laughter and clamped my hand over my mouth. I loved that even after our night had turned into such a disaster, you were still thinking about that stuff. A flood of fierce affection washed over me, and I bent to plant a kiss on your cheek. But as my eyes dropped to your chest I suddenly realised what a mess we looked, slumped on the floor in the semi-darkness, covered in blood, and for some reason it made me laugh harder, the hysteria bubbling up from my stomach.

'You hit pretty hard, you should start coming to training.' You didn't sound angry anymore, just tired and maybe a little sad.

'I'm so, so sorry.'

'It's OK. I deserved it.' You gave another sniff, but it sounded drier now. 'It's not your fault she's dead.'

I couldn't believe you could say it in such a calm, unflinching way. It made me shiver.

'It's not yours either,' I answered gently. 'And… it's not your fault she left.'

'I know,' you said, resting your head back against the tiles once more as you stared up at the top of the glass shower panel behind me. 'Sometimes I hate her, and other times… I forget, you know? I forget she even exists. *Existed*.'

That was the most you'd ever said about your feelings towards your mother in one go.

'When I was a kid, I just wanted her to come back. Even though I couldn't remember her… and I kinda hated her, for what she did to my dad… I thought, maybe if she came back, everything would stop being so hard… And then when I got older, I wished I could see her just to tell her what a bitch she was… You know, she's the reason I started fighting?'

'Yeah… your dad told me.'

'He did? Huh. Well, he thought it'd help, you know? If I had something to channel all my anger into. Back then I just wanted to hurt people – to hurt her… And now she's gone. And I'll never get to see her and tell her any of that stuff. And you know the worst part?' You looked at me suddenly, blinking as though you were emerging from a dream. 'I don't even care. Does that make me a bad person?'

I squashed myself in beside you, my shoulders wedged between yours and the cupboard below the sink.

'No,' I answered, pulling your hand into my lap and stroking your fingers. 'It makes you an honest person.'

You smiled and lifted my hand to your lips, your breath warming the skin. 'How come you always have an answer for everything?'

'I don't. You just always ask the right questions.'

'See?' You gave a helpless shrug.

I laughed. 'OK, well… maybe it's just because I'm a smart-arse.'

'You totally are,' you said, and I batted you lightly on the shoulder. You held up a hand in self-defence. 'Are you gonna beat me up again?'

'Shut up.'

There was a tentative knock on the door and we both looked up to see Matt standing there.

'Everything OK?' He switched on the light and took a couple of steps into the room, looking relieved to see you sitting calmly and quietly. 'How's the nose?'

'Sore.'

'Want me to take a look?'

'OK.'

We got to our feet, and Matt sat you down on the edge of the bath to examine your face. He felt your nose and you winced as he squeezed the bridge.

'Hmm… it's bruised but I don't think it's broken.' He stood back and rested his hands on his hips, frowning at you with concern.

'It's fine,' you said, shrugging. 'I think I might have found a new striking coach though,' you added, throwing me an impish grin.

Matt snorted and shook his head. 'I know, that was some punch. I think she should start training.'

'That's what I said!' you chimed in.

'Yeah, yeah.' I threw a clean towel at Matt and he faked terror before laughing at my indignation. 'You finish playing nursey while I go and find some ice for my hand.'

Well, I thought, retracing my steps along the trail of darkening stains on the hallway carpet, *I guess you know it's been a good party when there are bloodstains all over the floor.*

That night, despite our reconciliation and my exhaustion from all the drama, I couldn't get to sleep. I was troubled by thoughts of death and grief – of the fragile veneer of stability that could be cracked open so easily. I had begun to believe that we were unbreakable – that all the hardest parts were behind us and that the future was a certainty – and it scared me to realise that it could all be snatched away, with a single roll of the dice. I had found my way to you at a time when the Path was beginning to seem like more of a curse than a blessing; I'd almost refused its call and it would have cost me everything. And now I had decided that no matter what happened, I wasn't going to give you up. Was this the price of taking a stand? Was this the universe trying to force me to move on because it knew I had made the wrong decision?

I focused on the dim outline of your back and shoulder, watching the expansion and contraction of your ribs. I wanted to touch you but I was afraid of waking you, so I just lay there, keeping watch, worrying about you and about what the morning would bring.

Let this be the end, I remember thinking. *Let him be the last one – the only one. If I can't be with him, I don't want to be with anyone. Let me be free of it. Let me choose this life and keep it forever.*

I felt the cool trickle of a tear sliding down over my temple, and I wiped it away.

I knew the price of failure – the consequences of subverting the laws that governed humankind and made me what I am. I'd known it when I had stepped through the door that separated Hearthfire from the rest of reality, and I'd done it anyway. But what else could I have done? I'd been a child! A sixteen-year-old girl, with a head full of romantic notions about life in the outside world, and an inflated sense of self-importance that had been carefully cultivated by the only family I knew: the people I had trusted implicitly to teach me and sculpt me into what *they* said I needed to be. What kind of choice was that, really? How much free will can anyone truly exercise if every moment of their existence has led them to a single, inevitable conclusion?

I never asked to be what I am. I didn't have a choice in that.

I had never resented it until now, until you, and that resentment was rooted in fear; I didn't want to live in a world without you at the centre, and even the thought of it filled me with a mind-numbing dread. You were mine. You'd said so. We belonged to each other, in a way neither of us had ever belonged to anyone. Even at our worst we were made for each other, we balanced each other out and found a way through, even if it took everything we had to do it. If anything, what had happened earlier only made us stronger. We really could overcome anything, as long as we were together.

I'll always be here, I thought at you, willing the words into your mind and your heart so you'd never have to doubt it. We were a team, you and me. I'd fight for you with every scrap of breath in my body.

The next day, I cleaned up the glass from the door and called the repair company to get the panel replaced, then set about tidying up the rest of the mess from the party. The garden and the living room needed a lot of attention, and it took over an hour of scrubbing to lift the stains from the carpet.

You were subdued, spending most of the day in bed with the TV on and the curtains drawn. I checked in occasionally to see if I could fetch you anything. You were fairly uncommunicative, but in the afternoon when I poked my head in through the door you held out your arm in silent appeal, and when I plopped down next to you, you gathered me into a hug.

Your sister called in the evening and you had a long talk with her, sitting on the floor of the entrance hall with your legs stretched out in front of you. I kept out of earshot, not wanting to intrude, busying myself with making dinner and cleaning around the kitchen.

It turned out that your mother had actually died over a month before, but it had taken her new family a while to track your dad down and inform him. You had already missed the funeral. I wasn't sure if I was sad or relieved that you wouldn't have to attend.

I couldn't really offer any advice when it came to parental relationships. I'd done my fair share of soul-searching about what kind of people would just leave their child behind to be raised by strangers. Did my parents even know what Hearthfire was? Did they have any clue what would happen to me? Would they have cared if they did? The other thing that always bugged me was that, for all I knew, they could have been among the Elders there. There was simply no way I would ever find out the truth, and after all the years of wondering I had come to the conclusion that I probably didn't want to know anyway.

That night we sat out on the sunloungers in the garden, and you asked me if I could play you something on the guitar. My singing always seemed to soothe your nerves.

I played through a few of your favourite tunes and then plucked the strings idly for a moment, trying to figure out what to play next. There was something floating around in my head that was trying to come to the surface... I let my fretting hand settle where it wanted and struck a random chord. Then it came to me. I adjusted the tuning pegs, experimenting until I got them all at the right pitch, then shook out my fingers and began to play.

As soon as I started, I knew it was a Song. A current of tender sorrow – pain wrapped in sweetness – flowed outwards from my chest to my extremities, and then out through my pores into the cool night air. It felt like a gift – not just my gift to you, but also a gift to me from... wherever the Songs came from. It was 'Heartbeats' by José Gonzáles, possibly one of the saddest and most beautiful pieces of music ever written.

You sat in silence while I played, staring up at the sky. When I finished you turned towards me, a peaceful smile gracing your lips and your dark eyes liquid with tears.

'Thank you,' you said, reaching out your hand.

I took it and squeezed your fingers. There was nothing more I could say.

*

It was six weeks later that you got the next life-changing phone call. I was so pleased I could hardly speak when you told me the news; it was exactly what you needed to get back on track. You hadn't been the same since you'd heard about your mother's death. There was a sadness around your eyes that had been stubbornly refusing to lift, but on hearing about your upcoming fight the shadows seemed to vanish.

You'd finally done it. You were getting a chance to have a shot at the title. In five months' time you'd be fighting the guy who was currently ranked number one below the division champion, and the winner would go on to compete for the belt. You acted like you were taking it in your stride but I could tell you were massively excited.

'Hey, you know I'll have to train through your birthday.'

We were walking along the beach after dinner, hand in hand, watching the sun set over the water in a blaze of fiery glory.

'I'll have other birthdays,' I answered. 'You can spoil me after you win!'

'Hey, don't jinx it!'

'OK, sorry.'

You kicked sand across my legs and I smacked you on the arm, glad to see your playful side emerging again.

'Maybe we could go away for your birthday instead?' I suggested. 'It'll be a triple celebration.'

'I said don't jinx it!'

'No, I meant for our birthdays and our anniversary.'

'Oh yeah, I forgot about that. How long is it now? Ten years? Twenty?' I went to smack you again but you ducked away, laughing. 'Too slow.'

I pulled a face at you.

'Well, we'll already be in Vegas for the fight,' you mused, cocking an eyebrow. 'We could stay and blow my winner's purse.'

I grinned. 'Now who's jinxing it?'

'What do you think?'

I liked the idea. It would be fitting to celebrate our two-year anniversary – and your next win – in the city where it had all begun for us.

I nodded and squeezed your hand. 'OK. Let's do it.'

We carried on with our walk, talking about all the stupidly expensive and ostentatious things we'd do once the fight was over and our holiday could begin. You mentioned that you'd always wanted to go on one of those quadbike rides in the desert. I'd never been on a quadbike before and the landscape out there was incredible; what better way to explore it than on four wheels, racing over the sand like two rockets shooting through the air?

The night before the big day, I barely slept a wink. Along with the nerves and the hope and the excitement, there was a cold tremor of fear that shivered through my chest – the same sickly sense of dread I'd felt the night we heard about your mum – at the thought that everything we'd worked for, everything I'd come to care about could suddenly be yanked away. I'd been suppressing it, distracting myself in the hope that it would disappear, but it was always there, lurking: a shadow on the edge of my vision.

I went with you to the backstage area this time, for the first time since I'd met you. I knew it was probably unwise to break our usual routine, but I couldn't spend all those hours away from you knowing how much pressure you were under. I sat quietly and waited while you worked through your mental preparation process and started warming up with Matt.

We were in a small, beige room with blue grappling mats covering the floor. There were a few plastic chairs scattered around the sides but not much else – a couple of gym bags and bits of sparring equipment, a big pack of water bottles, a portable speaker and an iPod to pump out the music you liked to listen to while you were psyching yourself up. Today it was Metallica, the band that played the song you used for your entrance music, and James Hetfield's voice rang out from the speaker in a dangerous, primal roar.

The room was just for you and the guys from your team, and everyone was watching surreptitiously for the slightest hint that you might need something from them.

Joe came over and sat down beside me as you were getting your hands wrapped up.

'You wanna go out front? There's a seat for you.'

I studied you, sitting quietly with your arms resting over the chair-back, and wondered if my presence was a distraction or a comfort. You caught my eye and threw me a wink.

'No,' I answered. 'I think I'll stay here this time.'

We sat in silence for a while. I'd never seen this side of you before: the gradual drawing in that resulted in that warrior mask you wore when you walked down to the cage. I felt like I was being drawn in with you, tuning out everything that existed outside that room and focusing my whole being on what was happening right now.

Your five-minute warning came and you started working through some light striking drills with Matt, just enough to keep the blood flowing. My eyes were locked on you, absorbing every detail: the ripple of the muscles beneath your skin, the lightness in your feet, the angle of your arms and hands, and especially your eyes – your black, fathomless eyes that could be soft pools of shadow or coldly flashing flint. They were trained on Matt, never wavering for a second, but from where I sat I could see the light shining in them, and they had that particular sparkle that told me you were excited and nervous and joyful and peaceful all at the same time.

I loved you. God, I loved you so much. There was nothing I wouldn't do for you – no price I wouldn't pay to be with you. The feeling was almost frightening in its intensity.

And then it was time.

I stood up with everyone else and hovered next to Joe, waiting for him to point me in the right direction. Just before you left the room you suddenly turned back and kissed me hard on the mouth, and I was so surprised I didn't even have time to kiss you back before you were gone. I stood stupidly for a second, and then Joe was tugging me by the arm and I let him lead me down the hallway, through the double doors and out into the deafening noise of the arena. I was running completely on autopilot as I followed you and the rest of the team down through the crowd to the cage.

You stopped to shrug out of your hoodie and sweats, and you turned to give Matt a hug, and then Joe and the other guys. When you got to me you pointed to your tattoo, so briefly anyone else would have missed it, and hugged me hard, pressing your lips to the side of my head. Matt stuck your gumshield in your mouth and squirted some water in after. You had your face rubbed with Vaseline and were checked over by an official, and then you were stepping up to the cage and out of my reach.

I forced myself to breathe evenly, focusing only on the love that flowed between us, and it seemed for a second as though nothing else existed. It didn't matter that your mind was elsewhere, I knew your heart was with me.

I found my way to my seat, with nothing left to do but watch and wait. I strained to see every movement you made as you skipped lightly around the cage, knowing that inside your head you were composed, ready, the adrenaline coursing through your bloodstream and blocking out any sense of fear or doubt.

Your opponent made his entrance, but as usual I hardly noticed. All the formalities were observed, somehow taking aeons and yet over in the blink of an eye, and then the referee dropped his hand and the dance began.

The fight went back and forth. You were on your feet, on the ground, back up and against the cage. Matt was constantly shouting directions at you and I could see you were paying attention, responding almost as soon as he spoke. One minute the other guy was struggling to get a hold locked in, the next you were pushing to get past his guard.

The first round ended and a momentary relief settled over my fraught nerves. Matt and Joe dashed in to give you a drink and a brief, hurried talk, and I stole a glance around me. To everyone else this was just a fight – a great, exciting, edge-of-your-seat fight, but no more than entertainment – but to us, to you and me and the team, it was a fight to the death, a test of courage and endurance and skill, a rite of passage that could end in disaster or lead to ultimate victory.

The instant the next round started, my fragile tranquillity evaporated.

Your opponent managed to keep the fight standing for most of the second round, probably expecting to have a greater advantage there than on the ground since you were more of a grappler, but you didn't let it faze you and you managed to avoid any serious damage. In the third minute there was a moment when I thought you were going to catch him in an arm bar, but he twisted free.

You were both breathing harder this time as you took your corners, and I prayed that all the extra cardio would see you through if you had to go the full distance.

The klaxon sounded for the third round and I watched you stand up quickly and shake yourself. You began well, landing a couple of good strikes and finding your pace again, but then suddenly he caught you with a well-timed uppercut just as you shot forward to try for a takedown, and the blood ran cold in my veins. I saw you stumble and fall, and ashamed as I am to admit it I turned my face away, unable to watch any longer. The crowd was going nuts but I couldn't look; if you were knocked unconscious I'd be jumping the fence and climbing in with you.

The volume suddenly doubled and my eyes flew open of their own accord. All I could see was your body in a heap, the ref pulling the other guy away and the worry etched into the faces of Matt and Joe. The horn sounded and the crowd was roaring, and all I could think was, *Please be OK! The title doesn't matter as long as you're OK! Please, please, PLEASE!!*

Matt and Joe rushed into the cage to clean you up, and to pull your T-shirt and cap on for the cameras. I couldn't take my eyes off you as you rubbed your bloody face and let out a ragged growl of disappointment. Matt was talking in your ear and you were frowning as you listened, but when he patted you on the back I saw a resigned smile tug at your lips. I bit my cheeks to stop myself from crying.

The referee raised the other guy's hand as the announcer called his name, but I didn't care about that. I didn't care about anything apart from the fact that I could see you standing there, battered but alive, with your beautiful, bleeding face turned up to the ceiling and your chest heaving from the strain.

You said a few words to the victor, gracious in defeat, and then you were out of the cage and I was rushing across the floor and throwing myself at you. I don't think you registered that I was completely hysterical with relief, and you hugged me close for a minute before starting the long walk back to the locker rooms. I clung to your gloved hand the whole way there, and was pleased to hear shouts of approval and respect ringing out from the crowd. You'd earned it. They knew the same way I did that you were a winner, regardless of the outcome of the fight.

We got back to the room and Matt shut the door behind us, standing aside to let the medic take a look at your face and head. Joe was looking at you like he was wondering what would happen, and I realised this was the first time I'd been with you after a loss, apart from the first time we met.

Matt leaned against the wall and crossed his arms over his chest.

'You OK, man?'

'Yeah.' You winced as the medic felt along your jaw, but he seemed satisfied that your wounds were mainly superficial, and he left you alone with us.

Matt crouched down in front of you and started stripping off your wraps. 'You fought a hell of a fight, brother. Don't let this slow you down.'

You nodded and let out a long, quivering breath. A tear slipped down your cheek and you brushed it away with your forearm, clearing your throat impatiently.

'I know, man. It's all good.'

You were watching your hands as the wraps came off, but your eyes were seeing something else – I guessed you were replaying the fight in your head, trying to figure out where it had gone wrong.

'There was nothing else you could have done,' Joe chimed in. 'It was a lucky shot.'

You shrugged and drew your hands in to your chest, rubbing the knuckles. I saw your lips twitching downwards at the corners and I couldn't stand back any longer; I pulled you against me and wrapped my arms around your shoulders, wanting to take all your pain and disappointment and carry it myself so you wouldn't have to. You hugged me back, pressing your cheek against my chest as I stroked your head.

Your body shook a few times with silent sobs, but then your breathing quieted and your arms relaxed around me, your hands resting gently against my ribs.

You were so different to the man I'd met all those months ago: the one who had exploded at me in the hotel room and tried to shove me away. I'd become your safe place since then, and I was glad about that, but I was still sorry to know how much you were hurting.

'It's OK,' you murmured, sniffling softly. 'I'm OK.'

I looked down at you, holding your face and wiping away your tears with my thumbs.

'This isn't the end,' I said. 'You have so many great things ahead of you.'

'I know.' You smiled up at me and I kissed you, pouring my love into you as an antidote to the sorrow.

You got to your feet and let out another long breath, but it was steady this time, and your head was unbowed.

'You nearly had him a few times,' Matt said wryly, patting you on the shoulder. 'It was a close thing.'

You nodded. 'Yeah. Wish I'd have known I didn't have to make it to the end.' You threw Matt a rueful look. 'Could've skipped out on some of that goddam cardio.'

Matt and Joe laughed and the other guys seemed to heave a sigh of relief.

'Well, you can hang loose for the next week or so.' Matt winked at me and I smiled back at him.

'Hah!' you grunted. 'You seriously think she's gonna let me *rest* for a week?'

I pouted and everyone laughed, and the knot in my belly untwisted itself.

'We're still going quadbiking though, right?' you asked with a hopeful smile.

At one point I'd suggested that we would only go if you won, but I hadn't really meant it; I wanted to go just as much as you did. And besides, there was no way I could have refused that note of appeal in your voice.

I nodded, eliciting an excited 'yesss' from you and another ripple of laughter from the other guys. As if I could have said no; you'd had your heart set on it for months.

I wish I could say that I remember every moment of the days that followed with perfect clarity, but actually most of it is just a blur. The next morning is still pretty vivid, I guess because the fear of losing you was so fresh in my mind.

We had breakfast on the balcony and watched the people streaming past on the street below. You were quiet but you seemed OK otherwise; I was just happy to be near you, as always.

'I feel like I should be more upset.' You sat back in your chair after finishing your food, folding your hands behind your head and laying your bare legs across my lap.

I rubbed your shin. 'I think you're feeling whatever you're supposed to feel.'

'But I just lost the biggest fight of my life… I feel like I should be more… I don't know.' You trailed off, gazing across at the building opposite us.

'Babe, this is the beginning, not the end,' I answered, squinting as the sun shone in my eyes. 'I think the reason you're not upset is because there's so much to be happy about.'

You nodded absently. 'It just seems weird, you know? The last time I lost I was…'

'I remember.' I smiled, tweaking your big toe.

You looked confused for a second. 'Right, that was the night I met you… What the hell did you see in me?'

I arched my back in a stretch, patting my belly as it gurgled in satisfaction. 'A fighter,' I answered. 'Someone who wasn't ready to give up.'

Your eyes held mine and you smiled softly. 'I'm glad you saw that. I don't know if anybody else did.'

You leaned across and kissed me, and I savoured the smell of you as our lips met – that familiar blend of scents that was uniquely yours. You drew back and flicked a stray strand of hair away from my face.

'You still wanna marry me?'

'What do you think?' I placed my hands either side of your face, running my thumb across your cheekbone. 'Of course I do. It's all I want… *You're* all I want.'

'You changed everything for me. You know that?'

'You changed it, not me.'

'I don't mean the wins,' you persisted. 'I mean *everything* changed – *I* changed. Winning or losing, it doesn't matter anymore. Whatever happens in that cage, I've won. Do you get what I'm saying? As long as I have you, I've won.'

My eyes had teared up as you were talking and I didn't trust my voice to respond when you finished, so instead of saying anything, I kissed you; it was the only answer that came close to expressing how I felt about you.

My chair tilted under me as my weight shifted, and you threw out your arms to keep me from falling. Our kisses became interspersed with laughter as we delighted in the sheer joy of being us. I didn't think I'd ever felt as deeply whole and happy as I did in that second.

If I'd known, I would have counted down the days. I would have filled every minute with moments like that one.

The following Saturday dawned with the same gorgeous, blazing blue sky as all our other days in Vegas. We went for a run, ate breakfast on the balcony, and had a soak in the enormous tub in our bathroom before setting off for our quadbike ride through the Valley of Fire. You were totally pumped up; you had to avoid doing things like that on the lead-up to a fight in case you injured yourself, but this was your playtime and your excitement was infectious.

It was almost an hour's drive from the town to the quadbike centre, where the tours started. The rental car was a convertible and we rode with the roof down so we could feel the breeze as the sun beat down on us. The air smelled of melting rubber and hot tarmac, and the gritty sand scoured our faces as it blew over the windscreen and away. The landscape was incredible, like an alien planet, with burnt orange crags reaching their sharp, jagged fingers up to the brilliant blue above.

You were impatient, drumming your hands on the steering wheel as Pantera blasted out from the car stereo, tearing along the ribbon of road at a speed that would have terrified me if I'd been with anyone else. You spent the whole drive with this little satisfied smile on your face, and even though you were wearing shades I could tell your eyes were smiling too. I knew every expression you had by then; your features were more familiar to me than my own.

We slid to a halt in the car park at the quad centre, the wheels kicking up bone-dry dust and loose stones. You stood up in your seat and looked around, taking in a deep lungful of air.

'Now this is a vacation!'

I grinned and stood up next to you, surveying the immense expanse of rock and dirt and open air. I pulled off my sunglasses, but the light was so bright that everything was instantly bleached of colour and I had to put them back on.

You laughed and pulled me into a kiss, and I could feel the exuberance flowing through you where our bodies touched.

We hopped out of the convertible and made our way into the quad centre to join the rest of the group. There were around eight or ten of us altogether, plus the two guys who were leading the tour. We were all fitted out for helmets and overalls, and given a brief tutorial on a little circular course out the back. It was easier than I expected, although we were warned that the steering would be more difficult on rougher terrain. I grinned as you winked at me, revving your engine with thinly veiled impatience.

Two minutes later we were off. You were right behind the leader and probably would have sped past him if you'd known the way. I was next in line, keeping a safe distance but not wanting to drop too far back. The roar of the engines was thunderous in the still desert air, and I whooped with sheer exhilaration as we rode through the wild landscape, following your path as you shot down the trail.

At what I assumed to be the halfway point we stopped for a drink and a rest, giving everyone a chance to stretch their legs and rub knotted muscles. You strode over to me, pulling off your helmet, and I could tell by your huge, beaming grin that you were loving every second of it. We gazed out at the immense panorama, so massive it distorted all sense of distance and scale, seemingly stretching on and on to infinity.

Once everyone was rested and rehydrated it was time to move on. As you hauled me to my feet from my perch on a low rock, you kissed my sweaty forehead and laid a hand on my cheek.

'Remind me we need to talk when we get back.'

'We do?'

'Yeah.' You smiled enigmatically. 'I've had a crazy idea.'

Normally I would have rolled my eyes and groaned at that, but there was something in your expression that made me pause.

'OK,' I said instead. 'Can't wait to hear it.'

'I'll give you a hint. Hold out your hand.'

I did, and in the centre of my palm you placed a ring made out of a twisted piece of dry, yellow grass. Before I could figure out its meaning you flashed me a huge, sweet grin, gave me a lingering kiss and pulled your helmet back on. 'Let's go.'

I watched you walk back to your quad, puzzling over what you were up to. It must be something to do with the wedding, but I couldn't think what. I slipped the ring into my pocket and pulled my helmet on before climbing onto my quadbike. I was intrigued to find out what you were being all secretive about, but you'd tell me in your own time, like always.

I heard the growl of the other engines starting up and I turned the key in the ignition, creeping forward to take my place in the line behind you. It was going to drive me crazy staring at your back for the next two hours and wondering what you were thinking, but in the meantime I had the incredible view to keep my mind occupied.

I think we were about halfway back to the base when it happened, although I can't be sure. One minute you were speeding along in front of me as we raced across a high spine of ground, standing up a little in your seat to get a better view, and the next there was a jolt and a cloud of red dust, and all I could think was that you'd gone down a sudden dip in the trail... but then you didn't reappear.

I slammed on the brakes and came to a stop, too confused to be worried. Everyone else pulled up behind me and one of the tour guides was racing past me on foot and dashing off over the side of the path. It wasn't until I saw the fear on his face that I realised something must be horribly wrong. Suddenly I felt like someone was tightening a vice across my chest, and I leaped from my quadbike and tore off after him.

At that point the trail was on a narrow strip of earth that rose up from the desert, the ground falling away steeply on either side. I scrambled over the edge and felt a scream tear from my lips, and then I was plummeting down the treacherous slope, sliding and slipping in the sand, my eyes fixed in horror on the scene below.

I can hardly bring myself to describe it, even now. It wasn't that it looked gruesome, it really didn't, but there was something... wrong about it. Everything looked wrong. *You* looked wrong.

You were on your back on the ground with your legs sticking out in front of you in a crooked kind of way, and your arms were flung out to the sides as though you'd been flailing to find your balance in the moment you'd hit the ground. You still had your helmet on but the visor was open, and one of the guides was leaning over to talk to you, looking very, very worried.

I skidded to a halt on the shifting red sand and fell down beside you, ripping my helmet off my head. The fact that you didn't turn to look at me set alarm bells ringing in my brain, but your eyes were open and you were definitely breathing, your mouth sucking in air like you'd just gone three full rounds.

'Babe? Babe, talk to me!' I wanted to pull you upright and hold you against me, but I knew it wasn't safe to move you after a fall like that. I grabbed your hand and pressed it to my chest. 'Why isn't he saying anything?'

'Ma'am, you need to calm down,' the nearest guide was saying, pale-faced with shock.

'Don't tell me to calm down!' I snapped at him. 'I'll calm down when he's walking out of here! Somebody tell me what's happening!'

'OK, I think he hit a bump and... he must have come over the side.'

Your breath was coming in tearing gasps, and I could hear an awful, rattling wheeze shaking through you every time you inhaled. I laid my hand lightly on your chest, hardly daring to touch you but willing your lungs to respond, to heal and be whole.

'Babe, please! Look at me! Please tell me you're OK!'

'I think the quad must have come down on top of him,' the guide said, his voice hoarse.

I looked up and saw your quadbike lying on its side a little further down the slope, the tyres on the bottom half partially buried in the sand, like it had landed with force rather than simply rolling over. What had seemed like a big, exciting toy a few hours before now looked like a great mechanical monster. The thing must have weighed half a ton at least.

Oh God! I thought. *Oh God, no! Please.*

'You have to help him.' I looked up at the tour guide's frightened eyes and saw nothing there but panic. 'Please help him. Please. He needs a doctor. He needs to get to a hospital now!'

'Rick's calling someone right now. Just hang tight, OK? They'll get someone here right away.'

I nodded, desperately hoping he was right, and leaned my forehead against your helmet, watching your face for the slightest hint of recognition.

'It's OK, I'm here. I'm right here with you. They're gonna get help, OK? I just need you to stay with me. You fight for me, you hear? Don't you dare give up now. Babe? Don't you dare!'

You didn't reply. You just kept taking those ragged, gurgling breaths, which sounded so painful my chest ached in sympathy. Your eyes were looking up at me but I don't know if they were really *seeing* me. They had a sheen of moisture that made your pupils look like glittering black diamonds, and I let out a sob as a single tear ran down your face, leaving a streak in the dust on your skin.

I huddled closer to you, my fingers digging into your palm as I held your hand tightly to my chest. My whole body seemed to pulse with every heartbeat. I couldn't breathe. I couldn't think. My mind was crammed with a million words, churning over and over and over.

Why the hell did we have to come here? Everything was perfect. We should have stayed in the hotel and never, ever gone outside again! I should have known this was going to happen… Why didn't I know? Why didn't I stop him? He's dying right in front of me and it's all my fault…

I couldn't bear to hear any more so I pressed my face to your helmet and whispered to you, and kept on whispering to you. I don't even know what I said but I had to keep talking or the thoughts would come back again.

Somewhere in the numbness that was filling up the world I was vaguely aware that there were other people around me. I think somebody was trying to shelter us from the sun with their jacket or something, and I think I remember someone holding a bottle of water out to me, but I didn't take it. My eyes were locked on yours, my hands holding onto yours for dear life as I willed you to be OK.

But every breath you took sounded more and more painful, until all I could hear was that hideous rattling wheeze. I thought I would go mad with the sound of it. I noticed blood flecking the saliva at the corner of your mouth and I wiped it away with my sleeve.

'Don't go,' I whimpered, my throat full of grit. 'Don't leave me alone… please. I can't do this without you. You promised, remember? You said you'd always take care of me… And there was something you wanted to tell me, remember that? You have to stay so you can tell me, OK? Please promise me you'll stay. Please, I need you, I love you. Please, I love you so, so much. Please, please, please…'

My words choked off to a strangled whisper, and for a split second you were there – your eyes came back to life. You smiled, a tiny, sweet smile, like you were just seeing me for the very first time and the sight filled you with joy… but then your arm went heavy in my hands and all light disappeared from your eyes.

My fingers lost their strength and your hand slid down away from me, coming to rest over the spot where the doves were tattooed on your ribs.

I couldn't think.

I couldn't see.

I have no idea how long it was before the helicopter arrived. I don't remember the crew or what happened to the people from the tour. I don't know if I climbed into the helicopter or if I was carried. I really wasn't aware of anything besides the thick, grey fuzz that surrounded me.

The next solid memory I have is of sitting in the hospital. Someone had wrapped a blanket around me and I was in a room on my own with you, staring at your face. Your helmet had been removed. You were still and peaceful, lying on a bed. Someone had closed your eyes. I wanted to open them but I couldn't move. I wanted to see them flash at me – in anger or amusement, I didn't care – but they didn't open. You didn't move at all.

I studied the cuts on your cheek and lip, which had begun to heal after the fight. They seemed to be the only thing wrong with you. You were perfect other than that. Unblemished. It just didn't make sense.

I realised that the skin beneath my hand, which was resting on your dove tattoo, had grown cold. Reluctantly I pulled my fingers out from under your T-shirt. I didn't want to remember you like that.

People kept coming in and offering me things – water, coffee, even food, but I didn't want it. I didn't even look at it. I just looked at you and held my hand to my face with the engagement ring pressed against my lips, whispering prayers to it like other people do to rosaries. I don't even know what I was praying for; the one thing I'd ever truly wanted was already lost, beyond all hope of return.

Quite a long time must have passed. I think at some point someone tried to get me to move. I seem to remember them telling me that you wouldn't want me to be sitting there like that, all by myself, that you wouldn't want me to put myself through the trauma.

You don't know him, I thought. *You don't know what he wants. I know better. He wants me here next to him. He wants me here where it's safe.*

Sometime later I heard the door open and your dad came in. I didn't look up. I only know it was him because he fell down on his knees on the other side of you and sobbed like I had in the sand. I felt sorry for him, in a vague kind of way. It must be terrible to lose a son.

When your sister arrived she held me for a while, rocking me back and forth and crying into my hair. It reminded me of the morning after you and I met, sitting on the floor in the hotel room. But this wasn't the same. That time, you were healing. This time... I don't know. There was no healing to be done. There was nothing to be done anymore.

We buried you in LA. I don't remember the funeral or what happened after, except that at some point I ended up back at the house, alone.

I hadn't cried again since we'd left the desert. I thought I probably should, but the tears wouldn't come. What good would tears do anyway? They couldn't bring you back. If I'd thought that was a possibility I would have squeezed every last drop of moisture from my body – I would have cried myself blind.

Mostly, I sat out on the bench in the garden, staring emptily at the fluttering leaves on the trees and the ripples that chased across the surface of the pool. I felt like I'd swallowed a vat of acid that was burning me away from the inside. Nothing made sense, not the blue of the sky or the solid earth beneath me. Breathing made no sense… the world just didn't fit together right anymore.

Suddenly I remembered what you'd said – your crazy idea, the thing you'd wanted to talk to me about when we got back from the quad ride – and with a creeping, gnawing sense of utter devastation I thought I'd figured out what it was. We'd been talking about getting married for so long, but with everything else we just hadn't got around to it. But we were staying in *Vegas* – the place we'd met, the place your life had turned around. We wouldn't have had to worry about venues or flower arrangements or table settings or invitations…

When we get back. God, how those words haunted me!

My chest grew painfully tight, and I stood up, looking around at the space that had been ours. It meant nothing to me without you. I made my way across the lawn, back into the house and up the stairs to our room. I lay on our bed, stroking the soft bedspread that we used to lie under together. It still held the scent of you, almost as strong as if you were lying there with me, and I closed my eyes to breathe you in.

'Yes,' I whispered to the silence. 'Yes, babe, let's do it.'

There was no answer. The yawning chasm of emptiness swallowed me whole, and all that remained was darkness.

There was nothing left for me in LA, but before I disappeared back into the shadows of my half-life I decided to take one last trip to Vegas, just for old time's sake. I thought it might help, somehow – help me remember. Or help me forget, I don't know.

I pulled up on the street outside the dive bar and killed the engine, then sat in the car for a few minutes, trying to gather my thoughts. It had taken me a while to find the place, and after a four-hour drive my head felt heavy and dull, although it felt like that a lot of the time anyway.

I stared out through the windscreen. The dark doorway was just as inconspicuous as it had been on the night we met, and I'd driven around the block twice to make sure I was on the right street.

It was still only early – I think around four or five in the afternoon – so when I stepped inside the place was almost as empty as it had been that night. There were a few daytime drinkers dotted around, and the drone of the music muffled the odd murmurs of conversation. It was exactly how I remembered. Except, of course, there was one major difference: no you.

I walked over to the bar, retracing my own footsteps, and sat on the stool you'd been sitting on when I'd first laid eyes on you. It felt like I was a ghost in my own life, haunting the places that still held a vestige of comfort, unable to let go of the person I'd been. I envied her. She had you ahead of her. All I had was the past.

I asked for a bourbon and sat drinking it quietly, trying to recall the details of your appearance that night – the way you'd looked to my ignorant eyes, with your tatty clothes and swollen face, your snarl of disdain and sullen, unfocused gaze. You'd been so morose I'd almost left you there, stewing in your misery and loneliness. But then, that Song. I owed everything to that Song. It had turned something ugly and seemingly pointless into something… beautiful. Perfect. Even with the cracks it had been perfect – or maybe even more perfect because of them, like a piece of broken pottery repaired with gleaming veins of gold.

It was sometime later when the man came over to me.

I'd had quite a few drinks by then… OK, I was drunk, but not as drunk as I wanted to be. I don't know if it's possible to get as drunk as I wanted to be.

He leaned on the counter next to me and looked me up and down. He was young and clean-cut, all straight-ironed creases and neatly trimmed fingernails.

'You here alone, darlin'?' he asked, taking a deep gulp from a glass in his hand. 'You're way too pretty to be drinking all by yourself. What happened? Some asshole break your heart?'

I wanted to tell him to leave me alone, but a sudden wave of self-loathing swept up from my stomach into my chest and throat, where it stopped the words before I could utter them.

I knocked back the rest of my whiskey and licked my lips. 'You could say that.'

'You, er… you from around here?'

I let out a short bark of laughter. Nothing was funny.

'It's OK.' I turned to face him, wiping the back of my hand across my mouth. 'You don't have to chat me up.'

He smiled. It wasn't a very nice smile. 'How 'bout I buy you a drink?'

I suddenly felt sick to my stomach. Being here wasn't numbing the pain, if anything it was making it worse.

'I need to get out of here.'

'Whatever you say, sweetheart.'

I staggered outside to find that night had fallen, and began weaving my way down the street. I was losing my grip on reality, spiralling through time, the past and the present blending together until I didn't know one from the other.

I didn't hear the footsteps behind me, I only felt the rough clasp of a hand on my arm, and a sudden shove that sent me stumbling into an alleyway that was strewn with rubbish and stank of rotten vegetables.

In the half-light I could make out a young, clean-cut face, and I let out a yelp of protest as he grabbed both my hands and pushed me up against the wall. His breath was hot and yeasty, and his fingers were roughly pinching and prodding at me like he was trying to manoeuvre a piece of equipment into position.

I recoiled, shoving at his chest, turning my face from his and squeezing my eyes closed. 'No!' I said, as loudly as I could. 'No, stop.'

'What?' he demanded, panting against my ear. 'You wanted me to come after you, right?'

The numbing mist of inebriation evaporated from my brain, and I felt cold and sick, the rough bricks digging into my back. 'What? No, I didn't—'

'Don't lie. You know you want it, you little slut.'

'Let me go,' I said, my skin crawling. I was trying to stay calm but the panic was rising in my throat and my heart was thundering in my ears.

'I'm not gonna do that,' he answered, grabbing my wrists and slamming them hard into the wall, sending twin spikes of pain down my forearms and making my fingers prickle like a flame had passed over them. 'What you need is a good, hard fuck.'

'No!' I insisted again, squirming desperately to free myself. It only made him dig his fingers in harder.

I tried to bring my knee up to his groin but he was a step ahead of me, shoving himself between my legs so that I couldn't find my balance. My cheek suddenly exploded as he struck me across the face, and his hand clamped down hard over my mouth. I bit into it and he hit me again, the world veering sickeningly off-centre, then I almost doubled over as he punched me – a single, hard blow to the stomach. I retched, my head pounding and my lungs heaving, burning, but he held me fast, his forearm across my throat as I choked and spluttered. I wanted to scream and pummel him with my fists, but it took every ounce of strength just to catch my breath. Why was this happening to me?

And then, just as I thought things were as bad as they could be, I had a moment of blinding terror as I realised there was a gun pointing in my face. It was inches away, looming before my eye, and I couldn't look anywhere else. The fear – the massing, roiling fear – was a straitjacket anchoring me in place.

'Now then, that's better,' he said, bringing it to my cheek and stroking the barrel down towards my chin. 'Open your mouth.'

'Please,' I whimpered, 'don't do this. Please, just let me go.'

'I said, open your mouth!' He prodded the gun hard against my face, and I did as he said, staring at him in horror. He pushed the barrel in between my teeth – a bitter, oily, chemical taste flooding my mouth.

'This'll all be over in a minute. See how much easier it is if we all just play nice?'

His fingers were at my throat, gripping the neckline of my T-shirt, and with a sudden jerk he wrenched the fabric down, tearing it open.

I let out a strangled shriek that turned into a groan of despair as he ran his fingers over my skin, following the movement with his eyes. The gun was cutting into my lips, and my jaw ached as if it had been fractured into a hundred pieces.

'Damn, you are *fiiine*,' he said, looking into my eyes again as his hands moved further down my stomach. 'You'll thank me later, I promise. Whatever that guy did to break your heart, I'll make you forget all about it.' He laughed, like he thought he'd said something really clever, and any hope I had of escaping fizzled away into nothingness.

I stared at the dim outline of his head and shoulders, shuddering and petrified. What could I do? I couldn't let him do this; it went against every single thing I believed, everything I was. I had been put on this Earth to love and to be loved in return – this was sacrilege, a desecration of everything that was beautiful and holy and good.

This isn't supposed to happen; I'm not supposed to be here, I thought vaguely, just as his fingers found their way inside my shorts.

And then, in the midst of my terrified paralysis, I heard a sound… something familiar. It echoed down from somewhere above and behind me, faint at first but growing clearer. I listened harder, straining to pin it down.

Where is it coming from? And why do I feel like I know…?

Then it came to me, hitting me like a sharp slap to the face. I'd know that music anywhere. It was Metallica: 'Master of Puppets'. It was the song that always played when you walked out to the cage – your battle music, your game-face music. The message couldn't have been clearer if it had blazed in golden letters across the sky. Your face rose up in the darkness before me, bloody and determined, your eyes flashing with menace.

I can't, I whimpered inside my head, but even then I knew that I could. I would. I had to. Maybe I couldn't fight the same way you'd fought, but that wasn't what you were trying to tell me. You'd fought your battles your way and I had to do the same. I had to fight the way Aphrodite fights – the way a Keeper fights – with the only power I had at my disposal.

Reality blurred, fading to a misty grey, and I retreated inside myself as though my mind was drawing the shutters closed, sealing itself off from my body. I felt the long span of years stretching away, to the last time I'd reached inside and accessed that deep well of primal energy. There was a sensation like surfacing through a tunnel of water as it rose up inside me, and a tingling began in my bones, growing to a grating vibration. I felt like I would disintegrate if it wouldn't stop, but it carried on building, tearing through me like an avalanche ripping its way down a hillside.

The feeling began to pour out of me, seizing my attacker with intoxicating fingers, spilling into him and burrowing through his tissues. I felt torn in two, a part of me protesting such an appalling abuse of my Attribute, but the other part knowing it was beyond my control, that I had no choice and that it was the only way to save myself.

His grip on me loosened and he looked confused, and then the confusion turned to blankness and the gun slid out of my mouth, my lips and tongue afire and throbbing. I fixed my eyes on him, the ripples of heat rising up inside me, the fire gaining intensity as it fed on the need that grew in his eyes.

'You… you're…' He trailed off, his hands moving to the wall either side of my head as he gazed at me in growing wonder, slipping further and further under the spell.

'I'm Aphrodite,' I murmured, the sweat breaking out on my skin. My voice was a grating rasp of a sound, tearing from my throat.

I was dizzy with the glut of raw energy that was racing through my blood, and the fear congealed into a solid lump deep in my belly but it was too late to turn back now. I couldn't switch it off, even if I wanted to.

'You're... so... beautiful...' he said, reaching up to touch my face.

'Don't touch me.' The words choked out of me in a ragged whisper, and he flinched as though I'd struck him.

'Please,' he begged. 'Please, I'd do anything for you. Let me show you. Please, you have to believe me.'

Even in the shadows I could see the glistening line of a tear streaking down his cheek. The desperation in his voice robbed me of impetus for a second.

I felt that once, I thought. *I begged, I pleaded... but it didn't make any difference then, and it's not going to help you now.*

I felt a surge of blinding hatred and heard a keening wail from somewhere deep within me. The sound blended with the music that was echoing out through the night, although I was no longer sure if I was really hearing that or if it too was just a sound in my head – a reverberating thunder from the dim recesses of my mind.

I felt like I was breaking apart, like my heart was cracking open in the heat, spilling out the precious remains of the love I had shared with you.

There is no going back.

'I love you,' he whispered softly. 'I love you so much I can't take it.'

The fire sucked in the words and spat them out again, spewing out from me like a poisonous gas, reaching down, down inside him and withering everything but his longing for the one thing he couldn't have. And still he gazed at my face, adoring, overcome, besotted beyond any natural force of feeling.

There's a reason we're chosen, those of us who become Keepers. There's something more than human in us from the beginning, and during Forging that thing is hardened, tempered, made strong enough to withstand the primal forces that we bear with us and feed out into the world.

The power that I unleashed on him was far too great for any human body to endure. His mind began to crumble, cracking under the pressure, and then he was raising the gun towards his own face, calmly, unhurriedly, like he was moving through water. He held it to his head, gazing stupidly at me as though he couldn't bear to tear his eyes away.

And then he uncocked the safety and pulled the trigger.

The moment he went down I felt the roaring flames recede – suddenly, like all the oxygen had been sucked out of them.

What have I done?

I stood in the darkness, completely still, waiting for my heartbeat to slow back down to normal, waiting for reality to sink in. There was a crawling in my flesh, like some vile creature was burrowing through me, tracking its poison across my insides. I had revolted against my nature, and although I had done it to save myself I knew I'd committed a grievous sin.

I hadn't planned any of this, I hadn't asked for it to happen, but somehow I felt that I should have stopped myself. Once he'd let go of me I should have run away and never looked back, but instead, I'd stayed. I'd made him feel such an overwhelming hunger for me that nothing of him remained except the gnawing, aching need, and then I'd swept it all away and left him utterly empty. Utterly forsaken.

That was what I'd wanted, wasn't it? To make him feel how I'd felt as I watched the light fade from your eyes. To make him grovel in the dirt as I had in the hour of my deepest agony.

A trembling began in my legs and spread upwards into my arms, until my entire body was shaking. My mind went blank: I couldn't remember where I was, what I was doing, or any of the things that had just happened. When it came rushing back to me I swooned, collapsing against the wall. I just about managed to right myself but then nausea overtook me, and I bent almost double and spewed all over the concrete beside his ruined, lifeless face.

Then I ran. I ran out of the alleyway and down the brightly lit street, through the multicoloured glow of neon lights and between the clusters of strangers. I ran back to the car and opened the door with shaking hands, climbing inside and shutting the world out. That was when I noticed the blood on them.

I sat in the bath, staring at nothing, the water cloudy-pink and spotted with floating lumps of gore.

I was in a rundown motel off Interstate 15, seedy enough that the guy on the front desk hadn't asked any questions when I'd shuffled up to the counter in a hoodie with a cap pulled over my face and asked for a room. I'd managed to wipe myself down a little in the car, but my hair was a matted mess and my skin was tinted red with a film of dry blood. I'd been glad to find your gym bag still in the back – the cap and hoodie had come in useful and the towel had removed the worst of the filth from my face. Thank heaven for small mercies, I suppose.

Everything hurt. Half my face was on fire, and my shoulders were screaming with every movement. My ribs were sore all down my right side, throwing sharp shooting pains into my chest when I breathed in, and the back of my head hurt from being slammed against the wall. My thighs hurt too, where he'd forced himself between them. The pain was a dull, lingering ache that throbbed with every beat of my heart, and I was certain that the flesh would bruise overnight.

I rested my temple on my knee. I wanted to disappear. I couldn't face living in the real world anymore. I just wanted to escape and never come back.

I reached over the side of the bath and picked up your hoodie, rummaging through the pockets. I'd discovered your iPod in one earlier. I wasn't sure if it would have any battery left but I stuffed the earbuds in, my shaking fingers moving randomly over the buttons until something happened.

A song kicked in with a rumble of drums and I closed my eyes, hugging my knees as I listened, each beat driving a white hot brand through my head. The taste of whiskey rose up to overwhelm my senses, my breath gasping in and out as my body began to shake uncontrollably.

I had a flash of thought, a voice screaming in rage: *You're killing yourself! Can't you see that? Or is that the point?*

My voice. My rage.

My chest heaved as though I was surfacing from underwater, but I was still sitting in the same spot, the music pounding in my ears, and suddenly the memory of you filled my world, crushed me down and held me, emptied my lungs of air and my heart of any hope for future happiness. I couldn't bear it anymore. I'd tried, but it was no use. The loss of you had ripped me open and spilled my guts out on the floor, draining me of everything that made me who I was.

I looked down at my arms and saw the blotched and ugly finger marks, turning dark like ripening grapes. I examined them, remembering fragmented glimpses of an alley, of a fist, of a face overwhelmed with love, of the same face exploding in an eruption of bone and flesh.

What did I do? How could I do that to someone? Even knowing what he was didn't make it any better. *I should have run. I didn't need to… I killed him. I KILLED him.* He'd pulled the trigger but it had been my fault all the same. Another person dead because of me. Another pointless waste of life that could have been avoided. Why did everything and everyone I touched turn to ashes? What was the point anymore?

I saw a disposable razor on the shelf next to the bath and I seized it, tearing the blade away from the cheap plastic casing. I held it, feeling calm, the shaking in my hands subsiding to a deathly stillness. It seemed so obvious. Why hadn't I thought of it before? I'd thought I was trapped, helpless, with no control over what happened to me, but it wasn't true. I did have control. I could control this.

It wouldn't be that painful; I could take it, I was sure. All I had to do was jam the blade in and lie back, while the warm blood seeped out to mingle with the water. I imagined it would feel like going to sleep... a long, peaceful sleep from which I wouldn't have to wake...

Even now I think I could have done it – *would* have done it – if not for the Song: that precious, miraculous lifesaver of a Song. It was by Nirvana, one of your favourite bands, and it's called 'You Know You're Right'. It's not pretty, not comforting or sympathetic, but I needed it like I needed to fall.

The sound jarred against my eardrums, an ominous thudding that built to a screeching, angry guitar voice which penetrated the haze, jolting me from my trance. Every word stung as it cut into me, far deeper than any razor would, and it made me feel ashamed. That was what stopped me in the end: the shame. I was ashamed for giving up – for defiling your memory. Even in the deepest pit of your anger and pain you would never have done what I was planning to do, and you would have torn strips off me for even considering it.

I held the razor away from me and it slipped from my fingers onto the floor. I clasped my knees, rocking in the water, letting the Song deliver me from the blackness of my despair. I sat and listened to it, too frightened to cry, horrified by my own willingness to die after seeing you fight so hard – after feeling such helpless rage as I watched you slip away before my eyes.

After a while the water turned cold, and eventually I stood up from the bath, shivering. I caught sight of myself in the bathroom mirror and flinched, repulsed by my own reflection. I looked like I'd aged by several years and my skin had an ugly grey cast to it, but that wasn't the worst part. The worst part was knowing that beneath the surface I was a rotting, broken thing, soiled and unworthy.

All I'd wanted was to be close to you, to keep you near me, but what I'd found was another pathway into hopelessness. I'd been trying to find peace but now everything was even worse than before, perhaps so bad that I had lost all chance of redemption.

Country Boy

I didn't want to find you. I didn't want to find anybody, not after Fighter. I had barely managed to get through the experience in one piece, and I never wanted to feel that way again. I was exhausted and tormented by the memory of what had happened in Las Vegas. That city had broken me. I couldn't rid myself of the feeling that I'd betrayed my own nature – that I'd never feel clean again.

For the first time in my life I couldn't see any way forward, and I cursed everything and everyone that had made me feel that way. If I had never become a Keeper then none of it would have happened, and clearly someone had made a mistake in thinking I had what it took to shoulder that responsibility. My heart wasn't strong enough to endure the pain. I should never have been allowed to start along the Path, and my failure would have catastrophic consequences: I could prove to be the death of love. What hope was there for humankind if the Keeper of Love allowed it to be extinguished from the world? What hope was there for me?

I felt like my life was spiralling out of control, like there was nothing solid for me to grab onto except the slimy, poisonous guilt. I wanted to bury myself away but at the same time I felt like I was suffocating. I just needed some wide open space, somewhere I could breathe. I didn't want to die anymore, but I was looking for a way out.

Instead, I found you. And I found New Zealand. Maybe you could say I found a way back in.

I was working my way around the country, doing physical labour in the hope that I could tire myself out enough each day to drive the memories from my mind. I started off on the North Island harvesting onions and potatoes in the early months of the year, cradled in the autumnal wilderness that rose and fell in gentle, undulating peaks and valleys – a sea of tarnished copper and bronze interspersed with patches of dark green. In April I moved on to picking avocados, oranges, macadamias and olives, then spent the colder months at a kiwi fruit farm in Tauranga, sheltering among the laden branches and broad, downy-bottomed leaves, with the rich scent of earth rising up from the ground beneath my boots. After that I travelled down to Hastings where I stayed on an orchard in Hawkes Bay, and then got a job at a vineyard in the pinot noir region of Wairarapa. The work was hard, tiring and repetitive, perfect for rinsing my mind of all the things I didn't want to think about.

At the end of August I headed down to the South Island to bottle wine in Blenheim, with its endless rows of verdant green vines and volcanic mountain ranges, and then in the spring I helped with the vegetable harvest in Spotswood, picking lettuce and broccoli, my hands toughened but nimble as they adapted to their new occupation.

Finally, wearied from almost nine full months of slogging in the fields, I snagged myself some work on a ranch at the foothills of the Southern Alps in Canterbury, about a two-hour drive from Christchurch. I arrived there in November, and temperatures were slowly rising as the summer weather approached. I was staying with a family – a couple who had two sons and two daughters.

And yes, I'd managed it. Out of two hundred and sixty-eight thousand square kilometres of New Zealand earth and over four and a half-million people, I'd managed to find the one teeny tiny part of the world that happened to contain... you.

It's not that there was anything wrong with you – in fact, you were wonderful: sweet and funny and completely gorgeous in that offhand Kiwi way, and you had this soft, shy side that I found completely adorable.

What I'm trying to say is that you were totally loveable, in every way, and had I met you at another time in my life I would have been thrilled to find that you were part of my Path. It was just... I wasn't ready. And I was scared by the thought of what I'd do to you; I was scared *for* you, do you understand?

And I was right to be. I ruined everything, didn't I? You must think I'm a terrible person. If it means anything to you, it was heartbreaking for me too. I'm sure you won't take any solace from that, but I want you to know that it pained me to leave you, more than you can imagine.

And I did love you. I knew as soon as I saw you that my feet had carried me unerringly back onto the Path, even though I was trying as hard as I could to veer away from it. That's the problem with Paths you can't see: before you know it, they're right beneath your feet.

I didn't see you for most of the first day. I was getting a guided tour of the ranch with your younger brother, Luke, and finding out what my jobs would be. Since I hadn't ridden horses before I was mostly going to be earning my keep by working in the kitchen and the stables, but Luke promised I'd be riding like a pro in no time.

The ranch – or the farm, as Luke called it – was a sixty-acre chunk of alpine grassland, riven by myriad cold, fast-flowing streams, and flanked by a vast swathe of dense forest on one side and the feet of the magnificent Amuri Range on the other.

After the tour we stopped off back at the farmhouse: a low, sprawling structure of white-painted brick, with a blue slate roof and large, rectan-

gular windows that peered out across the landscape in every direction.
Despite its size it had an air of cosiness inside, like a ski lodge or a big
log cabin, and your mum made me feel welcome instantly, bringing
me a cup of coffee and sitting with me on the sofa in the living room,
which was covered in a soft crochet blanket that I guessed had been
homemade. She told me I should call her Ellen, and she wanted to know
all about me and where I'd come from. Although I was tired it was nice
talking to her; I felt like a child chatting to a kind, indulgent auntie.

She told Luke to show me to one of the guest cabins – indicating
that he should carry my bag for me – and handed me a key before
bustling off to complete whatever task I had distracted her from.

Luke and I left the house through the kitchen – a great big semi-
commercial affair – and crunched across the strip of gravel that separated
the building from the square yard at the back. As I followed him, my
gaze scanned the other structures that surrounded the yard: a row of
stables down one side; a huge, walled barn opposite the house; and a
communal dining hall which we skirted around so he could show me
the shower and toilet block at the back.

He asked me which number was printed on my key and led me
to the end of the little row of wooden cabins on the far side of the
communal building.

'Here we are, home sweet home,' he said, unlocking the door and
preceding me inside. He crossed to the bed and placed my bag on the
mattress, then gave a cheery smile and handed me back the key. 'It'll be
about an hour before Mum'll need you back at the house, so no rush.
This'll be yours while you're here so make yourself at home.'

'Thanks, this is great.'

It was a large room with a low ceiling and wood-panelled walls, made
snug by a few homely touches like the big rag-rug, and the patchwork

quilt on the bed. Everything looked like it had been made by hand, even the pine furniture and pressed flowers in frames on the walls.

'Well, shout if you need anything,' he said, offering a lazy salute. 'I'll leave you to get settled in.' His grin was open and friendly, and I smiled back before he left, closing the door behind him.

I let out a long breath and ran my hands down over my face, wondering if I had time for a nap. I caught a whiff of myself as I stretched my arms out, and decided I'd probably better take a shower instead. It had been a long day already, and I wasn't done yet.

When I thought an hour had gone by I headed up to the house, and was tasked with helping to peel vegetables for that night's dinner, lay the tables in the guest dining room and plate up all the delicious-looking food.

I waited on tables with Luke and your youngest sister, Maddie, while Ellen took charge in the kitchen. It was a really efficient team, made relaxed by long practice, and before I knew it the work was done and it was time for family dinner, an operation that was almost as involved as feeding all the guests.

The family dining room in the house was huge and airy, with polished timber floors of honey-coloured oak and exposed rafters. The table took up most of the floor space, with four chairs down each side and two at each end, and the walls were decorated with several framed collages of family photos, all crammed in together behind the glass like a school art project. I loved it the moment I walked in.

Apart from myself and your family there were two other summer workers – Nathan and Chris – who were staying in the cabins next to mine. I could see why you needed such a large table. How Ellen coped with feeding you all three square meals a day, I will never know.

You came in just as we were arranging the last of the serving dishes – weighty orange enamelled ones crammed with steaming vegetables:

mashed potato with chunks of caramelised red onion, carrots speckled with rosemary, buttered peas and plump broccoli. Two big shoulders of lamb rested at either end of the table, ready to be carved up once everyone had taken their places.

When I saw you the colour drained from my face, and the moisture evaporated from my mouth in a single instant. I'm sure that if I hadn't already been leaning my weight on the table as I reached across it, I would have stumbled against it. I took a deep breath, trying to steady myself, and made a fuss of squaring the dishes on the trivets while I regained my balance. I'd had no warning at all that I might encounter someone here – no inner pull, no tell-tale tingling down my spine, just bam! There you were.

It's OK, I told myself. *There's no need to freak out. Just breathe.*

'Sit here if you like.' Your eldest sister Kate patted the chair next to hers. We had bonded over the immense piles of potatoes and carrots we'd had to peel earlier, and she seemed happy to have someone new to talk to. 'These guys'll only be harping on about boring stuff all night, it's enough to send you to sleep.' She tilted her head towards you and your dad, her expression one of mock disgust.

I smiled at her and sat down, sneaking a quick glance over at you at the other end of the table. It was obvious just by looking at you and Luke that you were your father's sons: tall and dark-haired, with warm brown skin that hinted at Māori ancestry. Kate was dark-featured as well but Maddie favoured your mother, with coppery-red hair and hazel eyes, her nose and cheeks kissed with freckles that made her look even younger than her seventeen years.

I couldn't withstand the torrent of love that swept through me as you raised your eyes to meet mine; it engulfed me as surely as any desire I'd ever felt, but I didn't want it. My head wasn't on straight at all.

I forced myself to look away, schooling my expression as though nothing out of the ordinary had happened. I hoped that maybe if I willed myself to be invisible then your gaze might just slide right off me, but for the rest of the night, every time I raised my head, I could see out of the corner of my eye that you were following my movements, watching me across the table. The damage was done.

When it was time to clear up I rose with your sisters to help carry the empty plates and dishes through to the kitchen.

'Here, I'll give you a hand.' You stood up from the table, drawing puzzled glances from your siblings, and grabbed some empty plates while your mum sat watching you in astonishment.

'My God, it's a miracle! Hey, you can stay as long as you like, Aphrodite, if you can get these boys doing housework!'

I blushed, trying to suppress the conflicting feelings of dismay and delight that bubbled up inside me as I snuck a look at you.

Oh God, I thought, carrying an armful of dishes around the table. *I don't need this. Please! I really don't.*

We trooped through to the kitchen and deposited the dishes next to the sink, and your sisters began loading the dishwasher in a well-rehearsed routine. There wasn't really any reason for me to stay in there, other than that I was trying to hide. So much for that plan.

'Hey, we haven't met properly.' You emptied your hands of dishes and held one out for me to shake.

I took it hesitantly, not because I didn't want to touch you, just because… actually, more because I *did* want to touch you. Too much.

'I'm Aphrodite.'

'So I hear,' you answered, your large, warm eyes alive with interest. 'That's an awesome name. Are you staying long?'

I heard a noise that might have been a snort coming from Kate's general direction, but you ignored it. I was preoccupied with the sensations that were running through me from the contact with your hand, and with letting my gaze wander over the unfamiliar shape of you. You were a good couple of inches over six feet tall, with short, black hair and broad shoulders. Even your facial features were strong and definite, like they'd been carved out of the living earth… I didn't stand a chance.

'Umm, I don't know yet,' I mumbled.

'Do you ride?' you asked, one eyebrow raised inquiringly.

'No,' I gently extricated my hand from yours, 'but I think—'

'Oh, well, I'll teach you.'

'Mum said Kate was gonna teach her,' Maddie piped up from behind me.

I noticed Kate shush her and then turned back to see you throw her a quelling look.

'Yeah nah, it's cool, I'll do it.' You shrugged, like it was no big deal.

'Hey,' Maddie cut in again, 'but I thought you were busy with—'

'Don't you have homework to do?' You glared at her.

She gave you a 'what's-your-problem?' look, and then comprehension dawned on her face, quickly followed by a malicious kind of amusement.

'Oh right. Yeah. You *are* a good teacher. He's the *best.*' She winked at me in a mock aside and went back to sorting out the dishes.

I blushed again and tried to laugh it off, but I could feel myself falling fast.

Please, can't I just be left alone? I can't take this anymore. I don't know what I'm doing here and I really, really don't want to hurt him. He's so…

I looked at you and I knew it was too late; it was either hurt you now or hurt you later. What kind of choice was that?

I began the next day with a firm resolution to keep my distance, but it seemed the universe was conspiring against me. And I won't lie, there was a part of me that wanted to be around you, even if I was finding that difficult to accept.

After lunch you took me out riding and showed me more of the farm, and we chatted as the horses swished their tails and flicked their ears in curiosity, sploshing through the burbling streams with placid grace. Clouds drifted lazily across the bright blue sky, dappling the towering hillsides in shifting patterns of light and shade, and the wind swept in gentle currents over the golden grasses, which whispered and sighed beneath its caress.

You knew so much about the wildlife and the landscape surrounding us, I could have listened to you talking all day. You told me about the *Patupaiarehe* – the fairy folk who were said to live in the forests and mountains – and recounted a Māori legend from the North Island about four warrior mountains that did battle for the love of a fifth: Pihanga, a maiden mountain who was renowned for her beauty. The story seemed to be one that you were fond of, and the steady way you recited it made me think you had probably told it many times.

At one point we hopped down and walked for a little while – to give my legs a rest, you said – and you plucked a few wildflowers from beside the path, acting as though you were just teaching me about the local flora. I smiled as you handed them to me and felt my cheeks reddening, and for a moment I let myself imagine that everything was as simple as I wanted it to be.

'We'd better head back,' you said, squinting at the sky.

'Did you actually just tell the time by looking at the sun?' I laughed, glancing at you teasingly.

You broke into a grin and chuckled, shrugging as you met my gaze. 'Well, it's not an exact science, more of a rough guide.'

We came to a stop and you helped me climb back into the saddle, your hands carefully steadying me without lingering too long, as though you didn't want to overstep the boundaries. In some ways I wished you would; it was what we both wanted. If only I could escape the fear that I was carrying around inside me, I could even imagine being happy with you. For a while at least.

The following Saturday was Maddie's eighteenth birthday, and I was relieved of my duties in the kitchen so I could help with the preparations for her party, which was being held in the enormous barn. We chattered away while we worked, emptying the barn of horse jumps, and making seating areas out of straw bales that had me sneezing from the dust as it swirled through the dry air. Maddie was fascinated by my tales of adventure, and talking to her I was pleasantly reminded of the girl I had been when I'd first made my way out of my childhood sanctuary and into the unknown.

We spent the afternoon hanging decorations around the walls, taking it in turns to climb up the tall stepladder to hammer in nails and secure the strings. By the time we were finished there were balloons, bunting and paper lantern lights hanging from every corner, a disco ball suspended from the ceiling and a huge 'Happy Birthday' banner displayed proudly in the middle of the longest wall above the makeshift bar, which Luke had knocked together in an impressively short time.

We'd set up trestle tables at one end of the room for the food, and at the opposite end was a temporary stage complete with a brand new drum kit: Maddie's birthday present from your parents.

We all hustled to get showered and changed, and I caught myself humming as I did my make-up, surprised at the buoyant mood that had stolen over me since that afternoon. Maddie had lent me a dress for the occasion – a soft, strapless, peach-coloured thing, with a skirt made up of several layers of floaty material that ended just above my knees. It was the most feminine thing I'd worn in some time, and it felt a little strange after getting so accustomed to slogging in my scruffs.

I emerged from my cabin and looked out across the landscape, awed to see the broad sweep of the sky passing over my head and the vast, unbroken stretch of countryside rolling away into the distance. I'd seen many beautiful places during my wanderings but nowhere quite as magical as that view, which seemed too perfect to be real with its dark belts of forest and dizzying summits, like something from a children's storybook. How had I ended up somewhere so spectacular – so... *pristine*? I didn't feel worthy of it. Maybe if I could stay here long enough some of that purity would rub off on me. I could be happy here, in the clean, open air. Or at least peaceful, which seemed like the same thing as happiness given the upheaval that had gone before.

Before my thoughts could spiral into darker musings, I turned away and strolled down the gravel path that ran from the cabins to the house, humming again and anticipating the coming festivities.

The second I reached the door it opened, as if by magic, and there you were, standing just beyond the threshold and staring at me with a stunned look on your face.

'Whoa!' you said, and I giggled in response, doing a little curtsey.

I wanted to say something complimentary in return, but the words stuck in my throat, refusing to come out. You had discarded your work-worn attire in favour of smart black jeans and a pale grey shirt, which was open at the collar to reveal a string of wooden beads. You looked very dashing, but I just couldn't flirt with you. I felt like it would be selfish and dishonest, knowing that it could only end one way, and I wasn't prepared to play the siren, luring you to your doom.

You stood to one side and I stepped past you into the kitchen, feeling a crackle of electricity fizzle through the space between us. I said hello to your brother and your dad, receiving looks of surprised admiration from them both, and then the air was suddenly filled with twittering excitement as your mum and sisters came through from the dining room, along with a couple of Maddie's closest friends.

'Wow, you look great!' Maddie grabbed my hand and made me do a twirl. 'That dress looks way better on you, you should keep it.'

'Don't be silly,' I said, nudging her arm. 'You'd look amazing in a rubbish bag.'

She glanced at you, a wicked glint in her eye. 'What do you think, big brother? Doesn't Aphy look gorgeous?'

You flushed deeply, and she giggled at her own mischief before flouncing over to the door and summoning us all to follow her.

When we entered the barn a huge cheer went up from the assembled guests, and the band started playing straightaway, like they'd been poised and ready to go the second she came in. She squealed and ran towards the rest of her friends, looking impossibly young for a girl of eighteen, and then the party began.

The music was loud and lively, and Maddie and her friends skipped and strutted in the space in front of the stage, singing along with the words, tossing their hair and waving their arms around with uninhibited glee. There were three bands performing over the course of the evening – all young and inexperienced, but pretty good – and then after the live music finished Maddie's laptop was plugged into the PA system, and we were treated to a playlist of all her favourite songs on full blast.

The adults drifted in clusters between the tables and the bar, some sitting on straw bales to rest their feet, caught up in animated conversations. A few got up to join in the dancing, mainly sticking to the edges to avoid the flailing hands of the youngsters, and I laughed as I saw Ellen pulling Luke into an embrace while he screwed up his face in protest, before seizing her in a formal ballroom pose and leading her in a parody of a waltz around the thrashing teenagers.

For the first time in a long time, I really let my hair down, joining in with the dancing and occasionally stopping to nibble on some of the party food, especially the delicious homemade quiches that Ellen had provided, which were stuffed with sweet potato, spinach and tangy feta cheese.

The disco ball twisted slowly above our heads, glinting and reflecting the multicoloured beams that flashed from the stage, and the little glowing lanterns looked like ropes of fairy orbs, strung around the edges and criss-crossing the ceiling in a luminous web. Every face I could see was lit up with excitement or humour or interest, and I was surrounded by laughter and voices raised in merriment.

I saw you approach a few times but I managed to make myself scarce, and then I saw you dancing with someone else and I felt both relieved and disappointed. I wanted to be glad – the best thing for you would be to forget about me altogether – but the evening suddenly seemed to have lost its sparkle.

I made my way to the bar and stood alone for a while, sipping a drink and watching the proceedings. I didn't notice you approaching until it was too late. Your eyes brightened as they met mine and I felt my heart sink, even as it ached with longing; I'd seen that look many times, and it only ever meant one thing.

'Hey stranger,' you said. 'Where've you been all my… night?'

I chuckled and shrugged an exaggerated apology. 'Around.'

'Hmm…' You looked me up and down and took a swallow of your beer. 'Maddie's right, you do look gorgeous in that dress.'

'Thank you,' I answered, raising an eyebrow, amused by the uncharacteristic note of cockiness in your voice.

'I think,' you continued, laying one hand across your chest, 'you should come and dance with me.'

I shook my head, not in refusal but because I was at a loss.

'Is there something wrong with my dancing?' you asked, half-playful and half-anxious.

'No,' I answered quietly, resting my hand on your forearm. 'Your dancing is perfect.'

'Then what?' You were suddenly serious. You had obviously noticed that I'd been avoiding you all evening. How could you not?

My mind fuzzed up like static on a TV, then cleared. I had to tell you the truth. I couldn't give you what you wanted, no matter how good it would feel to give in.

'I'm just scared because… if I start dancing with you… I won't want to stop. And that wouldn't be a good idea for either of us.'

I held your gaze as I spoke, so you'd know it wasn't just an excuse. I waited a second longer and then picked up my drink and walked away.

It was another couple of hours before the party began to wind down. By 2.30 a.m. only the stragglers remained, and you, Kate and I began to clean up. No one would be in the mood tomorrow, and we all seemed to come to an unspoken agreement that we might as well get started on it while we were still standing.

After about half an hour Kate dropped her rubbish bag on the floor with a groan of defeat and looked over at me, shaking her head.

'I'm done, mate. I've gotta go to bed.'

'OK,' I laughed wearily. 'I'm not far off myself.'

She came and gave me a big, sisterly hug, then called goodnight to you before trailing out of the door.

I looked at you, frowning. You were standing on the stage packing away the sound equipment. One speaker was still plugged in, playing off Maddie's playlist, which had moved on to the mellow tunes she'd chosen to round off the night. My chest expanded softly as I watched you. There was something about you that soothed me – something solid and good – and I couldn't tear my eyes away.

You turned around and caught me watching you. 'Just us left?'

I nodded, raising my fist in a lame show of solidarity. 'We're hardcore.'

You grinned and let the lead you were coiling drop down onto the stage. I could feel it happening. I knew it was coming, and not just because it had happened so many times before. You jumped down and walked across to me, seeming self-conscious in that huge space. I awaited your approach with a fearful longing, paralysed with indecision.

You rubbed your neck nervously and I almost knew what you were going to say before you said it.

'I never got to dance with you.'

'No,' I replied, hugging my arms around myself.

The music changed and I heard my Fate ringing out across the beckoning space. For a moment the inevitability rose to choke me, but the music soothed it away. It was pointless to resist. You held out your hand with a conviction that I couldn't refuse, and I gave in to the enchantment of the Song.

You know the one. It's beautiful. 'Kiss Me' by Ed Sheeran.

I mean, what chance did I have?

We came together, drawn by invisible strings, and a sweet relief flooded into me from every place our bodies touched. Your arm circled my waist, your warm palm pressing against mine; it seemed like the best feeling there could be on Earth.

I looked up at your face. Your hair was scuffed a little out of place, with a tuft sticking up to the side of your temple, and I smiled at the air of boyishness it lent to your earnest expression.

'What?' you asked, watching my smile and beginning to echo it.

'Nothing. I was just…'

The hairs on my skin rose towards you, like flowers bending up towards the sun, and my heart was pounding impatiently as though it wanted to drive me forwards, closer to you, closer, closer, closer…

I inhaled through my nose and the air filtered through my whole body, a hit of pure euphoria. It was so good to be near you. I just wished it could be on my own terms – a genuine choice, not some divine mandate. I closed my eyes and sighed involuntarily, knowing that wishes were pointless.

It's going to be this way forever. No matter how much I love him, he'll never truly be mine. How can that be all there is?

I thought of Fighter, of the dreams I'd had that finally the Path had led me to a single, perfect person – that I'd found *true* love, the kind that lasts forever and refuses to fade, refuses to die. I was convinced that my thinking that had been the reason he'd lost his life. It was my fault, for not giving him up when I had the chance – for daring to demand something that I wasn't meant to have.

Tears pricked my eyes, and I struggled to contain them as the sudden rush of sorrow flooded my chest with pain. I don't know if you sensed that I needed comfort, but you hugged me tighter against you and tucked my head under your chin. You cleared your throat and I let the grief wash through me and away. Now wasn't the time to dwell on the past.

'I need to tell you something,' you murmured, and I felt your pulse quicken where my forehead rested against your neck.

You held me away from you a little, but your fingers pressed mine firmly as though you were afraid I'd slip from your grasp.

'I know,' I answered, diving into the soft pools of your eyes. 'I know what you're going to say.'

'Really? Because, I feel like there's this... thing between us. And... I dunno, we only just met so this sounds totally crazy but, I think... I'm pretty sure I'm in love with you.'

I tried to look glad, but there was a weight growing in my chest and it was choking the breath from my body. I glanced away from you, my gaze resting on the empty stage, dark and silent now.

'I know,' I croaked. 'I feel it too. But...'

'But?'

I looked back at you, reluctant to continue but dreading what would happen if I didn't. Your face had clouded over and it hurt my heart to see it.

'I'm not right for you,' I whispered, the words grating out through my unwilling lips. 'I'm no good.'

'What are you talking about? You're perfect.' You sounded so adamant, and in the low light cast by the paper lanterns I could see how sincerely you meant those words. Your shoulders were lifting and falling rapidly, as your emotions overcame your reserve.

'You don't know me.' I bit my cheeks to hold the tears inside. 'I'm not real.'

I was swept up in an undeniable longing as the music broke into the instrumental, and the sound seemed to swell around us, smothering all resistance. You searched my face, swallowed against your nerves, and brought my hand to rest over your heart.

'You feel pretty real to me,' you said.

And then you kissed me.

Now, I've been kissed many, many times. I've been kissed sweetly, and lovingly, and passionately and fiercely, but that kiss was like a distillation of all those things, a perfect fusion of every feeling behind every kiss there could ever be, and it captured me so suddenly that all the breath left my body in an instant, like a vacuum had opened up inside me.

And it didn't stop there; it started at full-on and kept going. I felt like a leaf being dragged up into a tornado, tumbling and twisting out of control, with no notion of which way was up, down or sideways. Your arms were the only thing holding me upright, and I hung onto you for dear life. My fingers were in your hair and my ribs were crushed against yours, and I could feel the pounding of our hearts as they beat in syncopated fury, pumping the blood around our bodies like the raging torrents of a spring storm.

And then, in the space between one heartbeat and another, I panicked. The tears I'd forced back earlier came surging to the surface again, and your arms became clinging vines that I needed to escape. You felt the sudden resistance and broke off, your confusion turning to shock as you saw the agony in my expression. You released me, immediately and completely, as though I had suddenly become electrified.

'Hey, what's wrong?'

'I…' I couldn't breathe. 'I'm sorry, I can't…'

There were flashes in my mind, images of love and pain and fear – smiles, dancing eyes, gentle hands and wrenching fingers. It was such a jumbled mess that I took a step away from you, battling against the maelstrom inside my own head. The tears filled my eyes and spilled over, and I couldn't control the deluge of emotion that flooded into me through some broken seal inside – a strained bulkhead that had finally given way. I clamped my hand over my mouth, holding back a scream.

It wasn't you, it wasn't anything you did, but the crushing claustrophobia was so sudden and so compelling that I ran from you, ran for the door, and the Song died away taking all our sweetness with it.

I reached the open air and looked up at the sky, my chest heaving and my head spinning with mingled grief and desire.

'Aphrodite!' you called after me.

I sobbed, shaking my head, furious at the intrusion of unwelcome thoughts as they swirled and spiralled around my brain.

You reached my side and laid a gentle hand on my back, agitation radiating from you. I looked up, silently imploring you to understand but knowing you never could, and then the panic took control of my feet and I dashed across the yard, along the end of the shower block and into the stand of scrubby trees that screened the cabins.

I'm not sure if I wanted you to follow me or not, but you did, calling out to me to stop, to wait, begging me to tell you what was wrong. I hated the idea that you would blame yourself for upsetting me, and although it took every scrap of willpower I had, I came to a stop and waited, gasping for breath.

You caught up with me and we stood beneath the trees, their branches swaying in the night wind and their tops illuminated by the floodlights that shone out across the yard.

'Aph, please, talk to me. I'm sorry, I didn't mean to—'

'It's not you,' I managed to choke out, grasping at your hands. 'Please don't ever think it's you, I promise you it isn't.'

'Tell me.'

You reached out, instinctively wanting to offer me comfort, but you couldn't protect me. No one could. How do you protect someone from themselves?

'I can't!' I wailed, covering my head with my hands. The whole world was spinning, buffeting me with chaotic primal forces, and I wanted to scream until my body shook itself apart.

But then I felt your arms around me, clutching me to your chest and encircling me with a protective wall of warmth. I clung to you, sobbing against your shirt, wanting so much to accept the safety you were offering, wanting so much to be supported, accepted, understood. You could never understand me, but in that moment all I wanted was to feel whole again – to feel like my life was more than a vast, empty pit of despair – so when you held me gently away from you, trying to find some hint of an explanation in my face, I gave up trying to fight it and let my hunger take over.

When our lips met for the second time you hesitated, clearly overwhelmed by the vehemence of my embrace. I didn't give you the chance to stop and think, overriding your uncertainty with my insistence and distracting you in every way I knew how. Your hands took a firmer hold of my back, and as you began to respond I crushed myself against you, clamping my body to yours and wrapping my arms around your neck.

I guess I underestimated your moral fibre; you were a better man than I gave you credit for. You stopped kissing me and pulled away so you could look at me, your ribs pressing against mine every time you breathed in, your fingers clenching around my waist like you were trying to regain control of yourself.

'Aph?' You leaned your forehead against mine. 'This is wrong. I can't do this.'

'It's not wrong.' I leaned back in your arms and looked up at you, willing you to give in to me. 'I was confused before, that's all.'

'You weren't just confused. Look at you.' Your fingers brushed my face, pulling the tear-soaked strands of hair away from my clammy skin.

'I'm OK now,' I lied. 'Please. Don't stop. I need you.'

You studied me a moment longer and sighed, shaking your head, and then you wrapped your arms tightly around me, surrounding me with your love. I forced the ugly, evil thoughts aside and focused on that – on your gentle, wholesome desire, on your willingness to fill me up with every scrap of joy and happiness you could summon – and even though you couldn't heal me, you were a balm to my torn and fractured heart.

Above us were the stars, blinking like so many faraway eyes gazing down upon us, as they have gazed down upon the doings of humankind for all of time, back and back and back, to the first stirrings of life in the furnace of creation.

You stared down at me and stroked my hair again, beautiful in your serenity.

'Come on,' you said. 'I think you should try and get some sleep.'

'Will you stay with me?' I asked, gripping your shirt. I was terrified of being left alone and your presence was the only thing that made me feel safe.

'Of course,' you murmured, taking my hand.

You led me through the trees back to my cabin, and I let us inside. We lay down on the bed, still in our clothes, and you wrapped yourself around me, your heart beating steadily against my back. I let myself be calmed by your soft breathing – its slow, regular rhythm. I must have dozed for a while, enveloped by your love.

When I woke up again a short time later, I knew what I had to do. You stirred a little as I rose from the bed, but didn't wake. I pulled on my work boots and collected my few vital possessions in the dim pre-dawn light that seeped through the window, taking care to be as silent as I could. If you caught me leaving I'd never get away, and seeing the hurt on your face would be more than I could stomach. It choked me up just thinking about it.

I knew you'd be upset when you woke to find me gone, but it was better than the alternative. It was better than the pain you would feel after weeks, or months, or years of building a life together. I couldn't let that happen. I couldn't watch it all fall apart, not again.

I took one last look at you, at your strong, beautiful face relaxed in untroubled sleep, and blew you a kiss before opening the door and stepping out into the night.

I'm sorry, I thought as I quietly closed the door behind me. *Please be kind, when you remember me.*

In the fading darkness I stole down the path to the house, shrugging my denim jacket on over my party dress. I hesitated, feeling a mounting guilt over what I was about to do. The keys to your dad's truck were hanging on a hook just inside the kitchen door, and I only had to poke my head in to reach for them and I was away.

I've never been more reluctant to drive anywhere in my life. I sped along the winding road that cut through the pale green landscape like a gouge in its skin. That green would deepen as the sun rose, but I wouldn't be around to see it. I would be gone, forever, and my eyes would never behold that sublime view again.

The silence pressed in on me and I flicked the radio on. I had a two-hour drive ahead and I needed to stay awake. I didn't want to stop for coffee, or take a break, because if I actually paused to think this through I'd change my mind.

I know it won't make what I did to you any better, but I mean it when I say that taking that drive broke my heart, it really did. But better my heart than yours.

I'm sorry. I'm so, so sorry.

The road rolled away, like it always does. I felt an ache deep in my guts, and for a while I thought maybe it would keep getting worse if I didn't turn around, but I kept going anyway. The radio kept me company, and as it switched from the graveyard programme to the early morning one, I watched the sky lightening slowly ahead of me. The stars were fading to nothingness – those same stars that had peered down at us as we'd poured our love into each other. I shivered, with memory more than the early chill, and turned the volume up to blot out my thoughts.

I laughed when it came. There's really no escape for me anywhere. I contemplated turning off the radio but what would have been the point?

Let Fate sing me its Song, I thought, arching my back against the seat. *Come on, do your worst.*

I was too tired to feel any sadder than I did already.

Since it was for you, I guess you should know: The Calling 'Wherever You Will Go'.

It echoed through the cab. I watched the colours change in the sky and the scenery scroll past as I rumbled on down the road, my eyes drained of tears and my heart too weary for sorrow. I felt empty, like a cracked glass with all the liquid drained out of it. The enormity of my loneliness pressed in on me from every side. There was nowhere to run from that, it would haunt me forever.

I listened to the Song, humming along and singing the bits I knew.

'At least I still have you,' I said, speaking to the music that seemed to follow me around, haunting my steps like a disembodied soul.

I arrived at Christchurch airport at around 6.30 a.m. I had no idea where I was planning to go from there. I found a space to park and killed the engine, my fingers limp and lifeless as they rested on the steering wheel. I was done.

All of a sudden a deep shudder rippled through me, and I groaned as convulsions wracked my body. It felt like my insides were being pulled to pieces and rearranged in a different order. I growled fiercely through clenched teeth – a grating, violent sound – and watched my knuckles turning pale as I gripped the steering wheel so hard I thought I might just shatter it. I was on the brink of screaming, but then the movement subsided and I sank back against the seat, reeling as I wondered how much more I could possibly take.

I'm not sure how long I sat there. It seemed as if the will that had kept me going for the past couple of hours had been sapped away. There was nothing pulling me onwards; I wasn't following the Path. The only pull I felt was back – back to you, to the farm, to the mountains…

There is no going back.

The only option was to go forwards, away from all those things, and towards… nothingness, I guess.

I heard a tap on the window and I jumped, my heart thundering in my chest, then turned to look outside, angered by the sudden shock.

There was a face at the glass. It wasn't one I recognised. I wound the window down, frowning with irritation.

'What?' My voice sounded like the croaking of an old hag in a fairytale, dry and withered as dead leaves.

The guy standing there was mid-height, maybe a few inches taller than me, with straight brown hair tied back in a short ponytail, slightly elfin features and a few days' growth of dark stubble on his cheeks and chin. He looked like a skater, or maybe a musician, and wore loose jeans and a band T-shirt over a long-sleeved top, with the sleeves rolled up to the elbow. His wrists were decorated with a collection of rubber bands, beads and woven bracelets, and he held a black guitar case in his hand.

Musician then.

'Are you OK in there?' he asked. His voice was clear and friendly. I couldn't place the accent.

I didn't understand what he wanted. His face was kind – his eyes a vivid blue, like glazed porcelain, and they shone with concern, luminous in their intensity. I nodded, irrationally annoyed by his solicitude.

'Oh. OK, cool.'

American?

'It's just… you looked a little…'

Irish?

'Anyway, never mind, just wanted to check,' he said, moving his hand away from the door.

I sighed and let my head flop back against the seat.

'Hey, do you need a hand… with your luggage, or anything?'

What do you want?

'Only, you seem sorta… well, not to sound rude, but…' He shrugged, gesturing at my appearance.

'Thanks,' I snapped. 'I'm fine.'

Glaring at him didn't seem to be working; he just stared back at me, patiently, like a parent waiting for a stroppy toddler to tire itself out. His air of quiet calm only served to make me more angry.

'You off somewhere, or…?'

I let out an aggravated growl, thrusting myself back into the seat and pressing my palms hard against the steering wheel.

'Hey, sorry.' He took a step back, raising his hand. 'Didn't mean to stress you out.'

He paused a moment longer, as though uncertain about what to do. After glancing at me a couple more times, tapping his hand against his leg, he waved an awkward farewell and gave a quick, sympathetic smile. 'See you round.'

I didn't respond. I just wanted to be left alone.

After he left I slumped again, dragging my fingers through my tangled hair. I looked an absolute state, but what did that matter?

I tried to imagine what had happened when you'd woken up and realised I was gone. Maybe you were still asleep, dreaming of the happiness we'd share in the days and years ahead of us.

Suddenly I found it hard to breathe. I pinched the bridge of my nose, trying to get a hold of myself. I desperately needed some coffee. And some sleep. I'd give anything for a proper night's sleep.

No Man's Land

The airport was already getting busy. The screens blinked steadily between one list of destinations and another, and I scanned the flickering lines of text waiting for something to jump out, but nothing did. I think it was at that moment that I realised I was very much on my own. I was off the Path, and if I was going to continue on this course I would have to do it alone.

I scrubbed my hand across my face and squinted again at the shifting sequences of letters and numbers. An ache was growing behind my eyes. I shouldered my bag and headed for the customer service desk; if I couldn't pick somewhere, I'd just have to ask someone else to do it for me.

After buying the first available ticket out of New Zealand, meandering blankly through security and finding my departure gate, I slumped down at a table in one of the nearby café areas with an overly sweetened coffee and allowed myself to relax – or as close to relaxed as I could get. I still had over an hour to kill before boarding started.

I cleaned myself up in the toilets and changed out of Maddie's dress into the clothes I'd shoved in my bag before leaving – which made me feel marginally closer to human again – then returned to the departure gate and sat there like a zombie for the next forty minutes. The wait seemed to go on forever, but eventually they were calling for passengers to board, and I numbly edged my way towards the counter before trudging through the tunnel to the plane.

The bustle of people squeezing along the aisles and reaching up to cram their bags into the overhead bins just seemed like a background blur in one of those time-lapse videos. I was vaguely aware of it all, but not a part of it. I was passing through it, like an invisible spirit or someone trapped between two dimensions, unable to fully exist in either. I didn't belong. I wasn't supposed to be there.

I looked at the seat numbers as I passed, shuffling down the aisle and trying to avoid swiping anyone with my rucksack. I was in 34H, an aisle seat somewhere near the back. I hoped whoever I was sitting next to wasn't chatty…

And then I found my seat, and my insides sagged.

Oh, for goodness' sake!

He glanced up and saw me. 'Oh, hey again!' It was the guy from the car park.

'Hi,' I answered abruptly, eyeing the guitar case that was propped against the middle seat.

'Are you my travel buddy?'

I glanced at the seat number again. There was no getting around it, this was my seat. For the next eleven hours until we reached Singapore.

'Looks like it,' I mumbled, slouching down with my bag on my lap.

'You look like you're having a pretty rough day,' he said cheerfully, twisting in his seat and laying a hand on his guitar case, drumming his fingers lightly over the surface.

I cocked an eyebrow involuntarily and he winced.

'I mean… sorry, that came out wrong.'

I smiled a little. It was kind of comical.

'It's OK,' I said, sighing as my muscles finally lost the battle to fatigue and my head fell back against the headrest. 'I am. Having a rough day, that is.'

'Yeah. I could tell.'

From the corner of my eye I could see him studying me, but I didn't care. He could spend the whole trip staring at me if he wanted, as long as he left me in peace.

'How weird is that, that we're on the same plane?' he asked.

I let out another sigh, wondering if I should just tell him outright to stop bothering me. But then I glanced over at him and for some reason the anger drained out of me.

'Life's like that sometimes.'

'True.' He nodded, shrugging philosophically.

My gaze dropped down to the guitar case leaning against the seat between us, and I shifted around slightly, trying to find a more comfortable position. 'Isn't that a bit big for hand luggage?'

He smiled, his fingers tapping softly against the faded black vinyl again, the pattern apparently random but still somehow rhythmic.

'Yeah, it would be, but this is actually my *other* travel buddy. She has her own seat.'

'You mean… you bought a ticket for your guitar?'

He nodded, blue eyes glittering with amusement.

'But…' I looked down at the case and back up at him, 'these seats cost hundreds of dollars!'

He couldn't be serious.

He was.

'Yeah. Well, actually, we're frequent flyers, so…'

I searched his face, looking for some sign that he was winding me up, but his expression didn't waver. 'So you just… fly around with your guitar. Like… this is normal for you?'

He laughed. The sound was softly musical, and I felt a little better, hearing it.

'Well, yeah. I don't trust them to look after her properly in the hold.'

'That must cost you a fortune.'

'She's a special lady. You could say she's one in a million.'

I twisted further in my seat and leaned my elbow on the armrest behind me. There was something strangely sweet about his expression as he gazed down at the case. It was almost as if—

'And,' he continued, breaking my train of thought, 'I get an extra meal.'

I laughed out loud at that but then caught myself; it was the first real laughter to pass my lips since— well, never mind.

He was nodding smugly, like the meal made it all worth it.

'I'll split it with you if you like?' he offered, wiggling his eyebrows.

I shook my head but I was still smiling. I couldn't seem to help it.

'Travelling light, are ya?' he asked, tilting his head towards the half-empty rucksack on my lap.

'Yeah.' I patted it. 'Got everything I need right here.'

'Hmm.' There was something in his expression that told me he disagreed, but he kept his opinion to himself.

We sat in silence for a while, and I shoved my bag down by my feet and leaned back into my seat. I didn't really feel up to making a new friend, but at least I wasn't sitting next to someone annoying. I mean, he should have been annoying, but somehow he wasn't at all.

'I'm Bran by the way,' he said, holding his hand out across the seat between us.

'Bran,' I repeated, giving it a shake. 'I'm Aphrodite.'

'Pleased to meet ya.'

I waited for the inevitable comment about my name that always followed introductions to new people, but it didn't come. Instead, he stretched expansively and started drumming his palms on the ends of the armrests.

'So, what'll we do for fun for the next –' he checked his watch – 'eleven hours and seventeen minutes?'

I shrugged, feeling my eyelids droop. I really didn't mind what he did, I was just glad to be able to rest.

By the time we were halfway through the journey, a tentative friendship had sprung up between us. Bran seemed to have a knack for lightening my mood. There were times when we sat in silence, or dozed in our seats, but every once in a while, when I felt the grief rising up to overwhelm me, he'd bat me on the arm and make a funny observation, or tell me another anecdote from his travels, and it was enough to distract me before I could spiral into hopelessness. I almost didn't want that trip to end. I was safe in our little bubble in the sky – the point between A and B, the no man's land between past and future.

As it turned out, we were catching the same connecting flight too – from Singapore to London – and when we boarded the plane we were both pleased to discover that we had been seated together again.

Somewhere over Central Asia Bran got his guitar out and we had an impromptu singalong. It was the first time I'd done any real singing since leaving LA, and the second I felt the pleasing vibrations filling my throat I realised how much I had missed it; the relief brought tears to my eyes.

Hello, old friend.

Bran seemed delighted that I was a musician too. Both of us sang while he played, adding in some soft, pattering percussion by flicking his fingers against the soundboard.

It really was a beautiful instrument. The front of the body had a pale wood finish, but the back and sides were stained brownish-black, with mother-of-pearl inlay in a delicate vine pattern. There were more inlays in a tree-of-life pattern all along the fretboard, and even the back of the neck had been lovingly detailed, with darker shades of wood echoing the same design.

And Bran was definitely worthy of it. He was really good – like, ridiculously good – and we were having a whale of a time until a flight attendant put an end to the fun by asking us to stop. Apparently, we were disturbing some of the other passengers. Bran just grinned impishly and slid the guitar back into its case. He seemed to take delight in getting himself into trouble, and I couldn't help but find that quality endearing. I had always played by the rules; it was fun to be one of the naughty kids for a change.

As we were passing over Europe, I began to get the feeling there was more to him than I'd first thought. I was better rested by then, and I think my senses had woken up from the dull catatonia that had settled over my mind. The longer I looked at him, the stronger the feeling became.

What is it that I'm not getting?

It was nothing like a Moment; I didn't feel a connection to him in that way and the Path wasn't pulling me on – if anything it was trying to yank me back the way I'd come – but there was something almost familiar about him, like a face seen in a dream.

He turned and saw me looking but he didn't seem surprised, and he didn't look away. Neither of us spoke. My skin began to feel like it was buzzing slightly, almost like a low-level current was passing through it. I hadn't noticed it before, but I thought perhaps it had been there the whole time and I'd just missed it in my miserable state. It wasn't uncomfortable exactly, just strange. I thought maybe it was the vibration from the plane; I was probably more sensitive to that kind of thing than usual.

He turned his face away and started humming, his gaze directed at a point outside the window. I was concentrating on his expression, which for all its blandness seemed to be concealing some underlying thought, and for a moment I didn't register the notes that were drifting from his closed lips. When I did I sat bolt upright, staring at him. It was the Song – the one that had been playing on the radio on my way to the airport.

He trailed off and I managed to regain my composure before he noticed there was anything wrong. It was a coincidence, that was all, just a weird, unfair coincidence. Maybe he'd been listening to the same radio station on the way to the airport. But the sound of that melody and the echo of the words in my head had scratched at the raw wound in my heart. The sadness weighed me down again. I wished it would leave. I wished I could forget the sweet, warm man I'd left behind. I think leaving things unfinished is even harder than seeing them fade.

I laid my head back and drifted, feeling the ghost of his lips against mine. His kisses had been so full of love, so full of everything I wanted. That last Song played on and on in my head, and I felt like he could hear me, all those miles away – like maybe he could hear my voice and understand.

Sometime later the pilot's voice came over the tannoy, announcing that our estimated landing time was in approximately one hour. Bran looked at me and blew the air out through his lips.

'Decided what you're gonna do yet?'

'No. Not really,' I said, scrubbing at my face to wake myself up.

He had mentioned – at some point during the last fourteen-hour stretch – that he was flying on to Dublin after London, and I had snorted in amusement and shown him the final destination on my ticket: Dublin. I wasn't sure whether to go the rest of the way, though, or just stay in London. Bran had simply shrugged in his carefree way and said I should do whatever I thought best.

I still hadn't decided by the time we landed, and I was tired and grouchy from the jetlag, not feeling up to making any important decisions. I studied the back of Bran's head as we shuffled down the aisle of the plane; the tenuous link between us was making me reluctant to curtail our friendship just yet. He was good company, and in my loneliness that meant a lot. The idea of spending even another hour on a plane seemed horrendous, but I'd never been to Ireland… and really, where else was I going to go?

Bran seemed cheerfully indifferent when I said I'd come along for the ride. He had a gig the following night, so his plan was to find a hotel and get some rest before making his way to the venue the next afternoon.

We got to Dublin at around seven in the morning, so muddled from the journey that it was all we could do to find a place to crash and… well, crash.

As I lay in my room waiting for the spinning to stop so I could close my eyes without feeling sick, I thought again about that odd buzzing sensation I'd felt on the plane. There was something niggling at me, scratching away at the back of my mind with spiky claws, but I was too tired to deal with it. Whatever it was, it would still be there when I woke up. Or maybe it wouldn't and it was just my imagination playing tricks.

*

I woke up to a knocking on my door, and when I opened it Bran was standing there, looking bright as a button.

'Hey,' I said sleepily, rubbing my eyes. 'What time is it?'

'Just gone five thirty. In the afternoon.'

'What?' I blinked at him. I couldn't possibly have been asleep that long, my head had barely touched the pillow.

'Yeah.' He smiled, sharing my disbelief. 'I was just erm… well, I'm heading out to get some food and I thought you might be hungry?'

My stomach gurgled noisily in response and I clamped my hand over it while Bran burst out laughing.

'Apparently I am. Can you give me a minute?'

'Sure,' he said, shifting his bag on his shoulder and leaning one hand against the doorframe. 'Take your time.'

I closed the door and turned back to the room, smiling to myself.

It hadn't occurred to me that we could carry on hanging out after getting off the plane. I don't know why; I guess I'd just assumed that once we'd finished being travel buddies we'd go about our separate lives again. I didn't know where he was going after playing his gig tomorrow night – home, presumably – but if he didn't mind me tagging along until then at least, I could postpone making any decisions about what to do next, which seemed vastly preferable to making a decision now.

It was almost December and the streets were slick with rain, but the Christmas lights bathed everything in a cheery glow, just like a scene from a Christmas card. The place thronged with shoppers and tourists, making their way between the market stalls that were festooned with winter greenery. The air was scented with mulled wine, cinnamon and warm gingerbread, and every stall was a magnificent grotto stuffed with unimaginable delights.

After skilfully navigating us out of the busiest part of town Bran took me to a welcoming little pub, with low ceilings and air that smelled of whiskey and age. We nestled into a corner near the fire to get warm while the barmaid disappeared off to place our order of lamb stew and fresh bread rolls. We chatted amicably – about travelling and music and the people we'd met along the way – examining our surroundings and sipping on pints of cider. I enjoyed the unhurried flow of our conversation, and the comfortable silences that occasionally settled before we went off on another tangent. It was as if we'd been friends for years, not new acquaintances that chance had thrown together only the day before. I liked Bran's gently teasing humour, and the wicked twinkle that surfaced every now and then as we talked.

A little later on some local folk musicians began to play, with fiddles and bodhráns and squeeze boxes, and a few guitars thrown in for good measure. Bran wheedled his way into joining in and easily outclassed every other musician there on almost every single instrument, although he didn't seem to be trying to show off. He was especially good on the bodhrán, which became a living thing in his hands, rumbling its rhythmic thunder in my ears.

We sang and laughed, enjoying the company, with no possibility of being told off for being too loud this time, but eventually we decided to turn in for the night. The warmth of the fire had worked its way into our bodies, making us both eager for our beds.

We giggled all the way out, and stopped on the street to let the fresh air clear our heads before starting the walk back to our hotel. There was a railing outside the pub and we leaned against it for a minute, gazing up at the canopy of glittering stars. I watched our breath sailing up, up into the night, and smiled wistfully as my thoughts grew still. Country Boy was out there somewhere. The last time I'd been out under the stars had been with him.

'Whatcha thinking about?' Bran asked gently.

'Impossibilities,' I sighed, letting my head drop onto his shoulder. 'Some things just don't work out, huh?'

'Hmm,' he said, the rumble of his voice vibrating against my ear. 'Maybe they just work out differently than you expect.'

I twisted my head to look up at him.

He studied me, looking like he was about to say something else, but then stopped himself and held out his arm instead. I took it and we walked back to the hotel, singing tuneless songs that didn't mean a thing and were forgotten by the morning.

I had a blessedly uneventful sleep, and when I woke I actually felt refreshed instead of groggy. My dreams were often plagued by the people and places I'd left behind – shifting from one to another, like a sad parade of vanished hopes and dreams – but not this time. I stretched luxuriously, waiting for the heaviness to descend again, but it didn't. Something had changed. I didn't know what it was, but I was glad of it.

When I knocked on Bran's door he invited me in to watch TV for a while before he got ready for his gig. He made us tea with the little kettle on the dressing table, and we sat on the small sofa under the window with our feet up on the coffee table. I wasn't really paying attention to what was on – I'm not sure where my thoughts had drifted to exactly – but it was nice sitting there with him. Cosy. I couldn't remember the last time I'd felt so at home.

Bran nudged my left foot with his right one. 'You've a hole in your sock.'

I glanced at my feet, and sure enough, there at the tip of the big toe on my right foot was a penny-sized hole.

'Oh yeah,' I said, shrugging, and went back to watching TV.

A few moments later, his foot nudged mine again. 'Isn't your toe cold?'

'No.' I shook my head, still focused the screen.

'What if it drops off?'

I turned to look at him. 'Does it really bother you?' I asked, wiggling my toes. 'Can't you cope with my holey socks?'

'I am just concerned for the wellbeing of your feet, as any friend would be.' He took a sip of tea.

Friend. I liked that.

'Why would my toe drop off?' I teased, poking his shin with the offending digit.

'I dunno. Maybe it'll catch a chill and fall off in the night.'

'Like frostbite?'

'Yeah, exactly. Frostbite. Or, maybe your toe will like, work its way through the hole and then the circulation will get cut off, and your toe will go all black and just… drop off.'

He was gesturing to illustrate the imagined toe catastrophe, and I watched his pantomime with unconcealed glee.

'Can that really happen?' I said, pretending horror. 'Really? Do toes go black when the blood drains out of them?'

He nodded sagely.

'That seems unlikely,' I argued, waiting for his deadpan expression to crack. 'Surely they'd go paler if there wasn't any blood getting through.'

'Well, it sounds to me like you're getting confused about the science of toe-damage. It's a very complicated subject, but the point is you really shouldn't wear socks with holes in them. They can wreak all kinds of unknown havoc.'

'I had no idea socks could be so dangerous!'

We regarded each other a moment longer before dissolving into laughter. I poked his leg with my foot once more and shook my head.

'You're such a weirdo,' I said fondly, before turning back to the TV screen.

And then he leaned over and kissed me on the cheek.

I looked at him, trying to puzzle out what was going on inside his head. 'What was that for?' I asked, still amused.

He shrugged and smiled lopsidedly. 'Just felt like kissing you.'

'Oh. I see.' My smile turned into a grin. Looking at him seemed to have that effect on me.

'And now I'm thinking I'd quite like to kiss you again.' His expression was as cheeky as ever, but there was also something sad about the way he was watching me… or maybe not sad, but… hesitant?

'Would you now?' I was overwhelmed by fondness for him, with his silly clowning and uncomplicated affection.

Our shoulders were touching, and I could feel his rising and falling as he breathed in and out.

'I would,' he said. He didn't seem to be joking anymore. 'But I know you… I know you haven't had the best time, and I don't want to make things awkward.' He looked down at his mug and scratched his fingernail around the rim.

I hadn't really talked about what had happened to me, except in vague terms, but clearly he'd picked up on it anyway which shouldn't have surprised me; he seemed intrigued by people. Apparently I wasn't as good at concealing my thoughts as I had hoped.

'Sooo…' he said, exhaling through his nose and raising his eyes to my face again, 'what would you think about that?'

I studied him, pondering. I liked him a lot, and when I looked at him there was a warm place in my chest where there hadn't been one before. Even the feeling of his eyes on me was pleasant, like the first rays of the sun peeking through the clouds. It was just…

'What is it?' he asked, a slight frown creasing the spot between his eyebrows.

I breathed out through my nose in a troubled sigh. 'I'm not…'
Allowed? Safe? Real? Ready?

'It's OK,' he said. 'You don't have to explain.'

I turned back to the TV and leaned my head against his shoulder, feeling unsettled. He rested his cheek against my head and sipped from his mug.

'I hurt people,' I said quietly, feeling suddenly very sad. 'I don't mean to, but I do. And I don't want to hurt you.'

He kissed the top of my head.

After a moment, he said, 'I'm gonna start calling you Socko.'

Despite myself, I had to giggle. I knew it would be OK.

That night I went with him to his gig in a bar across town. Helping him carry his equipment reminded me of old times, but I had no inclination to get back up onstage again; performing held too many memories and I wasn't ready to confront them just yet.

Bran set himself up at the front of the little stage, with a stool, an effects pedal, a mic on a stand and a single small amp, which fed into the house PA system. He was wearing his usual loose-jeans-and-baggy-sweater combo, with his hair pulled back into a ponytail, and he looked completely at home. His guitar gleamed softly in the pale yellowish light that pointed down at the stage, and he kept a pint of cider on a little table at his elbow to sip at between songs.

I sat at the front, offering the occasional good-humoured heckle and grinning every time he caught my eye. It was an education watching him perform, a lesson in stage presence as much as musical skill. He was born to be up there.

He came to sit with me between the two halves of his set. People kept coming over to tell him how good he was, and they were completely right: he was the best musician I'd ever met.

For the second half he switched from his clean acoustic sound to a more scratchy, distorted effect. He got rid of the stool and stood at the mic stand, with one foot operating the pedal. He played a couple of rocky tunes, picking up the pace from the earlier set. The crowd was receptive, and a few people started dancing in little pockets around the edges of the room.

A few songs in he paused to retune, and then seemed to hesitate for a moment before beginning the next one, his fingers hovering over the fretboard. Then he broke into a tune I hadn't heard before. It was mellower than the last few he'd played, but it had a jagged, skipping rhythm that worked well with the distortion.

I listened expectantly. It felt… special. It wasn't a Song – or at least, it didn't leap out at me in the way Songs usually did – and yet… it wasn't *not* a Song either. It made me feel completely still inside, like my body was on pause, its functions temporarily suspended.

I watched Bran's fingers on the strings and listened to the words. They were sad, so sad, and yet there was a fragile kind of hope in them, an unfinished story. His eyes were closed and he was totally lost in the music; I could tell that it meant something very personal to him. Whoever he was singing about must have been someone he'd loved very much.

Partway into the second verse I began to feel a buzzing under my skin, like I had on the plane. It was stronger this time, as if the current from the equipment on the stage was leaking out into the air and seeping into my flesh. I looked down at my hands but there was no visible sign of anything abnormal, and when I glanced around me no one else seemed to be feeling anything out of the ordinary. They were all lost in the performance, watching Bran with avid attention, a few with tears in their eyes.

The rhythm began to build and the feeling intensified, and Bran's features became set in a frown of concentration. His hands moved instinctively across the strings, and it seemed like he was channelling the music rather than producing it. It reminded me of the last time I'd sung on the stage in New York, and when I'd played in the garden of the house in LA – when music had become a feeling rather than a sound, experienced through another sense I couldn't put a name to.

The song swelled towards its crescendo and I could tell he was pushing his voice to its limits, singing with every fibre of his being to produce those raw, powerful notes. The effort was clearly visible from the strain on his face, but he didn't falter once. It was a masterful performance.

The last notes of the guitar rang out into the silence, and even though it wasn't the end of the set, everyone clapped.

I reminded myself to breathe.

When he finished I waited for him to pack up his equipment, and sat there smiling while he shook hands with person after person. I had a pint ready for him, and when he finally made his way back over to me he sank onto his stool in gratitude, clinked his glass against mine and swallowed almost half a pint in one long gulp.

I let him catch his breath, but then I just had to ask: 'Hey, who was that song by, in the middle of the set?'

'Which one?'

'Umm… it's hard to say without knowing the name of it.'

He chuckled, nodding. 'Yeah, I suppose. How did it go?'

I thought back, but I couldn't remember. All that came to my mind was the feeling.

'I don't know. It was the one everyone clapped for. It was amazing. Is it one of yours?'

'Ohhhh,' he said, his eyes lighting up, 'I know. Yeah, it's really cool, isn't it?' He gave no indication that there had been anything especially significant about it.

'Who's it by?'

'Erm… it's this guy called… James.' He smiled mysteriously. 'You wouldn't have heard of him yet, but you will.'

'Is he a friend of yours?'

'I guess you could say that.' He didn't seem to want to elaborate any further.

'What's it called?' I asked.

'The song? I'm not sure, he's still working on it. Maybe… "Scars"?'

He leaned his elbows on the table and clasped his hands around his glass, turning it slowly with his fingers. He seemed to be pondering something, but after a moment he broke into a smile and sat back on the stool, his eyes scanning the thinning crowd.

'Hey, let's get another drink, I think they're about to call last orders.'

As it turned out we still had another hour left before kicking-out time, and then we were invited to stay for a lock-in. We had a great time swapping stories with the locals, and hardly had to pay for a single drink the rest of the night.

*

The next morning I found Bran in a pensive mood, and after we had a late breakfast he said he was going to do some writing in his room.

'Unless you fancy having a jam?' he said, uncharacteristically subdued.

It had been a long, long time since I'd spent an afternoon fiddling with songs, and ordinarily I probably would have declined, but there was something about his solemn demeanour that made me agree; I didn't know what was wrong but I didn't like to see him looking so dispirited, especially after giving such a phenomenal performance. Besides, as he asked the question a little spark flared inside me, and I wanted to understand what it meant.

We sat on the bed and took it in turns to play guitar, replenishing the tea whenever we ran out. Bran didn't say anything about what was eating away at him, but his mood seemed to lift as we messed around with different tunes and worked out some interesting harmonies for songs we both knew.

Should I ask him if he's OK? I thought, strumming some random chords. The strings on his guitar seemed to have a life of their own, singing sweet lullabies as they lapped against my fingers. *Maybe he doesn't want to talk about it. We hardly know each other, really, wouldn't it be nosy to ask?*

I hummed along to the tune I was playing, not really concentrating.

'That's pretty,' he said, taking a slurp of tea and tapping his foot along with the beat.

He started drumming the rhythm against his thighs, and I started singing. Then I stopped. I'd realised what it was. That last Song again, the one that had played as I drove to the airport and… away.

'What's up?' he asked.

'Hmm. Just makes me sad.' I passed the guitar back to him.

'Oh.'

He adjusted the tuning pegs, not asking any further questions. His fingers found a tune and I listened, then began to sing along.

And then… *That's weird.*

'You don't know this one?'

'Yeah.'

It was 'Kiss Me'. My skin began to prickle.

I watched him for a moment, wondering how that had happened. He carried on, his brows creasing as he moved his fingers around on the strings, not like he was finding it difficult to play, more like he was lost in the music and trying to feel his way through.

It's got to be a coincidence, I thought. *What other explanation is there?*

He trailed off and strummed idly for a while, absorbed in his own musings. Then a third Song came – 'Heartbeats' – and I knew it was beyond a coincidence.

I leaned over and stopped his hand on the strings, my pulse beginning to throb in my temples. I felt disorientated, like I was still drunk from the night before. Bran didn't move. He looked down at my fingers, resting against his wrist. I realised I could feel a pulse that wasn't coming from my own body, it was coming from his skin beneath my fingertips.

'Do you know that one too?' he asked.

'Play another,' I said, a stillness growing inside me like the calm in the centre of a storm.

I let go of his hand and his fingers moved again. This time it took me a while to figure out what it was, and when I did I felt a cold fire sweep through me from my scalp to my toes. It was one of *my* songs, one I'd written: 'Home'. There was no way he could know that; it was impossible.

I didn't know how to ask what I wanted to ask. I didn't really know anything in those moments.

'Did you like them, those songs? Did they… help?'

And then he raised his eyes – those impossibly blue, eternally laughing eyes – and between one blink and the next, in less time than it took for my heart to skip a beat, he went from being *him* to being…

Keeper

…You.

You smiled and I just looked at you.

Neither of us moved.

Part of me heard the question, obviously, and part of me probably understood what it meant, but most of me was just frozen, in complete and stunned disbelief.

The world around us melted away. I felt the tingling in my skin, even stronger than before, and it seemed like I could feel the movement of every cell in my body, even down to the fizz of the oxygen as it coursed through my bloodstream, and the tiny beads of sweat squeezing out through the pores.

Your eyes were so blue. They were the bluest blue I'd ever seen. And they weren't laughing any more, they were dead serious, and bright with expectation.

Time stretched on. A thousand thoughts raced through my mind, and you just sat there, watching me. Waiting for me, like you could wait forever if it took that long.

Your fingers moved aimlessly across the strings of the guitar.

My thoughts were whirling. *You couldn't really know. It's impossible. There's no way you could know… is there?*

You began to play, so softly at first that hardly any sound came out. And then the gentle melody flowed out from the strings. It was 'Hallelujah'.

I saw your knowing smile.

'How?' I whispered, that one syllable holding more weight than any word I'd spoken in my life.

How could anyone possibly know about those Songs? I've never told anyone, and there's nothing linking them at all, apart from in my head… But you can't see inside my head… And you couldn't possibly know who I am – what I am – unless… unless…

Your eyes were glowing with a flickering light, so bright they seemed to illuminate the air around us.

'Bran?' I said, the sound sticking in my throat. 'Bran, as in…?' My mind raced back to Hearthfire, to the endless lists of names we had been made to learn by rote – names given to beings that had embodied our Attributes throughout human history. Bran the Blessed; Bran ap Llyr, who – among other things – ruled music, poetry and prophecy. How could I have missed it?

You nodded, only the tiniest movement of your head, your lips curving in a smile.

I took a breath, feeling like I hadn't breathed in years. 'You… you're… like me.'

You grinned, and the world came back into focus.

'Not quite, Aphrodite,' you said, your lilting Irish voice making soft, musical shapes from the word. 'No one's quite like you.'

I swallowed, stunned into silence.

'It's probably obvious now, but I'm—'

'Music,' I breathed, looking down at your guitar – that beautiful guitar, that one in a million. 'You're the Keeper of Music.'

All those stories of your travels, the sense that you weren't quite the same as other people, the reluctance to be parted from your guitar, being able to play any instrument like it was an extension of yourself…

'Yeah. That too,' you said.

'Too?' What else was there?

'Don't you remember?' you asked, with an anxious hope that made my heart surge with a desire to understand.

I tried to clear the fog, casting my mind back, all those long, long years, all that time between my life at Hearthfire and the person I'd become…

Who are you? We knew each other, didn't we? Everyone knew everyone. Why do I not remember? Keeper of Music…. who was the Keeper of Music?

And then I realised the answer – realised I should have known it all along. My mouth dropped open as everything suddenly fell into place. Every single, crazy puzzle suddenly made complete and perfect sense, and the only thing that seemed absurd was how long it had taken me to figure it out.

You'd been there the whole time. You'd been with me from the beginning, from that first, heartbroken melody that had sung to me from the shop doorway all those many years ago – that cry of a soul in agony, the sound of loss, of broken friendship, the tragedy of first love. It hadn't been mine, it had been yours!

First Love. My first step along the Path.

'No way,' I said.

And then you smiled, the light pouring from your eyes, and I grinned until I thought my face would split.

You got up and lifted your bag from the sofa, and from inside it you produced a plain black folder and held it out to me. I didn't recognise it but it was just like every other musician's songbook I'd ever seen, and I knew it would be full of music – guitar tabs and chords, and the words to go with them.

There they were, all laid out, in order, from the beginning.

You sat across from me as I flipped through the sheets, gaping in wonder at page after page after page of… Songs. All my Songs. Every single one of them.

'You?' I asked, my voice barely rising above a whisper. 'These were all from you?'

You nodded, scratching at a spot above your eyebrow with one fingertip. 'There's one more to go in there, after last night.'

I glanced at you sharply. 'So… when you said he's still *working* on it, you meant…'

You shrugged, your expression mischievous.

I didn't speak for a moment, trying to wrap my head around everything I'd learnt in the last five minutes.

'You were there the whole time,' I murmured, staring down at the pages beneath my hands.

You crossed your legs and edged closer to me, until your knee was resting on my thigh. We stayed like that for a long time, saying nothing, leafing through the past and somehow knowing, somehow *sharing* everything that had gone before, and the unburdening of my soul felt like a kiss of healing fire from heaven.

For the first time since we'd parted – practically as children – I was understood; I was *known*; I was myself. And you… I don't have the words to describe what you are to me. There aren't enough words in the world.

As we sat there, staring down at the pages, I felt the air around us pulsing like a heartbeat – keeping perfect time, perfect calm – and I knew I wasn't dreaming.

'So you see,' you said quietly, 'you can't hurt me. Nothing you do could ever hurt me.'

I turned to look at you, hypnotised by your voice.

You gazed back at me, your eyes burning with a blue fire, like flaming sapphires.

'The only thing that hurts is when I know you're in pain. I can feel it. Like an ache in my belly.' You clutched your fist to your stomach, and my throat grew tight.

I closed the folder and turned around to face you. The total absence of any sound was strange, but it seemed right somehow. We had stepped out of time, and the silence was the sound of the universe holding its breath.

'I'd like to kiss you again,' I whispered.

You smiled, as much with your eyes as your mouth. 'Would you now?'

'What would you think about that?'

'I wouldn't think anything at all,' you said.

I knew it was true. Thinking didn't belong in the space we'd created together.

I lifted my hand to your face and traced your nose with my finger, traced your cheekbones and your eyebrows and your jaw. I traced your lips with silent reverence, as though they were the lips of a sacred statue in some holy, hidden shrine. Looking with fresh eyes, I was amazed I hadn't seen you as I saw you now.

I bent forward slowly, watching you until the very last second, and then our lips touched and only feeling remained.

I liked the feeling of your unshaven cheeks, bristly, but soft. And I liked the shape of your ear when I felt it with my fingertip, the tickle of your hair where it brushed my knuckles and your warm breath on my face. I liked feeling the place where our mouths met – a warm, sweet feeling that ebbed and flowed like the tide. That feeling was my favourite.

My skin was buzzing again, like it had on the plane but more so, and the warm spot in my chest was there again too, only this time it swelled and expanded until it filled up my whole body, and then carried on expanding until the whole of the space around us was warm and sweet and full. And I felt that tingly feeling, like champagne bubbling through me, and just like the warmth it spread until it filled me up and my whole body fizzed with joy.

I felt your hands reach out around me, felt their warmth run down my arms, back up and around my shoulders, sliding over the skin and then stopping, pulling me closer. I unfolded myself and the warmth grew stronger as I shifted against you, closing the space between our bodies until there wasn't a space anymore.

I felt the thick strands of your hair as I laced my fingers through it, and felt your shoulder muscles shift beneath my other hand. I felt the loosening of my clothes, the freedom of the air on my skin, and the sharp and perfect sweetness that your hands had awakened. I felt the tensing of the muscles in your back, the expansion and contraction of your ribs, and the sudden, breathless wonder of my body becoming one with yours.

And then all I could feel was you. I could feel every heartbeat and every breath. I could feel the rapture of your mouth, the heaven of your hands, the surging, swaying harmony of our bodies and the echoes of ecstasy that sang through every nerve with every movement that we made.

I don't know if it was meant to be part of our Paths or not, but if it wasn't then we were forgiven, because nothing marred that perfect utopia of feeling, not a stray thought or a single doubt. We found freedom in those moments, something like a blessing from a god.

*

'When did you leave Hearthfire?' I asked as we lay in the little boat, gazing up at the night sky with a blanket tucked around our legs.

We were bundled up in layers of clothing, with thick fleece jackets to protect us from the chill rising up from the invisible deeps. Even though winter had passed, the cold was absolute out in the harbour, but we had love to keep us warm, and it was worth braving it for a while, just for the view.

The moon watched us from high, high above, robed in her rich mantle of stars. She looked like she was smiling.

'You know when,' you said, shifting your shoulder under my head and plumping up the blanket we had rolled up to make a pillow.

'Do I?'

'Guess.'

'Hmm… Was it when you sent me the Song?' I realised as I said it that I must be right, otherwise I would never have heard it.

'Yep.' You stroked my hair and planted a kiss on my brow.

I pondered for a while, wondering where you'd been and what you'd been doing on all the other occasions when the Songs had come to me.

'And where did you go after that?'

'That's two questions.'

'Oh.

'My turn.'

'OK.'

'Hmm…' You sighed, slipping your hand around my waist, gently tapping out a rhythm against my stomach while you thought. 'What do I want to know?'

'Is that your question?' I asked, teasing.

'No.'

'What if I answer it anyway? Then it would have to be your question.'

You poked me in the ribs and I squirmed, laughing.

'Clever clogs. OK, how about… which one was your favourite?'

'My favourite? Song or person?'

'Song. You can't have a favourite person.'

'*You're* my favourite person.' I snuggled against you, burrowing my cold nose into the warm spot where your neck joined your shoulder.

'Yeah, but I'm special,' you said smugly, wrapping your arms tightly around me to fend off the chill.

'Yeah. You are.'

We lay still, rocked by the gentle swell of the water.

'Are you going to answer the question?' you said.

'Oh yeah, umm… favourite Song… I don't know. Can I say all of them?'

'No. You have to pick one.'

'Oh.' I huffed. 'But I *do* love all of them. Apart from…'

You twisted your head to look down at my face, and I knew you could tell what I meant. You nodded. That was all that needed to be said.

'You know which one was *my* favourite?' you asked, your eyes dancing with starlight.

I propped myself up on one elbow, looking down at your face. 'Which?'

'"Voodoo Child".' You wiggled your eyebrows.

'Oh really?' I purred, sliding my hand under the blanket. 'I wonder why that might be.'

'Hmm.' Your lips spread into an amorous smile. 'I don't think there's any mystery to that one.'

I kissed you lingeringly, remembering the raw energy that had flowed through me that night in Pattaya. It had been pretty spectacular.

'Actually,' I said, 'you didn't know what I was doing, though, did you?'

You shook your head.

'So… how did you…?'

'Well,' you pulled me on top of you and rearranged the blanket around us, 'I couldn't *see* you but… I could *feel* you. You know, in a way.'

'Ah, I see.' I rubbed my nose against yours. 'You could *feel* me the whole time.'

I watched your face settle into languorous desire as I continued my manipulations beneath the blanket.

'Sometimes.'

'What did it feel like?'

'Not quite like this, but something similar.'

'Uh-huh. So you thought you'd have some fun at my expense.'

'That's three questions,' you replied huskily, opening your eyes and slipping your hands around my waist under my layers of clothing.

'It wasn't a question.' I grinned.

'I'm bored of this game,' you said, eyeing me hungrily.

'It was your game!'

'I've thought of a better one.'

You pulled me down and I lowered my mouth to yours. We didn't talk again for a while. You were right, though, it was a better one, although at times rather precarious in such a small, unstable boat.

*

We gradually pieced together the rambling pathways of our lives, bit by bit, step by step.

'I've been wondering something,' I said, one sunny spring afternoon as we sat eating a picnic in the sunshine on the bank of a shining river. 'If those Songs were all from you, how come they always pointed me in the right direction? How did you know what I needed to do next?'

I was surprised that I hadn't thought of it before, but the questions came and went like half-heard songs.

You finished chewing on the bite of apple you'd just taken, then swallowed it down and licked your lips. I loved watching you eat. I love watching you do everything you do.

'I don't understand the question,' you said, taking another bite.

'Well,' I leaned back on my hands, tilting my head to feel the warmth of the sun on my face. 'The Songs were like… signposts, right?'

You didn't answer. I opened one eye to look at you. You looked stumped.

'Weren't they?' I opened the other eye and studied your face.

'Were they?' you said, around a mouthful of apple flesh.

I mused over it while you finished chewing and swallowed again.

'Well, if they weren't signposts, what were they?' I asked, sitting upright and dusting the grass off my palms.

'They were… feelings,' you said. 'I felt what you were feeling and it just happened. On its own.'

'You didn't send them to guide me? They weren't meant to tell me what I should do?'

'How would I know what you needed to do?'

'I don't know, that's why I'm asking.'

'Aph… those Songs were a *response* to how you were feeling. They came to me because they fitted the way you felt, and… I don't know, somehow that just sent them to you. I don't know how else to explain it.'

I let out a long sigh and stared out across the opaque water. Every day it seemed I was learning something that completely blew my mind. There were puzzles inside of puzzles inside of puzzles.

You snaked out an arm and gathered me against you, pressing my forehead into your neck. I tried to think back to every Song, recalibrating my memories. All those times, they'd been a *reaction*. Which meant that none of the things I'd done or felt or wanted had been out of my control at all. Everything I'd done had been my choice; everyone I'd loved, I'd loved because there had been something about them that had spoken to my heart, not because I'd been destined to find them. I had been free. The whole time.

My mind wandered across the years... It didn't make me sad anymore, remembering. It was impossible to feel sad when I was with you.

'Did you know you'd find me?' I asked, laying my legs across your lap.

'I wouldn't say I *knew*, but I *felt* like I would. It felt like I was getting closer, in New Zealand.'

'Oh.' I pushed my fingers up through your hair, enjoying the smoothness of the strands as they slid against my skin.

'That morning, when I was on the way to the airport, I just... felt...'

'Different,' I finished for you.

'Yeah. Like there was a piece of me that was missing and I was really close to finding it.'

'So...' I said, watching your hand and my hand as they caressed each other, 'you thought you'd wander around the car park?'

You laughed, leaning back until you were propped on your elbows. 'No. I just followed me feet. And then I saw you, sitting in the truck. And you were *You*. With a capital "Y".'

Hearing it from you – that indescribable feeling that other people just don't understand – was music to my ears. No one could ever get it the way we do.

I love you, I thought. *I love you I love you I love you I love you I love you I love you I love you I love you I love you I love you I love you I love you.*

You gazed at me with your blue, blue eyes, and we grinned at each other.

'How did you know we'd end up on the same plane?'

You snorted. 'I didn't.'

'Oh. So you were just going to let me go? After all that, you would have just walked away?'

'Well, you weren't exactly being very friendly.'

I chuckled. 'No, but I mean, would that have been it, if I hadn't got on the plane? And what if I hadn't gone to your gig in Dublin? What would you have done?'

'Aph. You of all people know you can't force love. It either happens or it doesn't.'

'But what if I'd never realised—'

'Hey,' you soothed me, resting a loving hand on my cheek, your thumb stroking my cheekbone. 'I love you,' you said simply. 'I'd love you no matter what. That's… that's it. That's all there is to say.'

Tears pricked my eyes. You meant every word, and the certainty of your love filled every tiny piece of me with a glowing peacefulness.

My life became a Song. And every melody and beat of it is you.

Every day I woke up next to you, half-forgetting for a moment, and then reality expanded around me and I fell back into the dream. Only the dream was real.

We talked about Hearthfire sometimes – a past we'd never shared with anyone, a past no one else could hope to understand.

'When did you first fall in love?' you asked, while we lay in bed on a lazy Sunday morning, playing our game of taking turns to learn new things about each other.

We were in Galway, where we'd spent my thirtieth birthday. You'd bought me a new guitar and taken me to a folk festival, and my ears were still ringing from the clamour of drums and pipes and fiddles from the night before.

You had your head in my lap and I looked down at you adoringly, looping your hair behind your ear.

'The night of the apple wine,' I said, only then fully realising that was the case.

'Really? All the way back then?'

'Yes. All the way back then.'

'Even though I was going out with your best friend?'

I pouted at your cheeky smile. 'Hannah. I'd forgotten.'

'Yeah, Hannah. Who do you think she ended up as?'

'I dunno. Probably something clever. Maybe Intellect?'

'Hmm. Maybe.'

'What about you?' I asked, entranced by the soft pink curve of your lips. 'When did you first fall in love?'

'That was *my* question.' You averted your eyes, looking instead at the curtains, which were billowing in the fresh air that blew in from the Atlantic.

'I'm stealing it.'

You laughed, glancing back up at me and sighing in resignation. 'OK… Well, there are two different answers.'

'OK. Tell me the first one.'

'Alright.' You turned to face me, propping yourself up on one elbow. 'The first one is: on the night of the apple wine… I knew there was something about you. I just felt it.'

'Aww, that's so sweet.'

'Well, I'm not saying I felt it in my *heart*.'

You raised one hand in self-defence as I swatted at you, laughing at your own impudence.

'So, what's the second answer?' I asked, laying my hand against your chest so I could feel your heart beating.

'Well, it sort of comes down to semantics really.'

I gave you a withering look. 'Semantics?'

'Yeah, you know, the meanings of words and how—'

'I know what semantics means!' I swatted you again, knowing you were stalling but allowing you to have your fun.

'OK, OK! Well, basically… it sorta comes down to a bit of an issue with the phrasing of that question.'

I sighed. *Why are you so reluctant to answer?*

You reached up and ran a finger over my cheek. You'd grown serious again and I stopped baiting you. The air around us stilled, as if it too was waiting.

'I wouldn't really say it was the *first* time I fell in love. It was more… the *only* time I fell in love.'

Our eyes met again and my heart resumed its beating.

'Oh.' I couldn't think of anything else to say.

'See?' you added quietly. 'Semantics.'

I kissed you and the Song of my life became a symphony, filling my world with the sound of your words as they echoed in my ears, blending and rebounding with the joyous, harmonious beating of our hearts.

*

We stood outside the gates, hand in hand, like children. It seemed so small. So... ordinary. No sounds came from within, and somehow I knew that none would again.

You squeezed my fingers and I smiled up at you, knowing you understood the vague sadness I was feeling.

'Come on,' you said, pulling me away from the entrance and along the shining pavement that was still puddled here and there with the remnants of that morning's rainfall.

At the corner of the high brick wall we turned, following a narrow footpath that ran along beside it and was shadowed by the trees that bordered it on the other side. We emerged at the far end, finding ourselves on a broad strip of overgrown grass that rose before us until it met the shadows of the woods. No one ever came here, I knew it with absolute certainty. You took my hand again and we skirted the wall, heading into the trees, our bodies humming with anticipation as we smelled the familiar scents that had been lost to us for so long.

We found a tree with sturdy enough branches some way into the woods, and you jumped to grip the lowest one so you could swing yourself up. You lowered your hand and I grasped it, bracing my legs against the trunk, and then we were sitting on the branch together, grinning at our own daring.

'Ready?' you asked, swinging your feet and tapping out a rhythm on your thighs.

'No.'

You turned to scoot along the branch and I followed, knowing I'd follow you anywhere. I dropped into your waiting arms on the other side, breathless with wonder.

Home. The word hummed through my head.

I saw the same thought flit across your face, and then we turned and looked out over the old familiar landscape.

Is this where it began? I thought, trying to feel a connection through the ground, to link this place with the images in my mind. Somehow it wasn't quite the same, and I wondered if it had ever really been the way I remembered it. But then I felt your warmth beside me and I knew we had found everything we could ever hope to find, not in places or in memories, but in each other.

We crossed the broad sweep of lawn, unkempt and slightly eerie in the dying afternoon light, and reached the door in the side of the building that used to be the way up to the girls' dorms.

'Hmm,' I murmured thoughtfully. 'I don't know if you're allowed to come in this way. It's against the rules.'

You pulled me against you and wrapped me in your arms, watching me with your bright, adoring eyes, with the flecks of deep purple that made them that impossible shade of blue.

'I never liked rules,' you said. 'They always spoil the fun.'

This time you didn't tweak my nose and jog away. This time you laid your lips against mine, and I felt like we were somehow rewriting our own past, wiping away everything that had happened in between and starting at the beginning again. We broke apart and glanced back at the door, and then with a look of pure devilry you turned the handle and we made our way inside.

It was so strange being back. We wandered the halls, examined empty classrooms for traces of ourselves, explored the kitchen and the rec room, and peeked into the cellar where we all used to go and scare ourselves silly at All Hallows'.

At last we left the building and stood outside on the forecourt. The twilight was gathering now, and the walls loomed up into the darkening sky.

I glanced towards the gates, almost at the same moment you did, and without a word we moved together, our footsteps ringing softly in the echoing space. The gates opened with a gentle push, and before us stood the Forge like a vision from a dream – ancient grey stone, worn smooth with time, and the dark, weathered door with its faint and faded writing, in a language so old that few living eyes could read it.

Words rang inside my head – *there is no going back* – and I remembered Maia guiding me forwards, with the soft regret of a mother sending her child out into the world. It seemed like a hundred lifetimes had passed since then.

Surely it was just an empty room now, like all the rest.

I pushed the door open and we ventured inside, the fading light creeping across the threshold, unveiling the plain stone floor. Nothing happened. It was just an empty vault.

I moved deeper into the space, my whole body tingling. It seemed that nothing had ever been here at all. And yet…

The door swung closed, softly and deliberately, silent on its hinges. The air around us seemed to ripple, the darkness deepening then growing softer. I heard you breathing quietly beside me. A faint sparkle of light began to flicker at our feet, and then it grew brighter, slowly expanding until it engulfed us, bathing us in glowing hues of gold and silver and rich shades of violet. And then I was sinking down, down into darkness, and the only sensation left to me was the gentle, warm pressure of your hand in mine.

I can't say for certain exactly how long I floated in that nothingness. It could have been an eternity or no time at all. The next thing I remember is a blast of fragrant air, and its force was so strong that it seemed to blow right through me, lifting me up and away from the world, faster than I could comprehend, quicker than thought.

And then it seemed the universe was unfolding all around me, and brilliant starlight blossomed, lighting the darkness. I was aware of you – or rather, I was aware of the essence of you – and between us was a gleaming thread of energy, glowing with the same beautiful luminescence as the stars themselves. The thread strengthened and grew thicker, and then opened out into a web, and I felt myself being unravelled, dismantled into all my component parts and reassembled in a different order.

The lines of energy spread outwards from the centre of my being – tendrils of light that extended into space. I knew, beyond all knowing, that those shimmering, gossamer threads connected me to the great, vast ocean of human consciousness. From that point on, until the next generation of Keepers came forth, all love would be patterned after the blueprint of what we shared, defined by our connection to each other.

And what a love it is! A love based on friendship, compassion, empathy – on laughter and understanding, patience and selflessness; a love that's not delineated by time and distance, but by the strength of the bond upon which it is built – a bond that can never be broken.

I felt my inner power expanding out into the world, flowing through me from within, refracting into a spectrum of love in all its sacred perfection. It was a second Forging, and this time I passed through the starfire that had birthed me and emerged in a new form – still essentially myself but changed, made ready for a new phase of my existence.

At last, after an eternity of drifting in the tides of cosmic force, I realised that I could feel something again – not the strange floating substance of Spirit but something solid and corporeal. I was encased once more in the flesh and bone of my body. My feet were standing on solid ground. The darkness was all around, shrouding me in its presence, but I was whole again, bound up in matter, and your hand was still warm in mine.

'Bran?' I whispered.

'Yeah?'

'Did you feel that?'

The air shifted as you turned your body towards mine. 'What?'

I waited, my mind still reeling.

'Aphrodite?' you said, in your soft, musical voice. 'Did I feel what?'

I breathed in deeply again, rediscovering the sensation of inhabiting my body. It seemed impossible that you could have been standing so close to me and not felt the colossal shift that had taken place within me, but perhaps…

'I just…' I cleared my throat and ran my hand over my face. 'I think I just had…' What words could possibly describe what had just happened to me?

'Are you OK?' You sounded concerned, and I reached out to touch your face. You kissed me softly, carefully, on the top of my head.

I nodded. I didn't know what it all meant, but I knew I didn't want to stand there in the dark anymore.

Pale light spilled through the crack as you opened the door.

'Come on, let's get out of here,' you said, and we passed through into the courtyard.

I felt so different, like an enormous weight had been lifted from me. My stomach and chest felt light, as though filled with cool, clean air. I had no idea what it meant but it felt wonderful.

'Did something happen to you in there?' you asked, tucking my hair back behind my ear.

I nodded, knowing I couldn't explain, even to you.

'It's OK,' I said, slipping my hands around your waist and laying my head against your chest. 'I'm fine. I think… things will be different now.'

You enfolded me in your arms, and we stood like that, unmoving, as the stars began to wink out from the indigo backdrop of the sky.

'I love you,' you whispered. 'I know you get that a lot, but I really, really mean it.'

I hugged you back as tightly as I could, my head swimming with new possibilities. I thought I knew what had happened, but I couldn't be sure, and although I knew nothing could ever change the way you felt about me, I didn't want to share it yet. I didn't know what it would mean for us – for the future.

Darkness was descending quickly, and in the last remaining light we gathered kindling and firewood from the edge of the woods before dashing back to the house and huddling in front of the huge fireplace in the hall. The blaze was nowhere near big enough to warm the room, but we nestled together on the wooden floor right in front of it, and its cheery crackling at least gave us the illusion of warmth, while our bodies did the rest.

We didn't sleep all night, and when the morning came, creeping in through the windows, we realised there was still a world outside, waiting for us to return to it and continue on our Paths. Well, for you to continue on your Path; I had no idea what I would do, now that I had become…

Standing on the forecourt one last time, we watched the dawn light touch the red sandstone walls that were at once so familiar and so alien. The Hearthfire wasn't in this place anymore, and it no longer held any power over me.

'There is no going back,' I murmured – comforted rather than saddened by the thought. Ahead lay the future, with all its limitless possibilities.

We walked across the overgrown lawn, and found the path into the woods that led us back to the wall. You had to take a run-up but managed to grab the branch on your second try, and then you held your arm down to me so I could haul myself up beside you.

We found the footpath easily, and when we reached the pavement I stopped, turning to look at the outer gate that was set into the wall. That was where my Path had begun, the exact spot where I had started on my journey. I couldn't go now without at least setting my feet back on that same piece of ground.

You smiled gently as I moved to stand in that spot for a moment, and I knew you remembered the beginning as well as I did. You came to stand beside me and laced your fingers through mine, and we gazed out into the world like we had once before. Only this time it was different. This time we were together, and instead of blindly stumbling along an invisible trail, I could pick my own direction and go anywhere I chose.

You are everything to me, just in case you didn't know that already.
You are the sun rising in the morning.
You are the soft kiss of summer rain on my face.
You are starry nights over the ocean, mountain breezes and wild, playful winds.

You are the scent of damp earth, the taste of cherries, sharp and sweet.

You are the crackle of a camp fire and the dark surrender of sleep.

You are every song, and every Song, I've ever heard, and will ever hear.

You are Inspiration.

You are the beginning and the end, the alpha and omega.

You are me and mine.

We are one.

Epilogue

One morning I woke up from a deep and pleasant sleep, and Bran was gone. I could feel it, even before I saw that his things were missing.

I lay in bed, perfectly still, and stared at the lights dancing across the ceiling from the cars going past outside. I didn't feel upset, but there was an emptiness there, in the space where he'd been. I knew what it meant. I knew the same way he'd have known. No one else would understand.

After a while I got up and pulled on my big T-shirt.

I padded through to the bathroom, had a shower and got dressed.

I packed my bag, put my guitar inside its case and clicked the clasps shut.

I made the bed and opened the curtains. It was a pretty day outside, sunny and windy, with the soft scent of damp leaves.

I picked up the room key from the dressing table, and then I saw the note. And the iPod. My iPod.

I took them to the chair by the window and sat down.

I stared at the piece of folded paper. The outside only had one word written on it: *Aphrodite.*

Bran always likes to say my whole name. And I like it when he says it. It sounds different to the way everyone else says it.

When I'd studied my name in his writing for a while, I opened the paper out. There was more writing inside.

It said:

To my Aphrodite,

I'm not sorry for any of it. Especially not for kissing you that first time, before the world took you away.

We knew today would happen, we just didn't know which 'today' it would be. Well, it's this one. Looks that way, anyway. Lucky we went to Hearthfire when we did, really.

You know what I mean when I say I had to go. And you also know I'm not really gone, and I never will be again. That thought means more to me than I could ever put into words, and I'll carry it with me everywhere until our Paths cross again.

We still have more to come, I know it. You know it too. Don't forget.

I left you a present. It's not much but it's all I've got, so I know it's enough for you.

Don't be sad, and don't ever be lonely. I'm sure you won't, but if you feel like you might be, just be still for a moment and listen. I'm with you all the time, just like you're with me.

I know they say music is the food of love, but it works the other way too.

I love you.

I'll always love you.

Yours forever,

Bran.

I read it once.

Then again just to be sure.

Then I picked up my iPod. I knew the present would be there.

I stuck it in my bag, along with the letter, and my clothes, and my special book of Songs, and I picked up my guitar and left the hotel.

I didn't know where I was going, but I knew if I followed my feet they would take me wherever I needed to go. They would take me on adventures, lead me to people, to happiness, and yes, to pain as well, but eventually, if I followed them for long enough and let my footsteps guide me, one day they would lead me back to him. One day they would lead me home – the place where all Paths meet.

When I got to the airport I drifted along the wending river of people, past the crowds of travellers and the busy airport staff, past the newsagents' and the payphones, past the fast food counters and the cashpoints.

I walked straight to the nearest coffee counter and bought a cardboard cup full of coffee. Then I sat down on a plastic chair and read through the letter again, not to see if it had changed, just to hear Bran's voice speaking the words. I liked the way it made them sound. I like everything he does. I can't help it. He's a part of me now.

I pulled my iPod from my bag and looked at it. There were a lot of songs on it already. And all my Songs. Bran's Songs. Our Songs.

I flicked through the playlists until I found a new one. It said 'For Aphrodite'. I selected it and found all our Songs in order, like an audio scrapbook of memories. There was a new one at the end – a new one just for me.

I put the earbuds in and let my finger hover over the play button. Once I heard the Song, it would be real; it would be history, and another step away from the only person I would ever truly love.

We still have more to come... the words echoed in my head.

Don't think, just go.

I pressed the button.

I listened.

I'd never heard the Song before. It was new to me, and somehow I knew that it was new to the world too. I looked down at the screen. Wildwood Kin. I'd never heard of them. The Song was called 'The Valley'. I wondered if they even knew they'd written it yet.

I turned the volume up and sat back, closing my eyes.

It began with a guitar – nothing complex, but the simplicity was what made it beautiful. And then a sweet tremble of notes, soft, like the first tentative touch of a lover's hand. The voice that began to sing was a woman's, young and fresh as a spring morning, crisp with promise, unrefined but sweet and true. The music didn't have the usual sleekness of a fully studio-mastered track, but its rawness gave it a purity that couldn't be created through effects.

I listened, enraptured. Even though it wasn't Bran's voice I could hear him speaking to me through it, as I always have. I've always known when it was him, even when I didn't know who he was. No one else can make music sound the way he makes it sound.

The first voice was joined by two more, weaving around and through, a delicate, flawless interplay of melody and harmony that filled my chest with joy.

It was perfection.

It was us.

I felt the warmth of his love in my heart, and I knew he was listening too.

I didn't cry.

I didn't need to cry.

It wasn't like the sadness of an ending, because we haven't ended. We'll never end, will we? Until… until it all ends, I guess.

I didn't move.

I didn't think.

I just… felt.

I felt his words.

I felt his voice.

I felt his love echo through me.

I was swept up in his sweet sounds.

You're here with me all the time, just like you always have been.
You feel me too.
You know me like no one else will ever know me.
You're the alpha and the omega.
The beginning and the end.
I'll see you again, my love.
You're a Keeper.
My Keeper.

I sat in silence as the final, exquisite notes rang out.

I looked down at the letter in my hand.

It wasn't Bran, but it was of him, and that made it precious.

Sometimes it's good to remember, I thought.

I pulled the songbook from my bag and leafed through it. There was a new one at the end. I tucked the letter into an empty plastic pocket; it belonged with all the rest, even though there was no tune to go with the words.

Memories are important, like letters from the past, to remind us of the things that really matter…

I suddenly knew what I had to do.

I found a stationery shop and bought some paper and a pack of pens. Then I went back to my seat by the coffee place.

The people passed by on their way to lots of places. I knew that every single one of them had lines of force around them, connecting them to their loved ones, some of whom would still be strangers, until…

Even though I'm no longer a Keeper, I can still sense them around me – fine, gleaming threads that are woven through the spaces between people.

I know that being human again won't spare me from suffering, and yet… and yet, I don't feel helpless any more. I've been cast adrift in one sense, but in another I have become the master of my own fate. I have a purpose and a place. I have found Home – my own, inner Hearthfire.

I cycled back through the Songs in the playlist until I got to the very first one again, and stared down at the blank sheet of paper in front of me. It was terrifying in its emptiness, a void waiting to be filled…

*

That was almost a year ago now, when I started writing this… whatever this is. I've come a long way since then, geographically and mentally; I'm acclimatising to my new state of being and to the slower pace of life that comes with it.

I've been living in Greece for most of that time – it seemed the natural choice – and every morning I get up to greet the dawn over the Aegean, go for a run along the sand and bathe in the deep blue waters, before making my way home and sitting down at the table next to my living room window to write. And now it's done. Almost.

I wanted to give you all something to remember me by. I wanted you to have the same things that Bran gave me: my letter, my Songs, and the knowledge that I'll never be forgotten. It's not the same as having him next to me, but they keep the idea of him close. I know that once he finds the thing he's looking for he'll be free to come back to me again, and my ears are always open, listening for the perfect song – a piece of music to define a generation.

I've realised, in writing this, that all my loves have been tributaries to the one I share with Bran, feeding into the current from their many, distinct sources. The fact that they didn't last forever really doesn't matter, any more than the ever-changing nature of a river matters to its essential life force. It is their cumulative energy that holds the real power: they were all what they needed to be, perfect in their own way and their own time.

Perhaps in this age of humankind, love can be conscious and aware of its own transience without being diminished by it – valued and experienced in terms of depth, not length. Even a moment of love can bring about a change that will last a lifetime, and every person is the sum total of all the loves they've known, no matter how brief or long-lasting those loves may have been.

For all of you that I've been blessed to share my life with, I hope you'll understand, somehow. I hope this will find its way to you, wherever you are, and that you'll hear me speaking to you through the music in the world and the words on the page. Don't ever think you're any less precious, any of you, just because you weren't The One. I don't think there is a One, or else you all are. Every love is true love. Love by its nature has to be true, otherwise… I guess it's something else.

This is the end of our stories, but I know there will be more. There is always room for more love in the world. And every love story is different. They may have a common thread, but it's the details that make them precious, that give them meaning.

I wonder, as I sit here watching the people walking by along the beach, following their many, many Paths, whether maybe one of them is about to discover love – the greatest adventure of their lives. Maybe you are, whoever you may be. Maybe you've already seen the face of someone who will change your life forever, and you don't even know it yet.

Love always has something to teach us, once the pain fades away, and believe me when I say that no matter how much it can hurt, life is infinitely richer for having experienced it. It's up to you to find the meaning and let it guide you towards the next open door, the next new adventure, the next, vital step along your Path.

In any case, love will always be there, in some form, in some way. Soon there'll be another Keeper of Love, another Aphrodite, although she won't bear that name. That's mine now, to keep. After this, love will come under a new guise. There are a lot to choose from. It's a vast concept and it has many names in many places, just like the seas, and the heavens, and everything else that touches humankind… and even some things that don't.

She could be any one of them.

She could be Freyja or Ishtar.

She could be Venus, Hathor or Áine.

Perhaps Oshun, Parvati, Branwen…

She could be anybody. *She* could even be a *he* this time. The paradigms are shifting, and nothing is set in stone. That's the true purpose of the Keepers, after all: to bear the light onwards for the next generation – to be the trailblazers, marking out the Path for us all.

But know this: whoever is handed the torch, after me, is bound by love.

Love is their function, their reason for being. It's not just something they feel, it's what they are.

Everything they do, they do for love.

And they mean every bit of it.

And always will.

A Letter From Rose

Thank you for choosing to read *The Beginning and End of Us*. If you want to keep up to date with my latest releases, just sign up at the following link. I can promise that your email address will never be shared and you can unsubscribe at any time.

www.bookouture.com/rose-james

I remember hearing once, as a theatre student, that actors tend to prefer playing characters that are the least like themselves; there's something liberating about having licence to explore the hidden, unexpressed parts of yourself, and I certainly found that to be the case during my brief time treading the boards as a teenager.

This book came about in a very similar way, although I didn't realise it at the time. When the idea first came to me in around 2011 I'd been in the same relationship since I was sixteen, and a decade on there was definitely something missing. I began to daydream about the 'what-ifs' – those people who'd come into my life and flitted out again, unresolved attractions and missed opportunities. I tend to daydream on paper, so I traced out a story that would let me imagine what could have been, and – in hindsight – was probably an expression of my hope and desire for something more fulfilling.

For me, writing *The Beginning and End of Us* was all about wish fulfilment and escapism: I'd always wanted to go travelling and have adventures, both physical and emotional, but after getting a job straight out of college and settling down too soon, I wasn't in a position to live the life I had imagined I would. I think that sense of lost potential and regret lent a sadness to the story, but I hope in a way that enriches it rather than detracts from it.

Another idea that I really wanted to explore in the book was the impact of music on memory and emotional experience. I've been playing, singing and writing music since my early teens, and throughout my life there have been many songs that have become anthems that I associate with particular people or periods in time. I think most of us have songs that speak to us on a deeper level and represent something personal for us, beyond their obvious meaning. Some of the songs in this book certainly have very personal meanings to me, and a number of the scenes were written while I was listening to the songs that go with them, so I'd love to think that maybe some readers will play the songs when they get to those scenes too.

On top of all that, as a lover of all things magical and mystical, I've always been fascinated by different pantheons of gods – particularly the Greek and Celtic ones – and the way that we, as a species, have found so many ways to personify the same set of ideas, creating archetypal beings with human (and other) forms to represent the qualities we see as fundamental to our world. I wanted my protagonist to be someone who lived a little apart from the rest of society and wasn't entirely human, and it occurred to me that one way of doing that would be to make her a supernatural being with some of the attributes of a love goddess, but with human vulnerabilities and feelings. And so, from that blend of ideas, Aphrodite was born.

I'm far less of a romantic than I was when I started this book, but I still truly believe that love can be the most powerful and transformative force on Earth, if it's honest and genuine. The kind of love I wrote about in *The Beginning and End of Us* is idealistic and somewhat naïve, but I think it's fair to say that I was too when I started on this journey, and I will always enjoy Aphrodite for reminding me of the person I was before. Her love is unconditional, although I've learned that mine is not, nor should it be. I've become very fond of her after all the years we've spent together, and I hope she gives readers the same sense of hope, sweetness and maybe even closure that she has given me.

I'd love to hear from you if something in this book resonated with you, and of course I'd very much appreciate a review, as would other readers who might want to know what they're letting themselves in for.

Do get in touch – I'm often on Twitter and you can also contact me through my Facebook page.

Thank you so much for reading.

With love,
Rose James

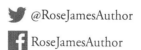

@RoseJamesAuthor
RoseJamesAuthor

Acknowledgements

First and foremost I want to thank three very special people, without whom this book would never have made it this far: Jenna for your Observing Eye, inappropriate humour, input and patience, and of course for inspiring the best portrait that was never painted. Rachell, I owe you more than I can say, for always believing in me, being unfailingly honest, and especially for never accepting less than my best. Granny James, you gave me a lifetime of inspiration and I'm so glad to finally be able to justify your faith in me.

I also want to say a huge thank you to my parents for imbuing me with a love of reading; to all my well-travelled friends for letting me mine your memories and experiences; and especially to Hillary, Matt and Clair for your insights and helpful notes.

Thanks also to my English teachers, Mike Ashley and Roger Calvert; I'm so glad I was lucky enough to end up in your classes during my formative years. And my lasting and sincere gratitude to the Open University and all my tutors, especially Tim Reeves for your feedback on my writing.

I would like to thank my editor, Kathryn Taussig, from the bottom of my heart for seeing the beauty in this book beneath its (very) rough edges. You've been my champion from the very beginning, and I'm so pleased we got to finish it together. Thank you also to the rest of the

Bookouture team for making my first publishing experience such a pleasure; you guys are brilliant in every way and I feel very lucky that I got to work with such lovely people right out of the gate.

To my agent, Thérèse Coen, thank you so much for your support, enthusiasm and humour. I still marvel at the serendipity that led to me sending you that first email. You're a joy to work with, and your encouragement and advice have been invaluable throughout this process. And thanks to everyone at Hardman & Swainson for making me so welcome.

Finally, to the rest of my friends and family – biological or otherwise – I want to say a massive thank you for building (and sometimes propping) me up, making me laugh, letting me cry, joining me on adventures both outward and inward, and showing me the magic in the world. You'll never know how much you mean to me, and I'm blessed to have you in my life.